T0274538

SALLY'S LAMENT

A TWISTED TALE

Sally's Lament

A TWISTED TALE

MARI MANCUSI

DISNEY • HYPERION
Los Angeles • New York

What if Sally discovered Christmas Town?

Published by Disney • Hyperion, an imprint of Buena Vista Books, Inc.
No part of this book may be reproduced or transmitted in any form or by any means,
electronic or mechanical, including photocopying, recording, or by any information
storage and retrieval system, without written permission from the publisher.
For information address Disney • Hyperion,
77 West 66th Street, New York, New York 10023.
Printed in the United States of America
First Hardcover Edition, October 2024
1 3 5 7 9 10 8 6 4 2
FAC-004510-24194
Library of Congress Control Number on file
ISBN 978-1-368-10450-0
Visit disneybooks.com

SUSTAINABLE FORESTRY INITIATIVE
Certified Sourcing
www.forests.org
SFI-01681

Logo Applies to Text Stock Only

To Leanna, who makes every day
feel like Halloween

—M.M.

CHAPTER ONE

Sally was having a very good night.

But then she always did on Halloween. It was, after all, the most wonderful time of the year. A night filled with frights around every corner. Shops stocked with slimy, slug-infested stews. Every ghoul and nightmare you could imagine—and some you couldn't—all gathering together and dancing in the streets, trying to out-scare one another with their own personal tirade of terror.

For three hundred and sixty-four days out of the year, Halloween Town prepared for this night. And on October 31, they all came together to put on a horrific holiday sure to scare even the most fearless of fiends. It was a glorious spectacle, both gory and grim, and the residents were not only creepy but rather creative. Like the Clown with the Tear Away Face. Or the moaning ghosts. Witches, vampires, zombies, sea monsters—you name it! Sally's town had it all. And on Halloween they put it all on display.

Sally loved every minute of it. Even if she wasn't supposed to be there.

Her eyes lifted toward her bedroom window, and she wondered if Dr. Finkelstein was still out cold. She'd played her own personal trick or treat tonight, enhancing the doctor's soup with some deadly nightshade she'd collected from her herb garden just outside of town. It wasn't actually deadly, you see. Sally wasn't that kind of doll. But it would, if properly administered, put the scientist to sleep for a long time. Enough time for Sally to sneak out of the lab and join in the festivities. Something Dr. Finkelstein would have never allowed, had he been conscious.

Sally sighed. To say the doctor was overprotective would be an understatement. Sure, she was his creation, a rag doll brought to life by his hands, and for that she'd always be grateful. But she'd never understand why he'd given her life only to keep her from actually enjoying it. She was always "too young" or "not ready," and it was always "better to stay in your room where you will be safe." Safe from what, Sally had no idea, and when she asked, Dr. Finkelstein would spout all kinds of nonsense, using large words that sounded very impressive until you realized none of them made any sense. But it didn't matter why, in the end. The verdict was always the same.

No Halloween for Sally. Not now. Not ever.

Sally had tried to tell herself it was no big deal. She had other interests, after all. She helped Dr. Finkelstein in his lab with his experiments. She read books in the library, devouring any she could find about botany. She'd gotten quite skilled at mixing potions, too; she barely ever blew up anything accidentally anymore. She'd even taught herself to sew and had made the most beautiful patchwork dress out of scraps she'd found in the dumpster behind the costume shop. She was wearing it now, in fact, and at least a dozen monsters had complimented her on how delightfully creepy she looked in it, which made her beam with pride.

But while that was all fine and good, deep down, she couldn't help longing for something more: to not only watch the festivities on that last day in October, but to take part in them herself. She wasn't inherently scary—at least not at first glance. She didn't have snakes for fingers or a Cyclops eye. She was just a simple rag doll, stuffed with dry leaves and roughly stitched together with coarse black thread.

But she was sure she could come up with something important to contribute. Like create more creepy costumes, for example, for those taking part in one of the many competitions. Or mix up some potions. Everyone knew the right potions could make or break a Halloween. And if that wasn't enough, well, she could just use her head. For what could be scarier than a creepy doll with a disembodied head?

In short, she would be great at Halloween, if just given a chance. But every time she tried to convince Dr. Finkelstein of this, he refused to budge. And Sally was prohibited from taking part in the festivities for another year.

It was enough to make a rag doll want to tear out her yarn.

Suddenly shouts rose in the air, assaulting her ears, followed by a flash of light that pulled her eyes away from the laboratory window. Sally turned, her breath catching in her throat as she realized excitedly what was coming next.

Who was coming next.

Her pulse quickened. The threads of her cloth stood on end. She clasped her hands over her heart, and her red-painted lips curled into an excited smile. This was it. The fearsome finale. The best part of every Halloween.

Jack Skellington—the Pumpkin King—was on his way.

The noise from the crowd rose to near-deafening proportions. Everyone began to rush the town square. Sally excitedly stepped out from the shadows and soon found herself swept up into the crowd, and she laughed in delight as she screamed along with them.

And then, there he was: a pumpkin-headed scarecrow emerging from the dark night, riding gallantly atop a horse made of hay, led by Behemoth.

"He's here!" cried Corpse Kid, clapping his hands in glee.

"He looks amazing!" declared his friend Mummy Boy, his one visible eye wide as a saucer as he tossed a loose wrapping over his shoulder. "He looks so cool!"

"He looks *terrifying*," two witches declared, sighing dreamily in unison as they watched him approach. Sally suspected the two ladies had a bit of a crush on Jack. Not that she could blame them.

Sally had always admired Jack from afar, ever since the very first day she'd seen him, giving a lecture in the town square on the importance of adding stink juice to dry ice to heighten the fright. He had been so confident, winning the crowd over with ease, and when he had finished, everyone applauded with such enthusiasm—as if he'd performed an actual miracle instead of just making smoke smell bad. It was something Sally could have done in her sleep had she been allowed to do it.

But Jack had all the freedom she lacked. And he took full advantage of this, well, advantage. With no limits on what he could do, he did it all. Effortlessly bringing everyone together under his gruesome glow. Inspiring them to be bigger and better and scarier versions of themselves each and every Halloween. He was self-reliant, self-assured. He was the Pumpkin King and he could do anything.

While Sally could do nothing at all.

The Mayor clapped his hands, bringing her attention back to the town square. His head swiveled to reveal a big smiling face. "Get back!" he cried, waving his hands at the excited crowd of creatures. "Make room!"

The residents reluctantly backed up an inch or two, just enough to allow Jack and his horse to be wheeled into the town square. Sally stared up at him, her leaves fluttering in her belly as she watched him reach down to pluck a lit torch from an excited volunteer. Jack lifted the torch triumphantly in the air, waving it at the crowd, then proceeded to light himself on fire.

Sally's eyes bulged from her head. *Whoa!* This was new!

She watched, admittedly fascinated, though a little terrified, as the fire spread quickly, catching the dry hay and causing flames and smoke to rise into the air. The crowd screamed in delight, clapping their hands in excitement. The witches blew kisses in Jack's direction. Lock, Shock, and Barrel, three trick-or-treating children in masks, jumped up and down in joy.

Jack, now fully engulfed in flames, leapt from his horse, singing and dancing and putting on quite a show for someone who was completely on fire. Sally clapped her hands along with everyone else, but inside her nerves jangled. Would Jack be able to put out the flames in time? Before they burned through the hay and scorched his bones?

But Jack never flinched, finishing his song and summersaulting into the goopy green fountain in the center of the town square, dousing the flames, then rising again a moment later in all his skeletal glory. The pumpkin head was gone. And in its place was a perfectly shaped bone-white skull with big hollow eyes and an even bigger smile stretching across his skeletal face.

The crowd went wild. Sally bounced up and down in excitement.

Oh, Jack, she thought. *You are truly magnificent.*

Jack leapt onto the fountain, giving a dramatic bow. Sally was shoved backward as everyone scrambled forward to congratulate him—and themselves—on another Halloween well done. Sally let them pass, contenting herself to stand on the sidelines to watch the aftermath, feeling proud but a little wistful. They all looked so happy. And well they should—it had been a terrifically terrifying night.

She just wished she could have been a bigger part of it.

"Great Halloween, everybody," the Mayor declared, slapping Jack on the back.

"I believe it was our most horrible yet," Jack agreed, leaping gracefully from the fountain onto the cobblestones below. His eyes roamed the adoring crowd, taking in their exultation. What must it be like to be so adored? Sally wondered. To be so needed. It had to be the most wonderful feeling in the world.

Suddenly she felt a hard tug at her wrist. She whirled around, her happy expression crumbling as she found none other than Dr. Finkelstein himself staring up at her angrily from his wheelchair. His ragged fingernails dug into her cloth and she winced in pain.

"The deadly nightshade you slipped me wore off, Sally," he growled.

Sally cringed. She'd been so sure the dose she'd given him was enough to last the entire night. Maybe his tolerance was increasing from all the times she'd administered it in the past. She'd have to go back to her books to recalculate her formula before next time.

But that wouldn't help her now.

"Let go!" she cried, trying to wrestle her hand away.

But Dr. Finkelstein shook his head, only tightening his grip. "You're not ready for so much excitement!"

"Yes I am!" she shouted, surprising even herself with

her boldness. Since when did she talk back to her maker? It never did any good and always just led to more punishment.

For a moment, she wondered if she should apologize—be a good girl, follow him meekly back home. The night was all but over anyway. She'd gotten to see Halloween. Shouldn't that be enough? Shouldn't she be content to return to reality now, however dismal hers might be?

But then she looked up at Jack, at the rest of Halloween Town partying without a care. A flicker of anger ignited inside of her, quickly growing as hot as the flames that had enveloped Jack moments before.

This wasn't right. It wasn't fair. Why should she have to suffer while everyone else celebrated?

"Come on, Sally! Let's go home," Dr. Finkelstein growled, beginning to wheel himself in the direction of his lab, still clutching her wrist in his hand.

Sally dug her heels into the dirt, resisting his pull. He scowled and yanked again, harder this time—so hard she could feel the stress on her threaded seams. She bit her lower lip, worried. If he kept pulling like this, he was going to pull her apart.

Which . . . might not be a bad thing?

Sally looked down at her arm, a shocking idea forming in her brain.

No. She couldn't.

"You're coming with me!" Dr. Finkelstein repeated angrily.

But then . . . why couldn't she? He was already furious. He was already planning to punish her for what she'd done. She could go back now and face that punishment.

Or . . . she could put off the inevitable just a little bit longer—and find a way to enjoy what was left of Halloween night.

Suddenly it felt like an easy decision.

Sally met his eyes with her own. "No, I'm not," she said in a steely voice. She reached down, pinching a thread in her arm and allowing it to unspool. A moment later her arm detached from her body with such force it sent Dr. Finkelstein flying forward, his wheelchair toppling to the ground.

He screamed in rage. "Come back here, you foolish—"

But Sally didn't stay to listen to the rest. She bolted in the other direction as fast as her stuffed legs could take her.

Elation rose inside of her as she ran, and suddenly she felt like laughing, even as fear threatened to choke her. What had she done? And how would Dr. Finkelstein make her pay for this act of defiance?

She shook the thoughts away. Who cared? At least for now. The deed was done and she'd deal with the conse- quences later. Right now, she was free. Completely free—on

Halloween night no less. Free to do whatever she wanted, just like everyone else.

The possibilities made her head spin. A giddiness rose inside of her.

This was going to be the best night ever!

She looked around the town, her heart pounding. Should she go door-to-door, trick-or-treating? Should she kick up her heels at the dance party forming in the town square? Maybe she could even go and congratulate Jack on a job well done like everyone else was doing. She'd never told him, after all, how much she admired his work.

But while all those options were tempting, she realized they could wait. She had the whole night, after all. And there was something important she still had to do. She'd used up all her deadly nightshade to put Dr. Finkelstein to sleep, which meant she needed to replenish her stash. Otherwise she'd be stuck in his lab from this point on, with no hope of future escape.

It'll just take a minute, she told herself. *Then I can come back and rejoin the party.*

Mind made up, she switched directions, heading toward the edge of town. She felt a spring in her step as she walked, as if her leaves were being whipped up by the gentle autumn breeze. But in her heart she knew it wasn't the wind that was making her feel so light.

It was the newfound sense of freedom.

If only it could always be like this, she mused, the thought making her a little sad. But then she shook it away. There would be time to lament her life later. Tonight she was free. And she needed to make the most of it.

She stepped under the archway and into the grave-yard, a contented sigh escaping her lips. She loved coming out here; it always felt so peaceful amongst the stones and weeds and feral cats that would wander between the graves hunting for field mice and spiders. Even though it was technically a place for the dead, being here always made Sally feel as if she were reborn.

She reached her favorite weed bed and knelt down to begin to gather her herbs, taking a moment to pet the scrawny black cat that wandered across her path and wishing it a happy Halloween. There were a lot of new nightshade plants, she noticed happily as she examined the patch. She should be able to gather enough to keep Dr. Finkelstein asleep for a very long time.

But just as she reached out to pluck her first plant, she heard a noise behind her. She leapt in surprise, her mind immediately going to the doctor. Had he followed her? Or sent his assistant, Igor, to collect her? Worried, she slipped behind a nearby gravestone to conceal herself just as a figure stepped into view under the light of the full moon.

Her eyes widened in surprise. Not Dr. Finkelstein at all.
But rather Jack Skellington himself.

Sally watched from the shadows, too shocked to move,
as the Pumpkin King entered the graveyard. What was he
doing out here? she wondered. And all alone, too, with none
of his regular gushing ghouls in tow. Usually Jack stayed
at the party till the break of dawn, dancing and celebrating
with his friends. How many times had she watched them,
enviously, from her bedroom window, wishing she could be
as happy and carefree as Jack?

He didn't look happy now, she realized as she watched
his usually confident steps begin to slow. His round head
began to droop. He didn't look free.

Maybe he's just tired, she told herself. *It has been quite a
night. And that fire stunt couldn't have been easy.*

But then . . . he didn't look tired, did he?

He looked sad.

Really sad.

Sally frowned. But why would Jack Skellington be
down—on Halloween night no less? The skeleton had everything he could possibly want! And the holiday had gone off
without the slightest hitch! He should be in his glory right
now, celebrating all his hard work.

Instead it looked as if he was about to cry.

She watched as Jack approached a small gravestone

etched with the word ZERO. He patted his leg with skeletal fingers, and to Sally's delight an adorable ghost dog emerged from the ground and floated up into the air, his translucent tongue hanging from his mouth. Jack tapped the dog playfully on his jack-o'-lantern nose, for a moment a hint of merriment back in his eyes. But it dissipated as fast as it came as he leaned his lanky body against a nearby gargoyle statue and sighed. Zero yipped loudly, circling the gargoyle, as if trying to cheer his master up. Jack only shook his head.

"Oh, Zero," he said. "You just don't understand."

His gaze seemed to go out into the graveyard, and Sally quickly ducked lower behind her stone, not wanting him to catch her watching. It was clear that Jack had come here to be alone, and she felt like an interloper, invading his space. There was no way Jack would want anyone to see him like this.

He was the Pumpkin King, after all. He had a reputation to uphold.

Of course, at that moment, he didn't look much like a celebrated holiday king. In fact, he looked more like a lost little boy. Something had clearly upset him tonight. But try as she might, Sally couldn't imagine what it could be.

Then, as if he'd heard her, he began to explain. His words tumbled from his mouth like a song. He was speaking to Zero, of course, but Sally couldn't help overhearing it all as she crouched behind the gravestone, unable to move without making her presence known.

You should have shown yourself while you had the chance, she thought ruefully. *Now it's too late. If he sees you now, he'll think you were eavesdropping.*

So she stayed as still as possible, listening to Jack's lament. About how frustrated he felt. How bored he was. How he longed for something more.

"I've done all that I wanted to do," he told the ghost dog, and Sally could hear the pain and wistfulness in his voice. "Why do I feel so empty inside?"

Why indeed? Sally felt an unexpected tug at her heart as he continued to pour his soul out to the little ghost dog. She never would have guessed, in a million years, that someone like Jack could feel as disconnected from his world as she did. She'd always assumed Jack's life was perfect, that he had everything he could have ever wanted.

But was that all an illusion? A show as unreal as the one he put on in the town square every Halloween? The real Jack, it seemed, was more than a flaming pumpkin head to be adored. The real Jack ached and hurt like she did. The real Jack longed for something more.

"Oh, Jack," she whispered, leaning longingly against the gravestone. "I know how you feel."

Suddenly there was a shift beneath her—the gravestone

crumbling under her added weight. She cried out in surprise, trying to move, but only managed to lose her balance in the process. She was flung from her hiding spot, tumbling forward into a wide-open space.

And when she managed to look up again?

She found herself staring straight into the eyes of Jack Skellington.

CHAPTER TWO

Hot and flushed under Jack's gaze, Sally scrambled to her feet. Why, oh why had she put weight on the gravestone? She knew as well as anyone how old and crumbly they could be. And now she'd been caught red-handed spying on Jack. How was she ever going to explain herself?

For a moment, she considered running away. Out of the graveyard, back to town. Maybe he hadn't recognized her. It was dark, after all. Maybe she could get away before he could.

"Sally?" His voice rose questioningly in the night air. "Is that you?"

She groaned. Or maybe not.

Swallowing hard, she forced herself to look up. To meet

his dark eyes again with her own. She expected to see anger. Or at the very least, annoyance. She wouldn't have blamed him for either. She would have been angry and annoyed herself had she been the one to be so rudely interrupted during a moment of such vulnerability.

But to her surprise, she could find no anger or annoyance in his expression. In fact, if anything, he looked almost relieved to see her. As if he was thankful for the sight of a familiar face shining through the fog of solitude that hung heavy in the dark graveyard.

And suddenly Sally couldn't help herself.

"Oh, Jack," she repeated. "I know exactly how you feel." And this time she said it loud enough for him to hear.

Jack's jaw dropped. He stared at her, his eyes seeming to search her face. Sally squirmed uneasily, wondering all over again if she'd made a mistake. He'd clearly come here to be alone, and she was invading his space. Butting her nose into his private affairs.

But then, she reminded herself, maybe that was exactly what he needed, whether he knew it or not. Someone to listen without judgment. Someone who would take his feelings seriously—and understand them. After all, how many times had she sat alone in her room, drowning in her sorrows, wishing she had someone to share them with?

Sally wasn't allowed to do much on Halloween. But she could do this.

Jack cleared his throat. She wondered if he was about to ask her to leave. Or tell her that he was leaving himself. Instead he slowly raised a skeletal hand, beckoning her to follow as he turned and crossed the graveyard, heading toward Spiral Hill.

Sally's shoulders slumped in relief. Okay then. All was well. Or if not, at least she had not been turned away outright. Drawing in a breath, she made her way through the stones, maybe a little too eagerly, as she followed Jack's path to the center of the graveyard, where he began to climb Spiral Hill.

Sally had always loved Spiral Hill, which looked just as its name implied: a small outcropping rising over the land and curling into a downward coil at the very top. It was a beautiful spot to sit. Quiet, peaceful, especially when backlit by a bright full moon. She would come here after gathering her herbs, whenever she could steal away from home, and sit as long as she dared, dreaming of a better world. A world where she could be free.

But she'd never dreamed of doing it with Jack by her side.

When they reached the top of the hill, Jack sat down, pulling his knees to his chest. Sally plopped herself down beside him, nervously tugging at the broken threads at her elbow with her remaining fingers. Jack frowned, observing her absent forearm for the first time.

"What happened?" he asked in a voice filled with concern.

Her face heated. "Oh, n-nothing," she stammered. "Just . . . a little accident. Dr. Finkelstein will give it back to me in the morning, I'm sure. He can restitch it, good as new."

Jack pressed his lips together, as if trying to swallow back words he knew he shouldn't say, and Sally squirmed again, feeling even more uncomfortable under his pitying gaze. Did he know how Dr. Finkelstein treated her? It embarrassed her to think that he might.

A sharp yip broke through the awkward silence. To Sally's surprise, Zero popped into view by her side. The ghost dog circled her once, then closed in, sniffing the spot where her arm had detached, his nose tickling her cloth. A moment later, he gave another cheerful bark, then zoomed off into the night.

Sally laughed. "What was that about?"

"I'm guessing he's gone to get your arm," Jack replied. "He's quite the retriever, you know. Once he's got the scent, he can find just about anything."

"Impressive," Sally remarked, glancing back toward

town just in time to catch a glimpse of orange light glowing from the dog's nose as he crossed under the archway. "Though I don't want him to get in any trouble on my account. Dr. Finkelstein isn't just going to give my arm back willingly to any ghost dog who shows up to fetch it."

"Don't underestimate Zero," Jack said with a twinkle in his eye. "He's not afraid of a little tug-of-war."

"If you say so," Sally replied. After wishing the ghost dog a silent good luck—he was going to need it—she turned back to Jack. "So . . ." she prompted with an expectant smile.

"So?"

"So what's wrong? Why are you out by yourself and not celebrating with the rest of them?"

"Ah. *That* so . . ." Jack looked bashful. "You sure you want to know? I warn you, it might ruin your good opinion of me."

Sally placed one hand on her hip, giving him a mock skeptical look. "Now what makes you think I have a good opinion of you, Jack Skellington?" she teased, unable to help herself.

Jack's head jerked in her direction. For a moment, he stared at her, speechless. Then, to her delight, he burst out laughing, so hard he almost lost his balance and fell off Spiral Hill.

"Well then!" he declared. "This changes everything. And I must say, I'm relieved to hear it. It's not easy, you know, having everyone think you're so wonderful all the time. In fact, I'd be literally dying for a critic—if I weren't already dead."

"It's a scary job, but someone's got to do it," Sally shot back, giving him a smirk, pleased to see the amusement dancing in his eyes, replacing his earlier sorrow. She couldn't believe she was being so bold. But then, whatever it took to lighten his mood.

"Now come on. Spill. What's troubling you tonight?" she pressed, growing serious again. "I promise whatever it is, I won't judge you. And I won't tell anyone, either. I'm good at keeping secrets. Mostly because I don't have anyone to tell them to," she added sheepishly. "But even if I did, I'd take yours to the grave, doll's honor."

Jack nodded slowly, his mirth fading. He turned to gaze up at the moon, watching a few bats fly by in a shadow play. For a long moment he didn't speak, and Sally worried he was going to get cold feet and make another joke, effectively pushing her away. But he turned back to her, a rueful look on his face.

"It's an odd feeling," he said softly. "And it comes on so slowly I don't always notice it at first. It doesn't come all the time, either. Just once in a while it will creep in, usually when I least expect it. Like when I'm lying in bed at night or maybe in the middle of a busy afternoon. I look around and everything is exactly as it should be. And yet, for some reason, I feel incredibly empty inside. As if something vitally important is missing from my life."

He scowled, squeezing his bony fingers into fists. "Which is ridiculous, I know! After all, I have everything I could ever want! My talents are legendary. I'm the scariest in the land. Not to mention charming and handsome." He grinned at Sally.

"You are the king of Halloween," she agreed. "Everyone always says no one can do it like you can."

"It's absolutely true!" he agreed wholeheartedly. Then he sighed. "And yet sometimes I just can't help wanting something more. Every year on Halloween it's the same old thing. Sure, sometimes we do variations. Sometimes I ride in on a unicorn. Sometimes we dye the fountain blue. This time I lit myself on fire. But despite these small touches, every year feels exactly the same. And, well, I honestly think I'm tired of it all." He yanked absently on his bow tie. "Sometimes I think I would give everything up just to go on some grand adventure. To try something completely new."

"Like what?" Sally asked, her curiosity piqued. An adventure sounded amazing. But then, just leaving her house constituted an adventure for her.

Jack frowned, kicking a small rock and sending it flying off the hill. Sally watched as it bounced off a gravestone, then fell to the earth with a small thunk.

"I honestly have no idea. That's the worst part of it. I mean, what else is there to do? Haven't I done everything there is to do already?"

"I don't know," Sally said honestly.

He groaned. "Sorry," he said. "I don't know why I'm telling you all this. It probably sounds so selfish. After all, I have a good life. I have acclaim, friends, respect. Why can't I be content with what I've been given? Why is it I keep longing for something more?" He fell silent, staring down at his feet in misery.

Sally gave him a sympathetic look, her heart squeezing at the unhappiness she recognized on his face. While she didn't understand everything he was going through, she did understand one thing: that frustrating feeling of wanting more out of life. That was a feeling she felt every day.

"I understand," she said. "I've felt similarly over the last few years. I get this horrible restlessness, even when I'm busy. Like something inside me is incomplete somehow. And all I want to do is go out, have adventures, play a part in Halloween. But Dr. Finkelstein thinks the world is dangerous and I'm just some silly rag doll and—"

"Just some silly rag doll?" Jack broke in, incredulous. "He really called you that?"

"Among other lovely terms of endearment," Sally joked bitterly, staring out into the night. "In truth, my whole life I've been treated as if I'm just some *thing* for him to control. Living for the whims of my maker, without any room for my own ideas, my own ambitions." She squeezed her remaining hand into a fist. "But I have so many dreams. So many things I would do if I was just given a chance."

Now it was Jack's turn to gaze on her with sorrowful eyes. "I'm sorry. I didn't realize. I just assumed you liked working in Dr. Finkelstein's lab. You seem good at it."

"I am good at it," she said. "But I think I could be good at other things, too."

"Oh, I'm sure of it," Jack agreed with a smile. "Why, I wager you could rival me for the title of Pumpkin Queen if they only knew what you could do!"

She snorted. "No thank you. I'm not ready to be that adored. Or to set myself on fire."

"Okay, the fire was probably a one-time thing. My bones are going to be aching for days." He shrugged impishly. "But you have to admit, it was a crowd-pleaser."

"It was indeed," Sally agreed. "Just maybe next time?

Think about what pleases you, not just them." She paused, then added softly. "Even the Pumpkin King has a right to be happy."

Jack nodded slowly, for a moment seeming lost in thought. Then he gave her a shy smile. "You know," he said thoughtfully. "We should talk more often, you and I."

Sally's breath caught in her throat as Jack met her eyes with his own. She'd never seen them so close up, she realized wildly. Or noticed how dark and deep they were. She felt a shiver down her back, not entirely unpleasant.

"I'd like that," she replied, her voice barely over a whisper. "I'd like that a lot."

They fell into silence. Not an awkward silence, like the kind that came when she was having dinner with Dr. Finkelstein and ran out of polite things to say, but rather something almost comforting. As if they were somehow sharing a precious moment beyond words, side by side, under the bright orange Halloween moon.

It was funny, Sally thought. If someone had told her yesterday she'd be out here on Halloween night, staring into the eyes of the Pumpkin King, she'd never have believed it. Up until now, they'd seemed worlds apart.

But she'd seen another side of Jack tonight. And for two people who were so very different, they were more alike than she could have ever imagined.

At last Jack reached his hands over his head, his mouth stretching into a wide yawn. Sally giggled. "Am I boring you?" she teased.

"On the contrary," he said, clamping his mouth shut with a sheepish grin. "You've been the most entertaining part of my night. But these long Halloween nights tire me out." He gestured in the direction of town. "Shall I walk you back home, Madame?"

She shook her head. "Thanks," she said. "But I think I'm going to stay out here a while longer. Who knows when I'll be able to get away next? Might as well enjoy my freedom while I have it."

Jack gave her a sorrowful look. "Would you like me to say something to him?" he asked. "I could, you know. Maybe he'd listen to me. I am the Pumpkin King, after all. That has to carry some weight."

Sally's leaves fluttered in her stomach at the kindness she heard in his voice. And a good part of her wished she really could send him in to fight her battles for her. But in the end, she knew it wouldn't work. Any attempted interference from the outside would only make Dr. Finkelstein tighten his grip on her, and cause her to lose any remaining chances of occasional freedom.

"I appreciate that," she assured him. "But it's my problem to deal with."

He nodded sadly. "The offer stands, should you change your mind."

"As does mine," Sally said. "If you ever need anyone to talk to, come find me. I may not be able to help. But I'll always be able to listen."

"Thank you, Sally," Jack said quietly. "That means a lot actually."

They looked at one another then. Just looked and looked as if, at that moment, there was nothing else in the world to look at beyond the other's face. And a strange feeling rose inside Sally, a warm fire deep inside that she'd never felt before.

Whatever happens to me afterward, this was worth it, she thought wildly. *Tonight was definitely worth it.*

At last Jack turned away with an awkward laugh. "Sorry," he said. "I was leaving, wasn't I?"

Sally grinned. "You did mention something about that."

"Of course I did! After all, I've got a lot to do," Jack said, back to his old bluster. "Next Halloween won't just plan itself, you know!"

And with that, he stood up and waved goodbye, then strode down Spiral Hill with a spring in his step. The kind reserved for someone as confident as him. To look at him now, you'd never know, Sally thought, that anything was

amiss. That Jack Skellington wasn't the most happy, confident, and content skeleton in all the land.

But now she knew differently.

Oh, Jack, she thought. *I wish there was some way to
make you happy. To make* both *of us happy* . . .

She sighed, staring out into the dark night. Maybe she
should go back to town as well. Maybe she could still catch
the tail end of the dance party in the town square. Or visit a
few houses for tricks and treats. Make the most of what she
had left of the night before she was forced to face reality at
the break of dawn.

Carefully, she began to descend Spiral Hill, back
toward the graveyard, trying to balance using her one arm.
But just as she got halfway down, her foot slipped on some
slimy moss, and she started falling forward. She yelped in
surprise, trying to catch herself, but it was no use. She was
falling.

And suddenly everything went black.

CHAPTER THREE

Sally was having a vision.

This wasn't unusual, in and of itself. Sally often had visions, usually when she least expected them. Like the one time she was sweeping up in the lab and suddenly had a premonition that the potion Dr. Finkelstein was mixing was about to explode. (Unfortunately, he didn't believe her until it actually did, burning off his eyebrows in the process.) Or the time she was picking flowers in the graveyard and one of them flashed, then burst into a loud dirge. And later that day, lightning struck the town square just as the zombie band took the stage. Thanks to Sally, the fire department was on hand to quickly douse the flames.

She didn't know where these visions came from or why

they would come. Perhaps it was a side effect of whatever process Dr. Finkelstein had used to bring her to life. Or maybe the old brain he'd stuffed in her head had been psychic when it belonged to its person. Or maybe it was just a rag doll thing; she had no other doll friends to compare to, so she couldn't be sure.

But while she didn't know *why* the visions came and she couldn't predict *when* they would come, she was sure of one thing.

They were usually trying to tell her something. Something important.

And she needed to pay attention.

She looked around, trying to discern her surroundings. She appeared to be lying in some sort of bed, her body cozily nestled under warm fuzzy red blankets. But she wasn't in a bedroom, she realized with surprise. She appeared to be outside, the bed surrounded by a grove of strangely triangular green trees. She was tossing and turning, too, feeling very restless—as if this vision version of herself was worried about something and couldn't sleep. Or maybe she was just excited—about something that was about to happen.

But what that could be, she had no idea.

Then something began to fall from the sky. Almost like rain, except it wasn't liquid but rather small white flakes fluttering down and landing on her blankets and face. She reached out, catching one of these flakes on her fingertip, and realized with surprise it was cold. Almost as if it was made out of ice.

How strange!

The vision shifted then and the white flakes seemed to dissolve, replaced by small round purple plums covered in ... sugar? But these plums weren't falling like the flakes had been. Rather they seemed to be dancing somehow. Slowly at first, then with added tempo. And soon Sally found herself watching what seemed like an entire ballet of these sugared plums, dancing around her head.

Sally smiled, enjoying the scene. One of the sugared plums tried to perform a rather elaborate pirouette. It spun out of control, landing on Sally's stomach. She scooped it up in her hand and held it out to look at it more closely. It immediately leapt out of her hand, shaking itself at Sally as if scolding her for her impudence, then floated off into the woods.

Curious, Sally slipped out of bed, placing her bare feet on the cold hard ground. She looked around, observing the trees and marveling how each seemed to be covered in soft green needles. Very different from the gnarled and bare-branched Halloween trees back home. The ice flakes began to fall again, dusting the trees and ground in a shimmering white. It was beautiful, Sally decided. Odd but definitely beautiful. And peaceful, too. *A wonderland,* something whispered in her mind.

Something different. Something new.

But just as the thought came to her mind, a darkness seemed to fall over the festive scene. The ice flakes stopped falling and the sugared plums stopped dancing, floating quickly into the distance as if something had frightened them off. Sally frowned, suddenly uneasy. What was going on here?

It was then that the dark shadow appeared—large and hulking, slipping between the trees. A sight actually less strange to Sally than the dancing sugared plums had been. After all, she was used to nightmares lurking everywhere; it was par for the course in Halloween Town. Yet there was something different about this particular creature, she decided, her cloth skin prickling with unease. An eerie sound it made each time it moved. As if each step was echoed by the ringing of a tiny tinkling bell.

Jingle.

Jingle.

Jingle.

And suddenly Sally was afraid. So very afraid. Though she had no idea why.

Jingle.

Jingle.

"Who's there?" she called out, trying to keep her voice steady. "What do you want?"

And then, just as quickly as it had come, the vision fell away. And Sally woke to find herself sprawled at the bottom of Spiral Hill, exactly where she had fallen.

Back to reality. Vision over.

Sally rose to her feet, blinking, still feeling a little creeped out. Which was usually a feeling she enjoyed, but something about the vision had left her cold and filled with dread. Brushing herself off, she looked around, trying to regain her bearings. She always felt a little faint after her visions. As if real life wasn't quite as real as it usually was, the dream world still so vivid in her mind.

Eventually the feeling passed, as it always did. And she found herself solidly back in the real world, standing in a dark graveyard on Halloween night. A very comforting place to be.

Still . . . memories of the vision lingered. What had it meant? Those strange ice flakes, those sugared plums dancing. Things she'd never seen before anywhere in Halloween Town. Where did they come from? Her mind flashed back to her and Jack's discussion. Their shared longing for something more.

Was her vision trying to show her this? To tell her there was something else out there, just waiting to be explored?

But then there was the other part of her vision. The menacing creature with the jingling bells. Was it meant to be a warning somehow? A symbol of the danger she would face if she attempted to chase the sugared plums?

She really wished, sometimes, her dreams weren't so open to interpretation.

Woof!

Sally startled at the sudden bark behind her. Lost in her troubled thoughts, she hadn't noticed Zero had finally returned to the graveyard. The ghost dog was wagging his tail proudly and carrying her arm in his mouth.

Sally grinned at the pup. "Good boy," she praised, petting him on the head as he dropped the arm by her feet. How he'd managed to steal it away from Dr. Finkelstein, she had no idea. She imagined the two of them playing tug-of-war over her arm and couldn't help a small chuckle. The doctor was going to be so mad. Served him right.

"*Very* good boy," she added, and Zero nuzzled her knee with his jack-o'-lantern nose.

Sitting down on a nearby gravestone, she carefully picked up her arm and set it in her lap. Then she reached into her pocket to retrieve the needle and thread she always carried with her for occasions like this. Carefully, she began to sew her arm back onto her body. It wasn't a perfect job by any means. It was awkward to sew with only one hand, and she dropped her needle twice into the dirt and had to search to retrieve it. Usually Dr. Finkelstein was the one to stitch her back up when she came apart at the seams.

But tonight she didn't want his help. She wanted to do it on her own, if only to prove that she could. That she didn't need him. That she did fine on her own. And if she decided to chase her sugared plums, well, she could do that, too. And no Dr. Finkelstein—or jingle bell jerk—was going to stop her.

She looked up from her stitching, staring out into the dark woods. "Do you think it's really out there, Zero? Another world, just waiting to be explored?"

Zero barked excitedly. He flew in a circle around her, then darted in close to lick her face. He spun, then flew over to the edge of the forest, where the Hinterlands began. When he reached it, he bobbed in the air, panting and looking at her with eager eyes.

Sally laughed, shaking her head. "I'm sorry," she said. "I don't have a bone to throw you right now." She finished her arm, biting down on the thread to break it in two before tying up the end. It didn't look great, she decided as she flexed her elbow to test it, but it was functional, which was all that mattered at the moment.

Zero zoomed back to her, summersaulting in the air and barking loudly. She reached out to pet him, but he dodged away, once again flying over to the forest's edge and giving her another expectant look.

"You don't give up, do you?" Sally asked, raising an eyebrow.

The ghost dog bobbed his head up and down. Sally giggled. "Okay," she relented. "I suppose you deserve a little fun." After all, she had no idea the trials and tribulations the canine had faced dealing with Dr. Finkelstein. It was the least she could do to thank him.

"Just for a minute," she added as she rose to her feet. Zero's nose glowed brightly in the darkness, and he gave a yip of excitement. As she ran toward him, he hovered at the forest's edge, as if waiting for her to catch up. But just as she was about to grab him, he darted away again, this time flying into the forest itself.

Sally stopped at the edge of the graveyard, her smile fading. "Zero?" she called out. "You're going too far. Let's just stick to the graveyard, okay?"

But Zero didn't answer. And he didn't return. Frowning, Sally peered into the woods. In the distance she could see a small orange glow, bobbing like an apple in water. She bit her lower lip worriedly.

"Come on, Zero!" she called. "It's dark in there. And I don't have your nose to light my way!"

The ghost dog yipped. But he didn't come back.

Sally shifted from foot to foot, not sure what to do. Should she just walk away? Leave him out there and assume he'd come back once he realized the game was over? But what if he got lost out there in the woods? Or something decided to make him into a ghostly snack? She'd heard too many tales of creatures lurking in the Hinterlands. And not the friendly kind, either, who enjoyed silly pranks on Halloween. If Zero ran into one of those, he wouldn't stand a chance.

But then again, would she?

Dr. Finkelstein's words seemed to ring in her ears. *You're not ready for so much excitement.*

Sally scowled. "I am," she muttered to herself, making up her mind. "And I'll prove it." She drew in a breath. "Hang on, Zero! I'm coming."

The first thing she noticed as she stepped into the forest was how dark it was; the moon always hung so bright over Halloween Town, they were never completely without light, even in the middle of the night. But here the gnarled tree branches formed a thick canopy above, blocking out almost all of the moon's glow and leaving the place in near blackness.

Delightfully creepy, she thought, *if difficult to see.*

She pushed onward, keeping an eye on the ground as she walked, not wanting to trip over an unseen rock or upturned root or snag her dress on thorns. Ahead, she could just make out the soft glow of Zero's nose and used it as a beacon to guide her way.

How deep does this forest go, anyway? she couldn't help wondering as she continued down the path. It was a thought that had never occurred to her before. She'd always been so desperate to be part of Halloween Town itself, she'd never given much consideration to what might lie beyond.

Something different. Something new.

She pushed forward, her steps lighter and more eager as she walked, a newfound curiosity bubbling inside her. Every rock and root felt like an adventure. Something that had never been seen before, never been appreciated for its own little miracle. Soon she found herself stepping into a large clearing encircled by a ring of strange-looking trees. It was brighter here, she realized, though she wasn't sure what was responsible for the added illumination.

She turned in a circle, taking in her new surroundings. Particularly the ring of trees, which were the strangest trees she'd ever seen. Each one had a small door cut into its trunk, shaped and painted in a particular design. A red heart, a fat bird, a painted egg, a four-leafed plant, a rectangular door with stars. Even one that reminded her of home—a big orange jack-o'-lantern, just like the one Jack would wear on his head on Halloween night.

It was the very last door that made her pause; it was shaped like a tree. But not just any tree, she realized in awe: a triangular tree with green needles, just like the one she'd seen in her vision. The tree was decorated, too, with shiny, colorful balls and tiny toys and cookies shaped like little men. And at its top was a golden star that seemed to shine brilliantly out into the dark night.

It was strange. But also beautiful. And Sally found she couldn't take her eyes off it. She ran a finger along the tree's edges, taking in the brilliant reds and greens and golds that seemed to reflect in her eyes like rare jewels sparkling.

Like sugared plums dancing.

What did it mean? she wondered. How could a tree from her dreams have suddenly appeared in real life?

Her finger stopped as it met a doorknob. And before she even realized what she was doing, she found herself wrapping her hand around it. *It'll most likely be locked,* she told herself, gearing up for potential disappointment. But it turned easily in her hand and the door swung wide open, uncovering a dark hole cut into the trunk of the tree.

And . . . something sweet?

Her nose twitched. What was that delicious smell? Was it coming from inside the tree? As a resident of Halloween Town, a place that celebrated frog's breath and worm's wort, she'd never smelled anything like it. Sweet, but with a touch of spice, too. She could almost taste it on her tongue.

Sally breathed it in, leaning forward to get a better whiff. But as her weight shifted, she lost her balance and started to tumble forward. Her hand shot out, grabbing the trunk of the tree just in time, preventing her from falling through. As she staggered backward, her leaves swirled in her stomach and suddenly she felt on edge again.

What was she doing here? All alone in the middle of the vast Hinterlands? Opening strange doors, smelling strange scents? No one even knew where she was. If something happened to her, no one would know where to look.

I've barely figured out what it means to be on my own in Halloween Town, she thought ruefully. *Let alone somewhere entirely new. I need to be smart about this. I need to prove I can make good decisions—keep myself safe.*

She reached out to close the door—

Woof!

Zero suddenly zoomed back into view, spinning around her madly. Sally's heart leapt in her chest.

"You scared me!" she scolded, leaning over to catch her breath. Then she wagged her finger at the naughty dog. "Now come on! Enough playing around. It's time to go!"

She reached out, trying to grab him. But Zero grinned

at her, dodging her easily, then floated over to the open tree door. Sally gasped in dismay as she watched him peer down into the darkness beyond, sniffing madly, his face alight with worrisome curiosity.

"Come on, Zero," Sally said. "Get away from that door."

For a moment, Zero appeared to obey. He pulled away from the door, heading back toward Sally. But just as she was almost close enough to grab him, something moved at the door, causing his attention to snap back.

Sally watched in shock as a fuzzy brown face poked out of the opening. It was some kind of animal—with strange-looking antlers on the top of its head.

What in the name of Halloween Town?

Zero's eyes lit up. He barked excitedly.

"Leave it, Zero!" Sally cried, alarmed. "You don't know what it—"

But Zero wasn't listening. He was too busy making a beeline for the door. The creature startled and quickly retreated, disappearing from view, but the ghost dog didn't seem deterred. Sally tried to leap into his path to stop him but only managed to trip over a root, which sent her flying through the air, straight toward the tree.

Through the doorway. Into the darkness.

With no idea of what she'd find on the other side.

CHAPTER FOUR

The first thing Sally noticed when she came to was how cold she was. And not the kind of vague coolness she was familiar with back home, the crisp air that arrived when an autumn storm swept in and whipped up the Halloween Town winds. This cold was different: a deep, full, body-aching cold. So cold it almost hurt. In fact, if she'd had bones, she was positive she would have felt this cold right down to them.

Opening her eyes, she blinked rapidly, trying to make sense of her surroundings. The last thing she remembered was tumbling headfirst into the strange tree's doorway after trying to grab Zero. She must have blacked out in her fall; she didn't remember landing. But here she was, lying in a deep pile of cold white powder—the dog nowhere to be seen.

She wasn't hurt, of course. That was one of the biggest advantages of being stuffed with leaves. An advantage that had come in handy over the years when she'd wanted to sneak out of her bedroom late at night to pick herbs in the graveyard. Dr. Finkelstein's lab sat far above the ground. But for Sally, it was a simple leap to freedom. No big deal.

The question was, where had she leapt to now? She rose to her feet, brushing off the white powder, which seemed to cling to her clothes and cloth skin. This was definitely what was making her cold, she decided.

It was then that she remembered the soft crystal flakes from her vision. They had been made of similar stuff. But while there had been only a few of those, flittering in the air, here they'd amassed into great piles, covering the ground completely in white stuff. It was actually rather pretty, she decided. It was too bad it was so cold. Curious, she put a finger to her mouth, tasting one of the flakes. It melted immediately on her tongue, confirming her theory that it was made of ice.

Trying to focus, she looked around, hoping to gain her bearings. She'd fallen into a tree, but she was definitely not inside one now. It appeared she was standing in another vast forest, just as she had been before she fell. Except here, the trees weren't twisted and barren and dead-looking. Instead they resembled the trees from her vision. The one on the door. Tall pointy triangle trees with long green needles poking out from their branches. The white stuff had settled on a few of them, giving them a frosty glow.

Worry gnawed in Sally's gut. She tried to tell herself she was just having another vision, but somehow she knew that wasn't the case. Wherever she was, it was real. And she had no idea how she was meant to find her way home.

Or find Zero, for that matter. She called out his name a few times but received no answer. Had he gone chasing the strange horned animal? And if so, where had they gone?

Then she caught a glimpse of something just a few feet away. Her eyes widened as they settled on a very familiar-looking clearing. Another ring of painted trees with little doors, just like the one in the Hinterlands grove. She ran over to it, finding the jack-o'-lantern one immediately, then pulled it open and peered inside. Her nose caught a whiff of something dead and she sighed in relief.

The door back home. It was right here. Ready and waiting for whenever she wanted to go back. That was something, at least.

She frowned, looking at the door, tapping her fingers on her chin. In all honesty, she should probably head back immediately. Go through the door, back to the safety of Halloween Town, and report to Jack what had happened to his dog. After all, she had no idea what she had walked into. It could be dangerous here. And she was alone.

Then again . . .

Her eyes lifted from the door, almost involuntarily. She looked out over the white-dusted forest, surprised as a strange sense of longing seemed to float up from her stomach and into her throat. She could go home now, yes. But if she did, what if that was it? What if she never found her way back here to this strange new land again?

She pictured herself walking home. Entering the lab, finding Dr. Finkelstein waiting for her. He'd definitely punish her for her disobedience. She might be locked in her room for a week. Or never let out of his sight again. Her first adventure over before it had ever truly begun.

She scowled. Was that what she wanted? To give up and return to her bleak reality? To go back to being the Sally Dr. Finkelstein believed her to be?

Or would she rather take this rare opportunity to be the Sally she knew she could be, if just given a chance.

Her heart began to thud faster. She squared her shoulders. Lifted her chin. Steeled her inner determination. *You've sat around your whole life waiting for something like this,* she told herself. *Now it's in your grasp. No way are you just going home.*

Also, she rationalized, she had to think of Zero. By the

time she got back and reported him missing and they sent out a search party, it might be too late. Who knew the dangers a ghost dog might face in this strange new world. She couldn't just abandon him here.

Mind made up, she stepped away from the Halloween tree, shutting the door firmly. It wasn't going anywhere, she reasoned. It had probably stood there for years. And it would still be there when she was ready to go home.

Sally headed out of the clearing, away from the circle of painted trees, scared but also strangely excited. As she walked, she called Zero's name once more but got no reply. Daylight was coming. She could tell by the way the sky was brightening above her, and she began to wonder if the ghost dog—who was definitely a creature of the night—would find some quiet little grave to curl up in and fall asleep. Not to reappear until dark fell again.

However, while Zero's nose remained absent from her view, another strange glow began to appear in the distance. Curious, she followed the light and soon came across more of the green triangle trees decked out just as the one on the door had been, in reds and greens and blues and purples.

At first she assumed these trees must grow this way. Like the glowing jack-o'-lanterns that sprouted from the pumpkin patches back home. But as she neared, she realized the lights weren't growing out of the tree trunks at all.

They were attached to thin ropes that had been draped over the trees' branches from top to trunk. In addition to lights, the trees also boasted little toys and shiny metal baubles, each seemingly hung with great care.

Why, they must be decorations, Sally decided. *Just like we decorate for Halloween back home.*

She felt a little bad for those who had gone to all the trouble. All this work and none of it had turned out to be particularly scary. Perhaps they were just learning, she thought. Perhaps they had been decorated by children who hadn't been taught yet how to properly string a spiderweb.

That said, she had to admit, as she took a closer look, that even though not a single tree sent the tiniest shiver down her back, they were quite lovely to look at all the same. Maybe they were meant to be this way, she considered. Designed to be admired, not feared. It was an odd thought, but a surprisingly comforting one, and she found herself staying longer than she meant to, examining each and every one in turn, appreciating how pretty they all were.

Until she heard a small yip coming from just beyond the grove.

"Zero?" she called out hopefully. "Is that you?"

She left the grove, following the sound of the bark. Soon the forest fell away, and she found herself at the top of a giant hill covered in the same white stuff she'd seen earlier.

Here, however, the drifts were a lot deeper, and she had to wade through them—which wasn't easy when your legs were made of cloth. When she finally arrived at the edge of the hill, she looked down, her jaw dropping as her eyes fell on the valley below. Or, more important, what was nestled in that valley.

"A town!" she exclaimed in surprise and delight. "It's a little town! Just like Halloween Town. Except . . ." She frowned, furrowing her brow. "Actually it's quite different."

While Halloween Town was consistently dark and dismal, and thus appropriately creepy, this town was bright and shiny and emanating a cheery glow. The houses were different, too: short and squat as if they were made for children, not grown monsters, with perky little chimneys popping up from roofs covered in white stuff.

Circling the town was a train track, and even from her perch high above, Sally could hear a sprightly *choo choo* as a small train exited a tunnel cut into the hillside, gaily circling the town until it stopped in front of a large building halfway up the hill. Sally could tell whatever was going on in that building was important—with smoke puffing out from multiple chimneys and people darting to and fro.

People and . . . flying animals? Sally's eyes lit up as she recognized what looked like an entire group of antlered creatures, just like the one that had popped its head out of the tree. They were in formation, flying around the building, even though not one of them had any wings. Very curious indeed!

She wondered what she should do next. Should she go check out the building or maybe the town? Would the residents be friendly? Would she be able to find Zero?

She grinned, loving the new freedom she'd found in getting to make decisions like these herself. If she wanted to check out the town, she could do just that. No one could stop her.

And so, mind made up, she began to carefully make her way down the hill, wondering if Zero had floated down already and was waiting for her at the bottom. Sadly, unlike Zero, she was stuck using her own two feet, which proved to be quite difficult when navigating the slick icy surface. In fact, it didn't take more than a few steps to lose her footing entirely, sending her hurtling down the hill on her bottom at alarming speed.

She screamed, the white stuff spraying in her face, blinding her as she slid faster and faster. She tried to grab on to a nearby rock or root while desperately attempting to dig her heels into the ground. But it did no good. As she barreled down the hill, the bumps sent her flying into the air, then gravity dropped her back to the ground. And suddenly, she was surprised to realize, she was enjoying the ride. It was out of control, thrilling, and quite a lot of fun.

Eventually the hill ended, and she rolled to a clumsy stop. She scrambled up, brushing herself off. She was soaking wet and freezing cold and absolutely delighted by it all. And bonus: she now found herself exactly where she'd wanted to be. On the outskirts of this strange little town.

Up close, the town was even brighter than it had appeared from the top of the hill, with almost every available surface covered in colorful strings of light. There were leafy green circles, too, hung on many of the doors, decorated with bright red bows. And while the roofs were heavily covered in white powder, the streets had been cleared, making them easier to walk down.

Excited and more than a little nervous, she headed into the town, her eyes darting all around, unable to focus on one thing before discovering another. The streets were lined with little shops with big glass windows, much like the streets back home. But instead of slugs and spiders and other scary wares, these shops displayed sugary-looking treats and stuffed teddy bears in their windows, as well as big packages tied up in elaborate bows. Sally paused in front of one such shop, observing its biggest box and waiting for the requisite monster to pop out of it—a spectacle she'd always enjoyed back home. Unfortunately, the package remained completely motionless and apparently monster-free. Perhaps it was malfunctioning.

"Good morning, dearie."

Sally whirled around at the sudden sound of the voice. There, standing before her, was the strangest woman she'd ever seen. For one thing, she was wearing the brightest crimson jumpsuit with forest-green buttons. She was very short, with snow-white hair piled in a bun on the top of her head, and her pale skin crinkled around her eyes when she smiled. Her cheeks were so round and rosy they reminded Sally of two ripe apples, and even her ears were strange— the tops pointed instead of round.

The woman raised her arm and Sally instinctively ducked, assuming she was about to throw a prank at her, a stink bomb perhaps or a fistful of spiders, as so often happened by way of greeting at home. But the woman only waved her hand from side to side, then dropped it again.

Sally raised her own hand awkwardly, trying to mimic the woman. "Good . . . morning," she said, hoping she was doing it right.

The woman smiled, then peered at her curiously. "Aren't you cold, dear?" she asked, looking worriedly at Sally's thin patchwork dress. She clucked her tongue. "Imagine walking about with no coat in all this snow." She gestured to the white stuff on the ground and Sally filed the word away in her head for later. *Snow. The white stuff is called* snow.

She realized the woman was looking at her expectantly. She shrugged. "I didn't bring a coat," she confessed. "I didn't . . . know about the snow."

"Oh, you poor thing. Hold on. I'll see what I can do." Before Sally could protest, the woman ran inside a nearby cottage. She emerged a moment later with a red woolen cape trimmed in white fur. She draped it over Sally's shoulders and fastened it at her neck by tying two strings into a little green bow.

"How's that?" she asked. "Better?"

"So much better," Sally agreed, feeling warmer already. "Thank you so much. That was very nice of you."

The woman practically beamed. "You are so welcome, dear girl," she said. Then she bobbed her head. "Merry Christmas," she added, turning and popping into the shop Sally had been observing a moment before.

Curious, Sally peered back through the window and watched the shopkeeper greet the woman, then reach to grab the large box in the display window and take it over to the counter, presumably to ring it up for sale. Sally wondered if she should warn the lady that the box might be defective, but then thought better of it. Maybe this woman preferred her boxes monster-free. Maybe that was even a selling point here! Everything was so upside down in this place, Sally had no idea what to think.

She shrugged, continuing down the street, feeling much warmer in her new cloak. She also fit in a lot better now, and as she passed other people similar to the woman who had given her the cloak—short with pointed ears and rosy cheeks—they threw cheerful greetings in her direction, as if she were one of them.

"Hello! Good day! Lovely weather, isn't it?"

"Merry Christmas!"

Sally found herself saying it back—"Merry Christmas also!"—even though she had no idea what they meant by it. Still, it seemed to please them when she said it, and they would smile at her and sometimes even offer her a sweet. One man gave her a small orange. A baby in a stroller handed her a piece of candy.

Maybe "merry Christmas" is the same as "trick or treat," she decided as she stuck the candy in her mouth and sucked on it. Though oddly no one here seemed to be playing any tricks. In fact, she'd never seen a place where everyone appeared so nice.

She continued walking along the path, calling out for Zero as she went. The town seemed to be full of oddities. Like the garden of strange snow statues, carved to look like little round men with jaunty black hats and carrots for their noses. And the leafy green bouquets with white berries tied up in bows hanging over archways all around town, often with two people smooching beneath them, as if the leaves were sprinkled with some kind of love potion. And then there was the large rotating contraption of wooden animals spinning round and round as jaunty music played from a hidden speaker. Even stranger, several children were riding on these animals, squealing in delight as they spun.

Looks like fun, Sally couldn't help thinking. She was tempted to go and see if she could try it herself. But then her eyes caught something even better beyond. Something that looked like a small swamp, but it was frozen over with ice. And instead of swimming in it like they did in the swamps back home, people were gliding on top of it, wearing some kind of special shoes that seemed to have blades on their soles. Some were laughing; others were barely standing upright. But they all looked as if they were having the time of their lives.

That's what I want to try, Sally decided. She took a step toward the pond.

"Oomph!"

Sally startled as she rammed into something solid. She had been so mesmerized by the frozen swamp, she hadn't been looking where she was going. She cried out as she lost her balance, tumbling to the ground in a pile of limbs. When she looked up again, she realized she'd walked right into an older man who had been carrying an armful of wrapped packages. Packages that had gone flying on impact and were now scattered all over the ground.

"Oh, I'm so sorry!" she cried. She scrambled to her feet and began trying to retrieve the man's packages.

"Bah! Think nothing of it!" the man replied cheerfully, though he was rubbing his knee as if it hurt. "These things happen! It'll all be fine."

"But your packages! Your knee!" Sally exclaimed in dismay. Some of the packages had landed in puddles and looked a bit soggy. "Is there something I can do?"

The man's hand jerked away from his knee, a strange expression washing over his face. In fact, if Sally didn't know better, she'd say he looked afraid. But afraid of what? That didn't make any sense.

"Are you sure you're okay?" she asked.

"Yes!" he blurted out, starting to sound angry. "I'm fine! Everything is fine. It's all *very* fine."

Sally felt a prickling unease at the back of her neck. Then she caught the man's look. He was glancing behind her, and his face had turned very pale. Slowly, Sally turned around to see what had frightened him. Her eyes widened as she caught a dark shadow lurking between two brightly painted houses. A tall man-shaped shadow. And it was holding something that looked like a cane with tiny bells on the top of it.

Jingle, jingle.

Jingle, jingle.

Sally's mind flashed back to her vision. She swallowed hard, her heart pounding. "Who is that?" she whispered.

The man grabbed her by the arm with a force that startled her. Pulling her around to face him, he looked up at her with wide, pleading brown eyes.

"Everything's *fine*," he repeated, emphasizing the word as if it was a secret code. "Just *fine*."

"Oh-oh-kay," Sally stammered. "You're . . . right. It's fine. It's all fine."

The man's shoulders seemed to droop in relief. He let go of Sally and scooped up his packages from the ground. Then he smiled up at her, though the smile didn't quite reach his eyes.

"Merry Christmas!" he said, before practically running down the street in the other direction.

Sally watched him retreat, utterly confused. She turned back to the spot between the houses where she'd seen the shadow. But this time, there was nothing there. Just two cozy cottages decorated in festive lights.

Everything's fine, she repeated to herself. Though somehow, for the first time since she'd arrived in this strange new land, she wasn't entirely sure that was the case.

She turned reluctantly away from the frozen swamp, deciding it might not be a good idea to try her hand at this gliding—in case she rammed into someone else and caused another scene. In fact, maybe she had already overstayed her welcome in this weird new place. Maybe it was time for this adventure to end. If only she could find Zero. . . .

She looked around for the ghost dog again, this time without much optimism. Just as she was about to give up on this area and start walking again, something caught her eye in a store window across the road. Something familiar. Something *purple.*

Were those . . . sugared plums?

CHAPTER FIVE

Sally ran over to the window, pressing her face against the glass and peering inside. Sure enough, the case was filled with all sorts of sweets. Canes made of red-and-white-striped candy, chocolates shaped like teardrops, marshmallows shaped like trees. But Sally only had eyes for one treat on display.

The tiny sugared plums.

They weren't exactly the same as those she'd seen in her vision. Those had been bigger and, of course, much more lively, dancing around like they had. But the resemblance between those and what sat in the glass case was too close to be a coincidence.

Was this a sign? But what did it mean?

Excited, she headed into the candy shop. She found a man with a salt-and-pepper beard, a big belly, and an even bigger smile standing behind the counter. He was wearing the ugliest sweater Sally had ever seen, and since she was from Halloween Town, that was saying something.

"Good morning," the man greeted, laying his hands on the counter. "I don't think I've seen you around these parts before. I'm quite sure I would have remembered such a . . . unique . . . doll."

Sally smiled at him, assuming he'd meant it as a compliment. "I'm just here on a visit," she replied, hoping he wasn't expecting a more detailed explanation for her presence.

"How lovely!" the man pronounced. "And what a wonderful time of year it is for visiting, too! What, with everyone so busy getting ready for the big event." His eyes twinkled. "Less than two months left, you know."

Sally cocked her head questioningly. "Two months?" she repeated. "Until what?"

The man's brow crinkled, as if he was surprised by the question. "Why, until Christmas Eve, of course!" He pointed to a calendar behind him that was currently displaying the month of November. The month after Halloween. He reached out and lifted the page, revealing December, then pointed to a circled date. *December 24,* Sally read. *Christmas Eve.*

She pursed her lips, thinking hard. Remembering all the pointy-eared people outside who had wished her a merry Christmas. Maybe it was more like saying "Happy Halloween."

Maybe Christmas was another holiday entirely.

Sally had never considered this before, but now that she thought about it, it made perfect sense. Why should Halloween be the only holiday in the world? Her mind flashed back to the circle of trees, each with its own symbol painted on the door. What if each one of them led to a different holiday town? A bird holiday, an egg holiday. Her head was practically spinning with the implications.

She realized the man was looking at her curiously.

"Oh, right! Of course!" she said with a laugh, trying to sound as if she knew all about this new holiday all along, so as not to arouse any suspicion. "It just . . . always sneaks up on me. Every year I ask, 'Christmas already?' And I'm never quite prepared."

"Believe me, I understand!" the man declared, shaking his head knowingly. "It seems to come quicker and quicker each year. Why, I haven't even finished filling my candy cane molds yet!" He stopped, then frowned. "But don't tell Santa I said that," he added, chuckling a little nervously.

"I won't," Sally agreed, mostly because she had no idea who he was talking about. But she did understand the idea of being behind schedule. It was something those back home complained about constantly in the days leading up to Halloween. Of course, somehow every Halloween it all came together. She hoped the same would happen here. He seemed like a nice man, after all.

The shopkeeper patted the top of the glass case in front of him, which was filled with interesting-looking treats. None of them, Sally noted, seemed to be made from scorpions, a particular candy delicacy back home. "Anyhow, how can I help you?" he asked. "Do you see something in here that catches your eye?"

Sally scanned the goodies in the case, pretty sure she'd be game to try them all. But then she remembered the reason she'd entered the shop in the first place and turned back to the case in the window.

"The sugared plums," she said, pointing to the purple candies inside, hoping she was calling them by their proper name.

"Ah! A classic choice!" the man exclaimed. "I'm glad to hear it. I don't get many people coming in and asking for those anymore. Why, my wife keeps saying I should stop making them altogether." He sighed as if pained by the idea. "Call me old-fashioned," he said, shaking his head. "But to me it isn't really Christmas without visions of sugarplums dancing through your head."

Sally startled. "What did you just say?" she asked, her voice a little hoarse. Visions, sugarplums, dancing! How did he know?

"Oh. It's from a famous Christmas poem," the man explained. "Surely you've heard of it." He peered at her strangely. "Where did you say you were from again?"

Sally swallowed hard. "Of course I've heard of it!" she assured the man. "It's my favorite poem. Which is why I love sugarplums. Can I get some, please?"

The man smiled, seeming appeased. He walked around the counter and pulled the tray from the window. "They're five coins a dozen," he said. "How many would you like?"

It was then that Sally realized she didn't have any money. Dr. Finkelstein never allowed her to carry her own, reminding her that *he* provided for her and therefore she should have no use for it. "Food, shelter—what else could a doll like you possibly want?" he'd jeer.

Well, besides some sugarplums, that was.

She began to back out of the store, her face heating. "A-actually, I think I'm all right," she stammered. "Sorry to waste your time. . . ."

The shopkeeper held out a hand. "Wait," he said. He reached up onto a shelf for a small white paper sack and began scooping sugarplums into it. "I don't let anyone leave my shop empty-handed! After all, that wouldn't be very *nice.*" He gave her a knowing look. "Besides, you seem like a lovely doll. And you appreciate classic holiday fare, which is more than I can say for most of the young toys around here." He pushed the bag into her hands. "Consider this a free sample."

Sally stared down at the bag. "Oh, no!" She shook her head. "I couldn't."

"You already have," the shopkeeper said, giving her a wink. Then he waggled his finger. "Besides, it's a gift. And it's not very *nice*, you know, to refuse a gift."

Sally nodded slowly, a little confused. The way he kept emphasizing the word *nice* was almost like the way the man outside had said *fine.* As if there was some secret meaning she didn't understand.

But she did want the sugarplums. So she shot the shopkeeper a grateful smile.

"Thank you," she said. "That's very . . . nice . . . of you."

The shopkeeper beamed. "Happy to do it!" he declared. "I hope you enjoy them. And I hope you have a lovely time in Christmas Town."

Christmas Town, Sally repeated to herself, realizing her hunch had been right.

Another holiday village. How fascinating!

She thanked the man and headed back out to the street,

the candies still clutched tightly in her hands. She walked over to a small bench and sat down, then opened the bag, reaching in to pluck a sugarplum from the pile and bring it to her lips.

"Mmm," she said in pleasure as her mouth practically exploded with sweetness. It was even better than she had imagined and nothing like anything she'd ever tasted in Halloween Town. She quickly chewed and swallowed, then reached for another.

Christmas Town was pretty delightful, she decided.

She looked around, taking it all in. She was near the center of town and could see another one of those overly decorated triangle trees. This one, however, was far bigger than the ones she'd seen in the forest and was ornamented even more elaborately, with hundreds of sparkling lights and shiny baubles. On its top sat a giant golden star that shone so bright it practically upstaged the sun.

Sally thought back to her own town's centerpiece. The slimy, goop-filled fountain that housed their resident Undersea Gal. She chuckled to herself. Definitely a different ambiance here in Christmas Town.

For a moment she watched the activity building in the town square. They seemed to be setting up some kind of stage. Perhaps there would be a show later? Sally wondered if she should stay to see it. She was pretty sure it'd be very different from any performance they put on in Halloween Town. The band might not even be made up of zombies.

Then she noticed the crowd gathering to the side of the stage, and her eyes widened in surprise.

Were those all . . . toys?

Sally rose to her feet, stepping toward the town square to take a closer look. Sure enough, the group appeared to consist of several life-size toys, though none of them were particularly scary, like the toys they had back home. There was a fluffy brown bear with jointed limbs and a clockwork bird, chirping merrily. Beside the bird stood a silly-looking clown and a fancy-looking robot and . . .

Dolls.

So many dolls!

Sally's jaw dropped as her eyes fell on the group of identically dressed girls, all standing in a circle, talking and giggling. They were unlike any she'd ever seen before and certainly very different from herself. Each one was practically its own work of art, with smooth skin of varying shades and long hair tumbling down their backs in waves or complicated braids. Their eyes shone like multicolored jewels, and their mouths were all perfectly bow-shaped and ruby red. Even their noses were impressive. Small and cute, several dusted with freckles.

And then there were their dresses. Fancy cotton confections of candy-colored frills and bows, with puffed sleeves and ribbon sashes. Sally had never seen such dresses before, and for a moment, she felt a little inadequate when she gazed down at her own homemade ensemble, rather plain in comparison.

But then, she'd made this dress herself, she thought. And who was to say she couldn't make one of theirs, too, if she just gave it a try? In fact, if she could find the right material, she was almost positive she could re-create one of these ensembles back in Halloween Town, adding her own special Sally touches, of course. For example, their sashes were practically screaming to be replaced by proper spiderwebs. And a few slashes with a serrated knife would give the puffed sleeves a lovely shredded flair. Her mouth curled as she imagined herself walking past the fountain in her hometown square, sashaying in a swish of silk and spiders. Halloween Town wouldn't know what hit them!

And what if, her mind whirred, others wanted a dress like this, too? She could take orders. Charge money. Maybe even eventually open her own shop. Support herself so she would no longer be reliant on Dr. Finkelstein.

She gasped at the idea. This could change everything!

Feeling almost giddy, she studied the dolls' dresses, taking the time to memorize every detail while happily munching on her sugarplums. Christmas Town was truly amazing, she decided. Even if it was very different from home. And while she'd always be a fan of the grim and gruesome, she saw now that fun and festive was actually pretty great, too. She was very glad she hadn't chickened out and gone home before seeing this place for herself. Perhaps she even owed Zero a thank-you for forcing her hand.

She wondered, for a moment, if this had been the pup's plan all along.

Then her mind flashed back to Jack in the graveyard. Sitting glumly on Spiral Hill. The desperate look in his dark eyes. The longing in his deep voice. His confession of feeling empty and bored and how he yearned for an adventure. And now here she was, having the most marvelous adventure of them all. If only he could have been here to share it with her.

But then, she thought, maybe it wasn't too late!

Her leaves began to swirl inside her as an idea formed in her mind. Why hadn't she thought of this before? She could return to Halloween Town and tell Jack all about what she'd found. How marvelous it all was. How different! How new! She imagined his eyes lighting up in excitement as she described the boxes with ribbons, the wildly colored candy, the frozen swamp that people glided on top of. Maybe he'd even want to glide with her!

Sally beamed. It'd be another adventure. And they could have it together.

SLAM!

Sally cried out as something hard and cold struck her cheek, jerking her back to the present. She whirled around to find a trio of children about the same height scooping up handfuls of snow and molding it into little balls, then lobbing them at one another, laughing as they did it. Sally raised a hand to her cheek, realizing she must have accidentally been struck.

The trio caught her watching them. One of the boys laughed and pointed and stuck out his tongue. *Okay, maybe not accidentally.*

"You naughty child," she teased. The kids were cute and they reminded her of Lock, Shock, and Barrel back home, though *they* were more likely to be throwing slugs than snow. She grinned at the boys mischievously. "Two can play that game, you know," she told them, leaning down to scoop up her own missile.

But before she could aim and throw, a shadow crossed over the street. She looked up, surprised to see the three children were now surrounded by a group of soldiers, seemingly made of tin. The soldiers carried sharp-looking spears, and each of them wore a hat with a bell on top of it that jingled as they walked.

Sally's eyes widened.

Jingle, jingle.

Jingle, jingle.

The boy who had stuck out his tongue at her had burst into tears, all bravado gone. "It was an accident!" he protested. "It wasn't my fault. She was in the way!"

"Are you blaming another for your behavior?" demanded one soldier. Sally noticed his hand tightening around his spear.

"Because that's not very *nice*," added a second soldier, taking a step forward. "Not very *nice* at all."

The boy's face paled. The other children began to back away from him, as if they'd never met him before and just happened to be standing nearby. The boy looked pleadingly at his friends, then at the soldiers, and then back at his friends again.

"Please!" he begged in a choked voice. "I didn't mean—"

But the soldiers weren't listening. They picked him up by his ears and stuffed him in a big red sack trimmed with white fur. The boy struggled to get free, kicking and punching the sides of the bag. But it did no good. The tallest soldier simply tossed the bag over his shoulder and began to walk away.

Sally had to do something. She ran up to the soldier, stepping into his path. "It's all right!" she told him. "He didn't mean it. And I'm not hurt at all. It was simply a prank." She bit her lower lip, her mind racing. "Everything's *fine*," she tried, remembering the man with the packages.

"Please step back, ma'am," the soldier said in a curt voice. "We've got it under control."

He stepped around her, continuing his journey, the others falling into line behind him. Sally watched in dismay as they marched in unison down the cobblestone street, their hats jingling merrily and yet somehow menacingly along the way. Past the red-and-white-striped lampposts, past the glittering Christmas tree. Past the shops with the sweets in their windows and past the people carrying their shiny packages. All of whom, Sally noted bitterly, seemed to avert their eyes from the scene in front of them. Turning away. Heading quickly in the opposite direction. Not one person tried to stop the soldiers. Or inquire about the boy struggling in the sack.

What was going on here? And what would happen to the boy?

Suddenly she felt a tap on her shoulder. She turned around, shocked to find that one of the dolls from the group she'd been observing had approached her from behind while she was watching the boy being dragged away. The doll had auburn hair and big green eyes. And she was looking at Sally with concern on her pale porcelain face.

"You shouldn't have done that," she said solemnly.

CHAPTER SIX

Sally stared at the doll, alarm bells ringing in her mind. She tried to force herself to appear calm. As if everything was *fine*. "What do you mean?" she asked. "What did I do?"

The doll shrugged her dainty shoulders, her auburn curls bouncing prettily as she did. "Sticking up for that boy," she replied. "I'm guessing you're not from around here."

Sally's hackles rose. "What was I supposed to do?" she demanded, trying to keep her voice even. "Just let them take him away? He didn't do anything wrong. He was just playing a prank. Is there some law around here about playing pranks? Is it not *nice* or something?"

The doll's already white face paled even further. She

looked from side to side, as if to see if anyone was listening. Then she grabbed Sally by the arm, dragging her into a small alleyway between two houses. Once they were alone, she met Sally's eyes with her own.

"Be careful what you say," she whispered. "They hear everything. They see everything, too. And trust me, you don't want to attract their attention."

A chill crossed over Sally that had nothing to do with the cold. Her mind flashed back to her vision. The shadowy figure lurking. The eerie jingle of bells. Was this what her dream was trying to warn her about? That beneath the cheery façade of snowflakes and sugarplums, Christmas Town had a dreadful secret?

The doll sighed. "Look, don't get me wrong. I thought what you did out there was really brave. But it was also really stupid. And it could get you in serious trouble. I just thought you should know, that's all." She shrugged, glancing behind her again.

"Well, I appreciate the warning," Sally told the doll, still wondering who the mysterious "they" were—the soldiers? Or did they have some kind of boss? And why would anyone care so much about how people acted? "Also, you're right. I'm not from around here. This whole time I've sort of been stumbling about, trying to figure out how things work. Let's just say this place is very different from where I come from. I mean, in Halloween Town pranks are practically a national pastime."

"Wow," the doll replied with a brittle laugh. "I can't even imagine." She paused, then added, "I'm Abigail, by the way. It's nice to meet you—despite the circumstances. You're a really beautiful doll. So different from the ones around here. And I really love your dress."

Sally looked down at her patchwork ensemble, surprised. "I'm Sally," she said, looking up again. "And honestly, I was about to say the same thing about yours," she confessed. "I've never seen a dress so fancy."

"I think the word you're looking for is *itchy*," Abigail remarked wryly, wrinkling her freckled nose. "Also, hard to play in and looks exactly like every other doll's dress in Christmas Town. Whereas yours . . ." Her eyes roved Sally's dress. "It has so many beautiful colors and patterns. It's like they shouldn't go together but they absolutely do."

"Thank you," Sally said, feeling a blush creep to her cheeks. "I made it myself, actually."

"You made that? Wow. I've never met a doll who could sew before." Abigail let out an impressed whistle. "Did you sew yourself together, as well?" she queried, examining Sally's stitches. "Sorry," she added quickly, putting a dainty hand to her mouth. "Is that rude to ask?"

"Not at all," Sally assured her. "But no, I didn't sew

myself together originally. Though I do sometimes repair myself when stitches come apart." She reached into her pocket, pulling out her needle and thread and showing them to Abigail.

"Wow," Abigail replied. "I wish I could do that. But porcelain doesn't exactly knit back together if it's broken." She cringed. "Which means we have to be really careful all the time. One crack and we're done for."

Sally bit her lower lip, suddenly very grateful for her cloth and leaves. She couldn't imagine how she'd manage to get through life always worrying about breaking. It definitely would impair her ability to jump out of a high window to escape Dr. Finkelstein, that was for sure.

Abigail sighed dreamily. "Seriously, if I were made of cloth like you? I'd be going ice-skating every single day."

Sally cocked her head. "Ice-skating?"

Abigail pointed to the frozen swamp where the people with shoe blades were gliding.

Skating, Sally corrected in her mind. They were *ice-skating.*

Just then the sound of a bell rang through the air. Abigail jumped a little. "Oh!" she cried. "I'm sorry, but I have to get back to the town square. It's almost time for the talent show and I have to warm up. I'm going to be singing," she explained. "Not every doll can sing, you know."

Sally didn't know. But she smiled encouragingly. "That's great," she said. "I've always wanted to enter a talent show. But . . . I was never allowed."

Her mind flashed to all the Talent Scare competitions back home in Halloween Town. Where the residents would show off their greatest frights, hoping to win a chance to play a part on Halloween night. How many times had she begged Dr. Finkelstein to let her try out, only to be told she wasn't ready?

"Well, we start in about an hour," Abigail said with a shrug. "If you want to try to sign up."

"Thanks," Sally replied. It was a tempting offer. But after what had happened with the soldiers, she wasn't sure it would be a good idea. "Maybe another time. Right now I have to get home. Just as soon as I find my dog." She bit her lower lip. "You haven't seen him, have you? He's all white—"

"With a glowing orange nose?" Abigail asked. "And he can fly?"

"That's him!" Sally exclaimed. "That's Zero. You saw him?"

"He was hard to miss!" Abigail exclaimed. "He was flying around town, leading a herd of Santa's reindeer. It was pretty impressive," she added.

Sally nodded, but her mind was still on finding Zero.

She scanned the sky, hoping to catch sight of him and the reindeer—which she assumed must have been those ant-lered creatures she saw flying around earlier—but came up empty. She turned back to Abigail.

"Do you know where they could have gone?"

"The reindeer have a stable up near Santa's workshop. You might try there," Abigail suggested. Then she paused and added, "Just remember what I said. Keep a low profile. Don't interfere. And above all . . ."

"Be nice," Sally finished for her. "Thank you. I understand."

Abigail looked relieved. She smiled at Sally. "Great," she said. "And if you ever find yourself back in town, look me up. We can go get a hot chocolate at Mabel's. They make the best in town." She pointed to a small shop with a red-and-white-striped awning. "And then you can tell me all about this Halloween place that you're from, where they wear beautiful homemade outfits and play all the pranks. I want to know everything."

"Sounds like a plan," Sally agreed, though she was admittedly a little baffled by the idea of wanting to acquire hot chocolate. Any chocolate she'd ever left out in the sun had melted and stuck to the wrapper, which didn't make it particularly appetizing. But to each their own, she supposed.

Abigail waved goodbye and headed back toward the

town square. Sally watched her go, then turned in the opposite direction, toward the hill that led to the workshop and
reindeer.

All right, Zero, she thought. *Adventure's over. Time to
go home.*

Luckily the path up to the workshop seemed to be covered in sand, which made it a lot less slippery to go up than
the opposite side had been to go down. As she walked, several people and toys passed her going the other direction,
giving her curious looks. Sally tried to appear as friendly
as she could, smiling and waving as if she belonged in
Christmas Town, and was relieved when no one attempted
to stop her.

The workshop at the top of the hill was larger than she'd
imagined it to be when down at the bottom, and decked out
in even more festive multicolored lights, giving it a bright
and cheery feeling. A feeling that quickly fell away as Sally
approached the front gates and discovered two tin soldiers
standing guard. Sally's mind flashed back to the kicking
boy in the red sack. She swallowed hard.

Just be nice, she reminded herself. *Act like nothing's
wrong.*

"Excuse me," she said politely. "Do you happen to
know where I can find the flying reindeer?"

The guards exchanged glances. "Who wants to know?"

the first one demanded. Which wasn't very nice, she noted. Maybe they were exempt from the rules.

"Sorry," she said. "My name is Sally. And I'm looking for my dog. Someone told me he might be with the reindeer."

The second guard pointed a finger to the sky. "Is that him?" he asked.

Sally looked up. Way up. Her jaw dropped as she spotted none other than Zero himself, his orange nose glowing brightly as he soared across the sky, leading what appeared to be a team of reindeer. Reindeer . . . and . . . some kind of strange wooden cart with rails on the bottom instead of wheels.

"Zero?" she cried. "What are you doing up there?"

"Looks to me like he's leading sleigh practice," came a new voice behind her.

Sally whirled around, looking down to see a small man with pointed ears staring up at her. He was dressed in green from head to toe, and the hair on top of his head was purple.

"Pretty good for a dog, I must say," the man continued. "That nose could really come in handy in a storm. Santa's always looking for out-of-the-toy-box ways to improve efficiency."

"That's Santa's—erm—sleigh?" she asked, bewildered. "It flies?"

"Of course! How else do you think he's able to travel the

world in one night? Teleportation?" The man looked at her as if she were an idiot.

"Right. Um, of course," Sally stammered, still confused. She turned her gaze back to the sky, watching Zero soar above her, his mouth open and his tongue lolling out. He looked as if he was having the time of his life.

"Zero!" she called out, cupping a hand to her mouth. "Come down here. It's time to go home!"

"I don't think he can hear you," the man said with a shrug.

Sally groaned, frustrated as she watched the ghost dog fly away with his new pack. She started to follow, but to her surprise the short man stepped into her path.

"Excuse me," she said, trying to move around him. But he shifted, continuing to block her.

"Hang on," he said. "You're not leaving just yet."

CHAPTER SEVEN

Sally felt her skin prickle with unease as she looked down at the pointy-eared man in her path. "Excuse me?" she asked, trying to keep the tremble from her voice.

To her surprise, the man grinned. "Sorry," he said. "Didn't mean to scare you. It's nothing bad, I promise. It's just, the big guy sent me out here to request an audience with you. And when Santa wants to see you, well, it's not very nice to refuse him.

Sally pursed her lips, unease rising inside her. The big guy? Santa? Was he the one everyone was so afraid of here? The one who heard and saw everything?

She wondered if she should try to make a run for it. But

then wouldn't the guards just chase her down? She didn't want to end up in any sack, thank you very much.

"Relax," the man admonished with a laugh. "Trust me, you're going to love him. *Everyone* loves Santa Claus." He held out his hand. "I'm Joey Mistletoe by the way. One of Santa's elf helpers. It's good to meet you."

Sally forced a smile to her face. *Be nice,* she reminded herself. She tentatively shook his hand. "Um, good to meet you, too?"

The elf smiled. To her relief it seemed genuine. "Now come on," he said. "He's a very busy man. We can't keep him waiting."

Together they headed past the guards and into the warehouse, which Sally noted was even bigger than it looked on the outside. The ceilings were high, and there was a buzz of machinery in the air. All around, there were various assembly-line stations, packed with people working on projects she couldn't identify.

"What is this place?" she asked, curiosity winning over her fear—at least for the moment.

"Christmas HQ," explained Joey. He waved his hand, gesturing to the room and looking quite proud. "Where all the magic happens, thanks to our crack team."

It certainly did appear magical, Sally decided as she watched the hustle and bustle. Not to mention quite efficient. In fact, everyone here—*the elves*, she reminded herself—seemed completely devoted to their tasks, giving 100 percent, with not a single slacker in sight. Christmas Town must run a tighter ship than they did back home, she thought with a rueful grin. But hey, Halloween Town always rallied and got the job done in the end.

"Come on," her guide said. "We can't keep the big guy waiting."

They headed out of the warehouse and into another hallway. Through the open doors they passed, Sally could see hints of a residence here and there and wondered how many people called this place home. There was a small living room with cozy red-velvet-cushioned chairs and a sweet-smelling kitchen complete with three steaming tea kettles whistling merrily on the stovetop.

Finally they reached their destination: a large receiving room of sorts, with a big cushy armchair draped in more red velvet set on a raised platform up against a far wall. On this throne sat an older man with a snow-white beard and a big round belly who was currently engrossed in a thick book with gold-leafed pages that sat on his lap—its title: *How to Get People to Believe in You.* He was dressed in crimson from head to toe—as if to match the room—and on his head sat a red stocking cap that ended in a white puffy ball that reminded Sally of snow.

This must be the big guy, she thought. *He doesn't look so scary. . . .*

The man looked up from his book as they entered the room. A toothy grin spread across his face. Such an infectious grin, in fact, that Sally found it difficult not to return it in kind, despite her nervousness.

"Ho, ho, ho!" the man cried. "You must be Sally! I've been hearing a lot about you. Why, you're the talk of the town!" He beckoned for her to approach.

Sally shuffled forward. Her leaves fluttered in her chest as she studied the man's face, searching for hints of unpleasantness. Some kind of secret agenda. But all she could find were sparkling blue eyes and a mouth that seemed permanently affixed with a smile. It made her feel oddly at ease.

"Yes, I'm Sally," she said. "And you're . . ." She struggled to remember his full name, assuming it wouldn't be polite to address him by his first without permission. "Mr. Clod?" she tried.

To her surprise, the man in the chair burst out laughing. His big belly jiggled with glee, as if it were made out of the slime from the fountain back home. It made Sally want to laugh, too, though she had no idea what was so funny.

"Mr. Clod. I like that!" the man declared. "And not entirely wrong, either. I'm definitely a bit of a clod sometimes—just ask the missus." He gave her a wink. "But officially it's *Santa Claus.* Or Kris Kringle if you're feeling feisty." He held out his hand. "It's nice to meet you, Sally. You are most welcome here in Christmas Town."

Sally relaxed as she took his hand in her own. She couldn't help it. He just seemed so jolly. So friendly. Her apprehensions began to fade. Whoever everyone was so scared of here, it couldn't be this guy.

"Thank you," she said, giving a small bow—just in case it was appropriate. He did seem to be the leader of the town, after all. Perhaps he was some kind of king. She bit her lower lip, then opened her mouth again. "Christmas," she repeated, forming the word carefully, not wanting any more embarrassing mispronunciations. "Is it . . . a holiday?" she asked, figuring it was as good a time as any to confirm her theory.

Santa raised his bushy white eyebrows. "A holiday?" he repeated incredulously. "Why, my dear sweet doll, it's the biggest holiday of the year!"

He stated this as if it were an absolute, undeniable fact, which was a bit offensive. After all, Halloween was a pretty big deal. But Sally didn't want to appear rude, so she continued her questioning. "And your town prepares for this holiday all year long?"

Santa nodded. "Christmas is a full-time job here and we take it very seriously. All the children of the world are counting on us to deliver them presents on Christmas Eve." He chuckled. "Well, at least all the *nice* children, that is."

Sally frowned. There was that word again.

"What do you mean?" she asked carefully. "Do only the nice children of the world get presents?"

"Of course!" Santa said, looking surprised. "Why would naughty children deserve gifts?"

Why indeed, Sally reasoned. Perhaps this was why they never saw Santa Claus in their neck of the woods. After all, while the young denizens of Halloween Town were all lovely monsters and nightmares in their own right, she wouldn't necessarily qualify any of them as particularly "nice."

She opened her mouth to say as much, but at that moment, a goateed man stepped into the room from a back door she hadn't noticed before. He looked a lot like the others in town, with the same pointed ears. But unlike them, he was quite tall—almost as tall as Jack himself. And his skin was a pale, milky color, his long fingernails bright orange. He wore a smart three-piece suit with printed silver bells all over it, and in his hand he carried a gavel. Which, Sally noted, had a single bell attached to the end of it.

The man sauntered up to Santa's side, then turned to smile at Sally. But his smile wasn't as nice as Santa's had been. In fact, it seemed a bit nasty. As if this man knew something Sally didn't—and preferred it that way.

Santa, on the other hand, seemed oblivious to Sally's growing unease. He grinned at the newcomer, slapping him on the back with such force that the man nearly fell off the platform. "There you are, Jingles!" he exclaimed. "And just in time to meet our lovely guest." He gestured to Sally. "Sally, allow me to introduce you to Mr. Jingles, the supreme court judge of Christmas Town."

"The pleasure is all mine," Mr. Jingles said smoothly, giving Sally a deep bow. As he did, his gavel jingled merrily, causing alarm bells to ring in Sally's head.

Jingle, jingle.

Jingle, jingle.

She swallowed hard. "Um, it's nice to meet you, too, Mr. Jingles," she stammered, shoving her hands behind her back so he couldn't see them tremble. Could this be the guy everyone was so scared of? Though Santa seemed to like him just fine.

The jolly ruler beamed at the two of them. "Mr. Jingles has become my right-hand man," he explained. "I used to do it all myself, of course. But I've gotten so busy lately with all the increased demands on my time. You wouldn't believe how much the population has grown in the past few years. And kids now have such high demands! It used to be I

could give them a tin horn or a toy drum and they'd be perfectly happy. Now they want electronics and video games.
Meanwhile, half of them don't even believe I exist. Do you
know how hard it is to prove to someone you're real?" He
shook his head sadly. "It's been giving me a bit of an existen-
tial crisis, let me tell you." Santa paused, looking off in the
distance, seeming far frailer and less content than he had a
moment earlier.

Sally grimaced pityingly. Suddenly he reminded her
a little of Jack and his graveyard lament. It must be tough
being in charge of a holiday. Maybe Santa needed a little
adventure himself.

"That sounds rough," she said. "I'm sorry."

"Don't worry. He's fine," Mr. Jingles broke in, laying
a hand on Santa's arm. "Now that he has me to help him
delegate."

"Yes," Santa agreed. "Mr. Jingles has become essential
to my operations. He keeps everything going. He even helps
me with the master list."

"Master list?" Sally cocked her head in question.

Mr. Jingles gave her a patronizing look. Lifting his gavel,
he walked behind Santa to a big poster Sally hadn't noticed
before. The poster was divided into two columns, one
labeled NICE and the other NAUGHTY. Under these columns
were long lists of names. Names like Mike and Akim and

Olivia. Sally even spotted a Sally Rose three names down in the nice column. She smiled. At least whoever her child counterpart was, they were doing well.

"We have a full staff monitoring the children all year long," Mr. Jingles explained, tapping the list with his gavel. "We watch them when they're sleeping. And, of course, we observe them when they're awake. . . ."

"Well, that seems a bit intrusive," Sally muttered, unable to help herself.

Mr. Jingles ignored her. "In short, we keep track of whenever they're naughty and whenever they're nice. And we're able to take that data and input it into our new-and-improved systems, which, at the end of the year, spit out a report, personally scoring each child. Those deemed mostly nice get presents. And those who are mostly naughty"—he smirked—"get a lump of coal."

Sally raised an eyebrow. She could think of a few monsters in Halloween Town who would be thrilled to be gifted an actual lump of coal. It made such lovely jewelry, after all, and was great for making one look filthy fast.

"So it's sort of like trick or treat," she ventured. "Back where I'm from."

"What is that?" Santa asked, looking intrigued.

"Well, kids go from house to house," she explained. "When people open the doors, they say, 'Trick or treat.'

The . . . nice . . . families give them candy. And, well, the others . . . don't." She pressed her lips together, hoping she was making sense.

"And if they don't?" Santa pressed.

"Well, then you're free to play a trick on them," she said with a laugh. "Not anything too serious. Just . . . a harmless prank. It's all in good fun!" she added hastily. "I mean, sure, some people take it too far. Like the time someone put a forgetfulness potion into the town fountain and poor Undersea Gal forgot how to swim and almost drowned!" Sally scrunched up her nose, remembering. "But mostly it's silly stuff like egging houses or toilet-papering trees. Nothing too"—she looked warily at the poster—"naughty."

Mr. Jingles gave a haughty sniff. "Well, that sounds all right for you. Unfortunately, we don't abide by that sort of thing here in Christmas Town," he said. "Let's just say we prefer a more . . . buttoned-up approach."

By throwing innocent children into sacks? Sally almost said, but stopped herself, remembering what Abigail had advised about keeping a low profile.

Mr. Jingles cleared his throat. "In any case, while this has all been very interesting," he said in a voice that told Sally he thought it anything but, "I must cut us short. Mr. Claus here, as you can imagine, is a very busy man. And we are on a tight countdown to Christmas. Which leaves us little time for casual chats, am I right, sir?" He turned to Santa, giving him a meaningful look.

Santa startled, as if he'd been in a trance. "What was that? Oh, yes, yes!" he said. "So few days left and still so much to do." He rose from his chair, nodding to Sally. "It's been a true pleasure to meet you. Please feel free to stay in Christmas Town as long as you like. And bring your friends, too!"

Sally caught Mr. Jingles rolling his eyes at this. But Santa didn't seem to notice. He was walking around his chair and heading to the master list, grabbing a pen hanging from a chain nearby. He knelt down to reach the very bottom of the list and carefully, with great penmanship, wrote Sally's name in the nice column. Then he rose to his feet again and clapped his hands.

"There," he proclaimed. "That makes it official."

Sally couldn't help grinning. "Thank you," she said. "I'm honored. Truly." Santa really was a nice guy, if maybe a little distracted, she decided. His supreme court judge on the other hand . . .

"Thanks so much for stopping by," Mr. Jingles said, putting an arm around Sally and shuffling her away from Santa. He thrust her toward Joey, who had been waiting in the back. "She's done here," he said with sniff. "Please show her out."

The elf nodded, leading Sally out. Sally took one last look at Santa, who was grinning and waving goodbye. She tried to wave back, but Mr. Jingles stepped in between them, effectively blocking her from Santa's view.

"So long, Sally," he said in a tight voice. His lips curled. "Be nice."

But the way he said it, it didn't sound all that nice at all. In fact, it sounded like a threat.

CHAPTER EIGHT

When they arrived back in Christmas Town, the talent show Abigail had mentioned was in full swing. The stage stood in front of the giant Christmas tree, and everyone was gathered in front of it, watching the show. Below the stage, a table and three chairs had been set up, on which sat three elves in identical striped pants and emerald coats, each holding a notepad and pen. The judges, Sally presumed.

As she watched a stuffed bear get onstage and start to dance, while the crowd clapped and cheered, Sally felt an unexpected tug at her heart. It looked so fun, she thought. Showing off what made you special. Actively participating in a long-standing tradition. Maybe she *should* enter. It might be her only chance to ever do something like this—without incurring the wrath of Dr. Finkelstein.

"What do the winners of the talent show get anyway?" she asked Joey curiously.

He looked surprised at the question. "A chance to ride on Santa's sleigh, of course," he said as if it were obvious.

"Santa's sleigh." Sally cocked her head. "Is that like a thrill ride or something?"

Joey chuckled. "It's a thrill, all right. And one everybody in town wants to experience once. It's the greatest honor a toy can be given, to be chosen by Santa for his annual trip around the world. If you're not chosen, you end up waiting another year, helping out with all the Christmas prep until it's your turn. Of course, some toys never get picked," he added with a shrug. "Quality issues, you know. Christmas gifts have to be perfect."

Sally nodded slowly, her gaze traveling the town square. There were toys all over, each labeled with a little number on their chest. They all looked excited, she thought, though some had a bit more desperation in their eyes than others. She wondered how many years they had been auditioning, only to be disappointed in the end.

It made her a little sad. She knew all too well what it felt like to be left behind. To be told you weren't ready.

She scanned the crowd for Abigail, catching sight of her in line just right of the stage. When she caught the doll's eye, she gave her a little wave, then a thumbs-up, hoping she was being encouraging. Abigail smiled back at her, though her eyes looked a little too wide and a little too bright. Perhaps it was nerves, Sally guessed. As much as she'd always longed to contribute to the Halloween Town festivities, she also knew it must take guts to have all eyes on you.

She watched as a happy-looking clown stepped onto the stage next. He pulled out a few red balls from his sack and began juggling them in the air. He was quite good—managing not to drop a single ball—and Sally found herself clapping enthusiastically for him along with the others watching.

The clown was followed by an impressive-looking robot who rolled onto the stage flashing multicolored lights and shooting laser beams here and there. The audience oohed and aahed at the spectacle and cheered loudly as he spun around in a clean circle. Definitely a crowd favorite.

But just as the robot was about to end his act and go offstage, his gears started spinning out of control. Soon he was sparking and smoking—malfunctioning in some way. And the formerly excited crowd hushed quickly, murmuring and tutting as three firefighters ran to the stage and dragged him off.

"No sleigh ride for him," Joey said wryly. "Fire hazards are a definite deal-breaker."

Sally looked over at the robot, who was now being hosed down offstage. He looked so defeated she couldn't help feeling sorry for him. The crowd was still muttering, a haughty disapproval veiled in the sheen of a polite hush, which was only making it worse. Sally turned to look at them, anger rising inside her. How dare they be so judgmental? She turned to the stage, hoping another act would go on to distract them. But the judges were still talking amongst themselves, and the stage remained empty. Allowing the crowd to keep focusing on the embarrassed robot.

No. Sally squeezed her hands into fists. Enough was enough.

"I have to help him," she exclaimed. "Distract them somehow."

Joey raised his bushy eyebrows. "What are you—"

But Sally didn't wait for him to finish. She pushed her way through the crowd and marched over to the empty stage. The audience fell into a shocked silence as she defiantly climbed the steps, taking her place under the spotlight. Then she turned to face them, her leaves fluttering wildly in her chest. All eyes were on her now, curious and questioning. Who was this doll who had come out of nowhere? they seemed to ask. And what was she about to do?

So much for keeping a low profile, she thought wryly.

Sally drew in a breath, preparing herself for her act.

She hadn't done it in a while, but she was pretty sure she remembered how it went. After all, how many nights had she practiced it back home the year she'd tried to enter the Talent Scare competition? Only to have Dr. Finkelstein uncover her plans just minutes before the show started and drag her back home, locking her in the basement and not allowing her out till it was over.

"You're not ready," he'd growled.

But she was now. And he wasn't here to stop her.

Drawing in a breath, she squared her shoulders. Lifted her chin. Then she reached up, grabbing her neck with her hand. With quick fingers, she snapped the threads, separating her head from her body, then triumphantly waved it in the air. Her yarn hair swished back and forth as she rolled her eyes into the back of her head and made scary faces at the crowd.

"Hello, friends!" she greeted as loud as she could from her disembodied head. "I'm Sally, the headless doll! It's so nice to *scare* you!"

To Sally's delight, everyone screamed. People and toys bolted from their seats in terror. Soon the entire town square had erupted into sheer panic as residents pushed and trampled one another, desperate to get away. Sally grinned happily from her spot onstage, still clutching her head in her hands.

She'd done it! She was scaring them all! Just as she'd always dreamed of!

Who's not ready now, Dr. Finkelstein?

She gazed adoringly at the frenzy beneath her. At all the delightful looks of horror, mixed with disgust. She curtsied prettily to the gobsmacked judges, winking at them with her disembodied head before skipping offstage.

Mission accomplished. With some added flair, if she did say so herself.

Offstage, she plopped down on a nearby chair, pulling out her needle and thread to reattach her head to her body. Once she'd finished, she looked up, wondering if anyone was going to congratulate her on a job well done.

Wouldn't it be funny, she thought, *if they asked me to ride on Santa's sleigh?*

Of course she'd have to decline. She had to get home, after all. But it would have been nice to be asked. To go back home knowing she'd won. Maybe she'd even get a medal or something. Something she could wear proudly around her neck to remind her of her grand adventure.

She frowned, scanning the town square, puzzled. Where had everyone gone? The entire place was barren. Even the judges had abandoned their posts. Had she missed the show's finale while she was sewing her head back on? Had they already announced their winner?

Her eyes fell on an elf who was frantically trying to disassemble the stage. She tapped him on his shoulder to get his attention. "What's going on?" she asked. "Who won?"

He turned to look at her. His eyes bulged from his head. "Don't hurt me!" he begged, putting his hands over his face as if he expected Sally to strike him.

She frowned. "Why would I hurt you?" she asked, confused.

"Because you're a monster!" he exclaimed.

"What? No, I'm not," Sally corrected. "Monsters have fangs and tails with spikes on them. Also, they usually drool a lot and smell pretty bad." She smiled at him pleasantly. "I'm a rag doll."

But the elf just moaned in terror before bolting in the opposite direction. Sally watched him go, utterly confused. She glanced around the empty square. Maybe she'd gone too far. Though she hadn't even been that scary. Imagine if they'd seen the Clown with the Tear Away Face.

A sinking disappointment settled in her stomach. She hadn't realized up until that moment just how much she'd secretly wanted to fit in here in Christmas Town. Sure, it was very different from back home, but she liked it all the same. She liked the bright and shiny things here almost as much as she liked the dark and dreary ones there. And shouldn't that be okay? Shouldn't there be a way to have both?

Suddenly she felt a strange prickling at the back of her neck. The kind of prickling that usually happened when a cat crawled over your grave.

Or . . . you were being watched.

She swallowed hard, her eyes darting around the empty square. There was no one there, she told herself. Everyone had fled. But still her leaves refused to settle in her chest. Somehow, some way, she knew something wasn't right. Someone *was* there; someone was watching. Even if she couldn't see them.

Then she caught movement out of the corner of her eye. She whirled around just in time to see a tall dark figure slip into the shadows between two cheery cottages. She swallowed hard as her ears picked up a faint tinkling in the distance.

Jingle, jingle.

Jingle, jingle.

Oh, no. No, no, no.

Her mind flashed back to the boy struggling in the sack. All he'd done was throw a snowball.

That's not very nice. . . .

And now she'd gone and scared away half of Christmas Town.

Not very nice at all . . .

She backed away slowly, taking one step, then another, her eyes never leaving the figure in the shadows. He stood still as a statue. Watching, waiting. But she had a horrible feeling if she tried to run, he'd follow. And where would she go, anyway? Where would she hide? There was no one around anymore, thanks to her stunt. Which meant there would be no losing him in the crowd.

Sally turned and walked with purpose, then tried a nearby shop door, but it was locked. She tried another, but it was locked, too. All the shops, she realized in dismay, that had once seemed so welcoming and friendly had drawn their shades. Barricaded their doors.

Leaving her nowhere to go.

Jingle, jingle!

Her heart leapt to her throat as Mr. Jingles stepped out from the shadows.

"Mr. Jingles," she said in a shaky voice. "You gave me quite a fright."

The tall elf did not reply. He stood there, his arms crossed over his chest as he silently shook his head.

"Look, I'm really sorry," Sally tried again, her voice now sounding like a small squeak. "I wasn't trying to hurt anyone. It was just a silly trick!"

The judge raised his gavel in the air and shook it. Once.

Twice. And suddenly Sally found herself surrounded by three tin soldiers, just like the ones who had taken the boy away. Two of them lifted their spears. The other pulled out a large sack.

"No!" Sally cried. "I'm nice. I'm really nice!"

The soldiers stepped closer. Sally winced, her whole body shaking in fear. In a moment they would reach her. They would grab her. Stuff her in a sack.

She had no choice. She turned and ran.

CHAPTER NINE

Sally dashed through the slippery streets of Christmas Town, trying not to lose her balance on the slick icy cobblestones. She could hear the tin soldiers behind her, marching in unison down the streets, their spears clicking every time they hit stone. Sally tried to pick up the pace, but she'd always been a little unsteady on her feet. She took a sharp right, following a road that seemed to lead out of town. But halfway down, it twisted and she found herself passing the hot chocolate shop again, near the center of town.

She groaned in frustration and changed course, skirting around the frozen swamp this time, then heading down another street. How was she going to lose them? Even if she managed to get out of town, she'd be a sitting duck trying to climb that hill to get home. Plus she couldn't leave Zero in this place alone! Her heart beat faster and she tried to swallow her rising panic.

Suddenly she came to a dead end. A towering fence, too tall for her to climb. She stopped short, slipping on an ice patch, her legs sliding out from under her in both directions, sending her slamming down onto the ground in a straddle. As she attempted to scramble to her feet, her ears picked up the sounds of the soldiers on approach. Any moment now, they would turn the corner.

And Sally would have nowhere left to run.

She looked up at the fence. There was no way to scale it. She tried a few more doors—but they, too, were all locked. Her insides coiled into knots and her whole body started to shake as she realized this might be the end. No going back home. Ever.

No more Halloween.

No more Jack.

Then she heard a hissing sound behind her. She whirled around, shocked to see none other than Abigail herself, standing in a doorway she could have sworn wasn't there a moment before. The doll's green eyes were wide and anxious as she beckoned to Sally with a porcelain hand.

"Come with me!" she cried. "Quickly!"

Sally let out a breath of relief. She dashed toward the

open door and dove through it. Abigail slammed it shut behind her, turning the lock on the handle. Then she motioned for Sally to get down, to hide behind a nearby sofa. Sally did as she was told, collapsing onto the ground, chest heaving. She could see shadows through the sheer-curtained windows. The soldiers had arrived and were searching for her. She could hear them cursing under their breath, asking one another where she could have gone.

Abigail turned to Sally. "That should buy us a little time. But we have to move."

Sally nodded woodenly, grateful for the kindness she heard in Abigail's voice. She knew she was risking a lot by helping her, breaking her own rule of keeping a low profile. With effort, Sally forced herself back to her feet, then followed the other doll as she headed purposefully through the house, making her way through an old-fashioned kitchen that still smelled like cookies and out a back door into another alleyway. Sally tried her best to keep up with Abigail's quick steps, praying they wouldn't run into any more soldiers before they reached safety.

They headed down alleyways blanketed in pine needles, around red-and-white-striped poles. Past shops and houses with windows displaying ceramic villages, trains, and lit-up Christmas trees. Finally they came to what looked like a small factory—a miniature version of Santa's workshop on the hill. Abigail unlocked and opened the door, then slipped inside, calling for Sally to follow her.

Sally steadied her nerves and headed into the building. Once inside, she turned and locked the door behind them.

"All right, I think we've lost them," Abigail said, peering out a small greasy window before covering it with a curtain. "We should be safe. No one comes here anymore, now that Santa moved his operations. Most people think it's haunted." She made a face, telling Sally what she thought of that notion.

Sally smiled, hoping the place *was* haunted; she could use the help of a few ghosts right about now. She found a nearby chair, covered in comfortable-looking dust, and sank down into it. The dust bloomed and she breathed in deeply, rejoicing in the familiar musty scent. For a moment, she closed her eyes, allowing herself to reset. *Safe,* she told herself. She was safe.

She opened her eyes again, realizing Abigail was watching her carefully. "Thank you for saving me," she said simply, though it sounded like such an insignificant platitude after what the doll had done for her.

"You're welcome." Abigail shrugged uneasily. How could Sally blame her. What had she risked by sticking her neck out for her—a practical stranger?

"You didn't have to, you know," Sally added. "I mean, you probably shouldn't have."

"I know I shouldn't have," Abigail said, making a face. "But what else could I do? Leave you to those barbarians? Let them take you away? You didn't do anything wrong!"

"Neither did the boy who threw the snowball," Sally pointed out. "Evidently that doesn't matter much around here."

Abigail sighed. "I couldn't believe it when I saw you step on that stage!"

"Yeah." Sally blushed. "Well, you did suggest I enter."

"Right. Except . . . well, I was thinking more you might sing or dance or maybe play a harp or something," Abigail said, shaking her head in disbelief. "Not take off your head."

"Where I come from, that's about as tame a scare as you can get," Sally said with a groan. "I thought I was being entertaining."

"Oh, it was *very* entertaining," Abigail assured her. "Especially when everyone ran off screaming." She snorted. "They're all such scaredy-cats! Afraid of their own shadows!" She laughed again and Sally found herself smiling at the memory, seeing it through the other doll's eyes. It had been pretty great, she realized. Until Mr. Jingles and his soldiers had shown up.

She sighed. "I really didn't mean to break any laws. I was just trying to stop people from laughing at that poor robot."

"Well, as I said before, no good deed goes unpunished in Christmas Town these days," Abigail said with a groan. "Not now that Mr. Jingles is in charge."

"I'm confused," Sally said. "I thought Mr. Jingles oversaw the children of the world. Not the residents of Christmas Town."

"That's what we thought at first, too," the doll said. "But then people here started disappearing, and there were whispers that his duties had . . . expanded. That he has spies everywhere," she added, glancing at the window as if half expecting someone to be peeking inside. "It seems they roam the town, looking for those who dare step out of line. One wrong move and BAM!" She hit the wall lightly with her fist. "You're on the naughty list. Which means we all have to be nice. Always. Or else . . ."

Sally shuddered a little at the ominous tone in the doll's voice. She thought back to the folks she'd seen in Christmas Town. How sweet and happy they'd all seemed. Was it an act? Their way of escaping the ever-watching eyes of Mr. Jingles and his henchmen? "What happens if you get on his list?" she asked. "I assume it's not coal in your stocking like the kids around the world."

Abigail wrinkled her nose. "To tell you the truth, we don't actually know," she confessed. "All we know is you're taken and never heard from again."

"Wow," Sally said. She gave a low whistle. "That's terrible. And kind of overkill, don't you think?"

"Definitely," Abigail agreed. "But what can you do? Speaking up is not an option. It'll just get you on top of the list. Most people and toys don't want to risk it. So they just turn a blind eye and hope they're not next."

Sally could understand this. After all, she'd been living under her own personal tyrant her entire life. She knew full well it was sometimes easier to just play the game and not cause a fuss.

But it never got you anywhere in the end.

"Anyway, it's probably best for you to get back home," Abigail said. "I mean, at least until things cool down around here."

"What about you?" Sally asked. "Are you going to get in trouble for helping me?"

Abigail shrugged. "I'm hoping no one saw me," she said. "And honestly, I don't know if it matters at this point anyway. I missed my chance to audition. Which means no Santa's sleigh for me this year." Her eyes closed, her thick lashes brushing against her cheeks.

Sally cringed, realizing what Abigail didn't want to say.

She'd missed her chance to audition because Sally had accidentally stolen the show.

"I'm sorry," she said. "I really didn't mean to cause you all this trouble. All you did was try to warn me. And then, when I didn't listen, you saved me anyway. And now you might have ruined your chance to win?" She sighed. "You're probably wishing you never met me at this point."

"Not at all," Abigail said firmly. "You're one of the nicest people I've met in a long time. And I mean, actually nice, not just fake nice for show. You care about other people and you're willing to stick your neck out for them. No matter what happens to me, I'm glad I was able to do the same for you."

Sally nodded slowly, giving Abigail a wistful smile. "Well, just know it's much appreciated. And if I can ever return the favor, please let me know."

"Absolutely," Abigail said. "Now come on. I know a back way to Santa's stables. Now that the workshop moved up the hill, we should be able to get there without being seen. You can get your dog and you can go back home."

Sally nodded, feeling a sense of relief at the idea. Though she had mostly enjoyed her trip to Christmas Town—there was so much to like about it!—she was definitely feeling it was time to head home. Maybe she could come back again, when the dust settled. She'd love to spend more time with Abigail. To try some of that hot chocolate. Maybe even go ice-skating.

And, of course, bring Jack along to experience it all, too.

She followed Abigail out the back door of the warehouse, then down a path that wound through a thick forest of green triangle trees. The path soon curved, heading up the other side of the hill. Shielded by the trees, they were able to climb unseen by the town.

"So tell me this," Sally said as they climbed. "What's the big deal about Santa's sleigh anyway? Why does everyone want to go on it so badly?"

Abigail smiled, as if the question amused her. "It's like winning the toy lottery," she explained. "Every year Santa picks only the best toys in town and wraps them up in big packages. Then he travels all around the world, stopping at every child's house to leave these packages under their Christmas trees."

"So wait, he just abandons the toys?" Sally asked, horrified. "For how long?"

"Oh! Forever!" Abigail replied.

"Well, that doesn't seem very nice," Sally muttered.

Abigail laughed. "You don't understand," she said. "It's a toy's greatest dream to have a child of their own. Someone to love them and care for them." She gingerly scrambled up a boulder, then reached down to give Sally a hand. "If you get a good child, they'll even take you to fancy places. They'll throw parties for you and serve you tea in tiny porcelain cups with matching saucers. Some dolls even get to travel the world with their child." She hugged her arms to her chest. "It's the best thing ever. And I can only hope that someday I'll prove worthy of boarding Santa's sleigh."

Sally tried to imagine herself in this situation. Leaving Halloween Town forever. Being forced to say goodbye to everyone she'd ever known. All to go live with a stranger for the rest of her life? She wasn't sure any amount of tea was worth that kind of sacrifice.

But while she didn't understand Abigail's dream, she did understand the sentiment behind it. The feeling of wanting something more than the life you'd been given. Of finding a connection with another person. After all, didn't Sally long for the same thing herself? Wasn't that how she'd found herself in this strange land in the first place?

"Anyway, it's not a big deal," Abigail continued as they resumed their hike. "I'll just audition again next year. And in the meantime, I'll find a job or something. One where I won't accidentally break."

She sounded optimistic, but Sally could hear a thread of desperation in her voice. She was really worried, Sally realized, even if she didn't want to let on.

"Maybe you can go to Santa," Sally suggested. "Talk to

him. Explain what happened. I met him today, you know. Perhaps if he hears the whole story, he'll realize it wasn't your fault. Maybe he'll give you another chance to audition."

Abigail seemed to consider this. "Do you really think he would?"

"I don't know," Sally said honestly. "But it's worth a try."

Yip!

Sally startled as her words were interrupted by a familiar bark, followed by a cold breeze against the back of her hand. She looked up, delighted to find Zero hovering above them, a big sloppy grin on his ghost-dog face. He wagged his white flowy tail and flew around the two of them in circles, yipping happily.

"Zero!" Sally cried. "I've been looking all over for you!" She considered scolding the pup for taking off but, in the end, decided to hold her tongue. After all, there was enough punishment for naughty behavior in Christmas Town already. And Zero was only having fun on his own adventure. He hadn't meant to cause her worry.

She grabbed the ghostly mutt and snuggled him in her arms. "Good boy," she whispered. "Are you ready to go home?"

Zero barked appreciatively. Sally booped him on his jack-o'-lantern nose. Then she turned to Abigail, giving her a sheepish smile.

"I think this is my cue to return to Halloween Town," she said. "Before I get either of us in any more trouble."

"Probably a good idea," Abigail said, wrinkling her nose. "Though I am glad we met. If you ever find your way back, my offer for hot chocolate stands."

"If you're still here, that is," Sally reminded her with a sly smile. "And not in the loving arms of your forever child. Which I'm going to assume you will be. After all, anyone would be lucky to be friends with a doll like you."

"Thank you," Abigail said, giving Sally a fond look. "I have to say, for someone who just got here, you really seem to understand the spirit of Christmas. Maybe more than some of those who actually live here." She rolled her eyes, then smiled at Sally. "I hope you don't mind if I call *you* my friend."

Sally swallowed hard, trying not to feel overwhelmed. *Friend.* Had she ever had a real one of those before? Just the idea made her feel warm inside. A kind of warm that even the snow couldn't chill.

Christmas Town may have its flaws, she thought. *But it's rather magical in its own way.*

"I'd love it if you could be my friend, too," she said, not quite certain how this exchange was supposed to go. "I hope you don't mind that you're my first."

"On the contrary, I'm honored," Abigail assured her. "Now come," she added, pointing to the reindeer barn. "Before you go, let's duck into that old shack over there. There's one more thing we need to do."

CHAPTER TEN

Sally had never felt so glamorous. Or so nervous.

After agreeing to Abigail's suggestion that they swap dresses so Sally could better slip through town without being spotted, she had donned the lacy garment and covered up her hair with a big floppy red hat that Abigail insisted was practically a Christmas Town uniform. Abigail had, in turn, put on Sally's dress and was now marveling at her reflection in the window.

"This is so pretty," she said. "You're sure it's okay if I keep it?"

"Of course," Sally said. "I can easily make another. If I don't decide to wear this for the rest of my life, that is," she added, giving a little twirl, loving the way the skirt spun out as she did.

"You won't, trust me. It'll be so itchy, by the time you get home, you'll be ready to tear it into a million pieces," Abigail assured her, and Sally laughed.

After instructing Zero to meet her outside of town, Sally headed back down the hill into Christmas Town, trying to seem nonchalant as she strolled past residents who greeted her with a cheerful wave and a "Merry Christmas" just as they had when she'd first arrived. Even the soldiers she passed scarcely gave her a second glance, and she was thankful for Abigail's foresight. It wasn't long before she met back up with Zero under the archway that led out of town.

After that, it was simply a matter of heading up the hill to get back to the grove of holiday trees. As Sally climbed, Zero floated up ahead of her, barking as if he was impatient with her slow progress on the slippery slope.

"I hope you had fun," she playfully scolded the ghost dog. "Because you almost got us in a lot of trouble." Still, she decided, she couldn't be too cross with Zero. After all, without him, she never would have discovered this place to begin with.

When they finally reached the grove of trees, Sally made

a small circle, observing each trunk with new eyes. What kinds of adventures were waiting behind their doors?

It was a question for another day. Right now, she was far too exhausted to think of anything beyond going home. So she opened the door shaped like a jack-o'-lantern, and she and Zero climbed through—this time feetfirst. A moment later, she was spiraling into a familiar darkness. And when she came to, she was back in the forest again. But this time the trees were all brown and bare, just as they were meant to be. It appeared to be late afternoon, with a hazy orange sun hanging lazily in the sky. And while the air had a small chill to it, it was not very cold and there wasn't a hint of snow to be found.

Sally smiled. She was home.

Zero spun around her, barking excitedly. Clearly, he was as happy to be back as she was. And together they headed down the path until they reached the graveyard.

For a moment, Sally stopped just below Spiral Hill, looking up at it with a wistful smile. Had it been last night she'd been sitting there, side by side with Jack, longing for something more?

Well, she'd certainly found it. And then some.

Zero hovered over his grave. Sally walked over to pet him on the head. "Thank you," she whispered. "For everything."

The ghost pup yipped happily, his glowing nose seeming to brighten for a moment. Then he dove into the dirt pile in front of his headstone, disappearing from view. Even ghost dogs, it seemed, could sometimes use a rest.

Sally watched him go, then started the trek to town. Through the graveyard, past the scrubby patch of weeds, under the archway, and back into Halloween Town.

Home sweet home—for better or worse.

The town was a lot quieter than when she'd left it. But then the day after Halloween usually was. Everyone had worn themselves out with the festivities and all monsters were tucked away, visions of . . . well, not sugarplums— maybe sugarworms?—dancing in their heads.

She passed a few monsters who hadn't quite made it to their beds, curled into fetal positions on the sides of the road. A vampire snoring loudly. Corpse Kid sucking his thumb. But when her eyes involuntarily lifted to Jack's window, she saw a light flickering inside.

He was awake.

She shouldn't disturb him, she told herself. He was probably busy, already making plans for next Halloween. Besides, she needed to get home. To try to make nice with Dr. Finkelstein before crawling into bed to get a good day's sleep like the rest of the town. Goodness knew she was exhausted after being out all night and into the day. And she was pretty sure if she just laid her head on her pillow and closed her eyes, she'd easily sleep for a week.

But somehow she found herself turning toward Jack's place, pushing through the pumpkin gate, and climbing the steps until she was standing outside his front door. She stood there for a moment, then gave in, pulling on the spider bell.

Her leaves fluttered in anticipation—and with nerves— as she saw the shadow in the window shift at the sound, then disappear from view. A moment later, Jack was opening the door, a big grin crossing his skeletal face. "Sally!" he cried in a voice rich with delight. "So good to see you this afternoon!"

Sally sighed in relief, feeling silly that she'd been so nervous. "Hello, Jack," she said. "I saw your light and figured you might be awake. I hope I'm not disturbing you."

"Not at all." Jack peered up at the orange haze peeking over the rooftops, signaling the coming evening. "You're up early. Well, for the day after Halloween anyway."

"I never went to bed," she confessed with a bashful grin.

"Ah!" Jack nodded knowingly. "I completely understand. I can never fall asleep on Halloween night. Even when everything's over and it's quiet and everyone else has gone to bed. I'm just too wound up. And my brain is already poking me with pesky ideas for next year."

"I can't wait to hear about them," she said politely.

"Ah!" He held up a bony finger. "I could tell you, but then I'd have to kill you." His eyes twinkled merrily. "So what have you been up to, Sally? Don't tell me you've been busy plotting our next holiday, too. If so, you must tell me everything! After all, I'm already dead, so if you have to kill me, it won't make much of a difference."

Sally snorted. "Actually, I do have something to share. If now's a good time," she added quickly, not wanting to interrupt whatever it was he might be working on.

"It's perfect!" Jack exclaimed. He dramatically stepped out of the doorway, bowing gallantly as he invited her inside.

For a moment she hesitated; she'd never been inside Jack's house before. Few had. But he seemed genuinely welcoming, so she forced her feet to move, one after the other, and stepped into his chambers. Jack closed the door behind her, then ushered her into a parlor just off the main hall.

Sally looked around, taking everything in. The room was small but tidy. Beautifully draped in silvery spiderwebs. Two lamps in the corners gave off a dull orange glow, and the furniture was heavily coated in dust. It was dark. It was gloomy. About as different from the homes in Christmas Town as could be. Sally found herself wondering what it'd be like to combine the two towns' aesthetics—and come up with something entirely new. A little cheery, a little creepy. She could definitely see it.

She settled down on the coffin-shaped couch against the wall, folding her hands in her lap. Jack held up a bony finger and retreated into an adjoining room—the kitchen, she realized as she took a peek—then returned a moment later with a steaming cup of what turned out to be rotten mushroom tea. She took it from him gratefully, breathing in the salty scent before taking a long, deep swig.

"So good," she murmured after she'd swallowed, then took a second sip. She hadn't realized how hungry and thirsty she'd been. The sugary snacks she'd eaten earlier hadn't filled her up. But this was the kind of cauldron concoction that stuck to your bones (if you had any, that was).

She realized Jack was watching her from his spiky armchair across from the couch. She felt her cheeks heat at the weight of his stare.

"What?" she asked. "Don't tell me I have mushrooms in my teeth."

He shook his head, then peered closer at her. "You just look . . . different somehow," he explained. Then his own cheeks brightened. "I don't mean in a bad way!" he amended quickly. "You're as beautiful as you've always been. But still . . ." He tapped his finger to his chin. "There's something else about you now."

She looked down, suddenly remembering she was still wearing Abigail's clothes. "It's the dress," she told him. "It's borrowed. And perhaps a bit too fancy for an afternoon chat."

"I don't mean the dress, either," Jack said, shaking his head. "It's something in your face. It's almost as if you're glowing somehow." He pressed his palms together, giving her a thoughtful look. "It's as if you have some big secret practically bursting at your seams. And you're dying to tell someone all about it."

She laughed. "Actually, that's not far from the truth."

Jack leaned forward, placing his elbows on his knees and tucking his chin into his hands. "Go on, then," he said. "I'm listening."

It was all Sally needed to hear. She leaned forward, her eyes sparkling as she readied her tale. Jack was going to be so excited when he heard all about her adventure. Maybe even a little jealous, too, that he hadn't come along.

"Have you ever ventured into the forest beyond our graveyard?" she asked. "Past the curve of Spiral Hill? To a certain clearing deep in the Hinterlands, surrounded by a circle of mysterious trees, each with a painted door?"

Jack slowly shook his head from side to side. "I'm certain if I had, I would have remembered it."

"It's not something you'd forget," she agreed. "And that's only the beginning."

Jack's eyes widened. "Tell me everything. And don't leave anything out."

So Sally started to share, slowly at first but then picking up momentum as she relayed the more peculiar details. About stumbling into the grove of doors while chasing Zero. About opening the one with the colorful painted tree. About how Zero—naughty pup!—had leapt in and how she had fallen in after him, waking up to find herself in a strange new world.

As she spoke, Jack's eyes grew wider and wider. He leaned forward in his chair. So far forward that at one point he almost lost his balance and tumbled to the floor.

"This is incredible!" he declared in a voice filled with wonder. "Another world?"

"Another holiday," she amended with a smile. And then she continued her tale, describing the beauty of Christmas Town. The sugary sweets. The brightly colored packages wrapped up in bows. The jolly Santa Claus and the sweet Abigail, whose dream was to ride on Santa's sleigh and someday have a child to call her own.

"And Christmas Town is just the beginning," she added as she finished her tale. "There's a lot more trees in the grove and I think they each represent a different holiday. There's an egg holiday and a clover holiday and even one that looks as if it might explode if you celebrate it."

"Incredible," Jack breathed. "And here, all this time, I thought we were the only ones. But of course we're not—we couldn't be." He rose to his feet and began pacing the room, his eager steps eating up the distance between walls. "This changes everything," he muttered.

Sally cocked her head. "Does it?" she asked, not quite sure what he was getting at.

He turned to her. His eyes were bigger than she'd ever seen them. And suddenly Sally knew exactly what he meant. And exactly what he was about to say.

Uh-oh.

"Sally," he cried, reaching down and grabbing her hands to pull her off the couch. His big hollow eyes met her own as a pleading smile slowly stretched across his face. "You absolutely have to take me to Christmas Town! Right now."

CHAPTER ELEVEN

Sally swallowed hard. She should have known this would be his reaction. On some level, in fact, she'd *hoped* this would be his reaction. Christmas Town was amazing on so many levels, and hadn't she thought again and again while she was there how much she wanted to share it with him? How much he would love such an excursion?

But then, was it safe for them to return immediately, after the way she had left things? She wasn't exactly on the nice list anymore. And would someone like Jack really be able to keep a low profile? Jack's high profile was kind of his defining trait.

"I don't know, Jack," she said finally.

Jack gave her hands a little squeeze, a silent plea. His

eyes shone with a quiet desperation. "But don't you see, Sally?" he asked. "This is exactly the kind of thing I've been searching for. Something different. Something new. And you found it! You found it for us!"

The way he said *us* made something tingle inside her. But she forced herself to pull her hands from his and turn away. "I know," she said. "It's just . . . complicated."

Jack's shoulders drooped. He sank back into his chair, scrubbing his face. For a moment, he didn't speak and the silence—awkward this time—grew between them. Sally wrung her hands, knowing she should say something—she should explain somehow. She had a million reasons, after all, why they shouldn't return to Christmas Town right this moment. But the look on Jack's face . . . Seeing his initial hope crash into despair—it felt as if it would break her. In a way no stitches could ever repair.

"It's been less than a day since Halloween ended," Jack said at last, his voice dull and wooden. "And I've spent the entire time pacing my workshop, trying to motivate myself to get started on next year's holiday. But somehow I can't seem to bring myself to jump back in. To face yet another year of the same old thing." He shook his head. "I wish you could know what that feels like."

Sally ached at the pain and frustration she saw on his face. "I *do* know, Jack," she said gently. "And I want you to see Christmas Town—I do. Believe me, when I first found the place, all I could think of was bringing you back with me." She bit her lower lip. "But then something happened. Something bad. And I'm not sure it's safe for us to go back . . . at least not just yet."

Jack sat up in his chair. He cocked his head. "What do you mean?" he asked. "What happened?"

Sally reluctantly told him the rest. Starting with the talent competition. Her taking off her head. The whole town scattering in fright.

"But that's not even that scary!" Jack protested, looking indignant. "I mean, no offense, of course. It's a very fine trick and all. But—"

"No, I get it," she assured him. "Here in Halloween Town, no one would bat an eye—not even the bats. But there? It was so bad, they put me on the naughty list."

"The naughty list?" Jack's eyebrows rose. "What's the naughty list?" He grinned wickedly. "Sounds like fun, if you ask me."

Sally snorted. Of course it did. "Well, it's not fun if you're from Christmas Town," she clarified. "People who are deemed bad are taken away by Mr. Jingles. And they're never heard from again."

"Dun, dun, dun . . ." Jack sang dramatically.

"I'm serious, Jack!"

He held up a bony hand. "All right. Let me get this straight. You don't want to take me to this fabulous fantasy land because you're afraid some resident scaredy-cats who run away at the mere sight of someone's disembodied head will somehow manage to capture the two of us and lock us up in some horrible naughty prison and throw away the key?"

Sally sighed. It did sound a little ridiculous when he put it like that.

But then he hadn't been there. He hadn't seen the fear in the man's eyes as he stared at the shadow lurking between the houses after his packages had spilled in the street. He hadn't heard the desperate cries of the boy being dragged away in a sack. He hadn't felt the chill in the air as the bells jingled menacingly, the soldiers closing in on her.

Jack seemed to catch her expression. His face softened. "I'm sorry," he said. "I'm not trying to make light. Whatever happened, clearly it disturbed you." He gave her a rueful smile. "And I'm not trying to push you into something that will make you feel uncomfortable, either. I'm just excited. Intrigued at the chance of seeing something new. This whole new world, just waiting to be explored. If it's even half as magical as you say . . ." He shrugged, looking sheepish. "But I don't want to drag you back there against your will. If you prefer to stay here, I'll go myself. Zero can take me—sounds like he knows the way."

Sally squirmed uneasily. She knew this was his way of letting her off the hook. Giving her an easy out. She could leave his house, go home. Get some sleep, which she definitely needed. She'd already had her adventure, after all. Did she truly need another so soon?

But then she found herself glancing back at Jack. Could she really let him just wander into Christmas Town all by himself? He knew nothing about the place. He wouldn't blend in, that was for sure. How long would it take for him to attract the attention of Mr. Jingles and his henchmen? And, unlike her, he wouldn't have Abigail to help him when he did.

"You really want to do this, don't you?" she asked, resigning herself to her fate.

"I do," he said simply. "In fact, Sally, I think I need to."

And there it was. Naked and vulnerable just as he'd been the night before on Spiral Hill. The hint of desperation in his face. The longing in his voice. He was the Pumpkin King and he had everything. And yet he was desperate for something more.

Something only Sally could give him.

Besides, did she actually want to go home right now and face Dr. Finkelstein?

She cleared her throat. Squared her shoulders. Lifted

her chin. "Never mind Zero," she said. "I'll take you to Christmas Town."

Jack cheered. He grabbed her and hugged her tight, then danced her around the room so fast her feet barely touched the ground.

"To Christmas Town!" he sang. "We're going to Christmas Town!"

"You're going to make me dizzy!" she protested as he spun her round and round. But deep down she didn't really mind. Jack's enthusiasm was contagious, and she was starting to feel excited, too.

It would be something different. Something new.

Something they could do together.

CHAPTER TWELVE

Once they'd made the decision to return to Christmas Town, all that was left was to plan the trip. After a long nap on Jack's couch to catch up on her sleep, Sally woke at midnight to a stale cup of moldy coffee and began to lay out the ground rules.

"If we're really going to do this," she said. "We have to do it right."

Jack nodded as if he were an obedient schoolboy. "You're the expert. You let me know what I need to do."

"First," Sally said, counting on her fingers, "we need to find a way to blend in. It wasn't as bad for me the first time since I look like a doll and there are dolls in Christmas

Town. And then I had Abigail's fancy dress and hat. But a skeleton walking around is going to cause a scene."

"Hmmm, a fair point," Jack conceded. "Let me dig into my costume closet upstairs and see what I can come up with."

Sally was impressed by the idea of a costume closet, but she forced herself to stay focused. She raised another finger. "Second, you must promise me you'll behave yourself while you're there. They don't like tricks. They don't like scares. Anything you do that might be considered sneaky or mean-spirited will get flagged."

Jack put his hand to his skull in a salute. "I'll be on my best behavior," he told her. "Scout's honor."

Sally was pretty sure Jack had never been any kind of Scout. But she simply nodded, telling herself she'd have to take him at his word.

"Lastly," she said, "we don't overstay our welcome. Two hours max. Then we head back. This way by the time they realize we're there, we'll be gone."

Jack nodded, a little less enthusiastically this time. However, luckily he didn't argue and simply asked if she had anything else on her list. When she said no, he leapt up, telling her he was off to assemble his disguise.

It took a few tries to get the costuming right. Everything

Jack owned appeared to be black or gray or both. In the end, Sally decided it would be better to start from scratch. Using the cape she'd gotten from the sweet lady in Christmas Town, she tore out the stitches then reassembled it using Jack's sewing machine. As Jack watched eagerly, she constructed a crude red one-piece suit, cinched with a black belt from the costume closet. (Jack had a lot of belts, though it was tough to find one not ornamented with a spider.) The suit was long enough to cover all his bones, and once he added gloves, boots, and a hat, along with a snow-white beard made out of cotton balls, Sally had to admit, he looked the part. A very skinny Santa Claus.

"Excellent," Jack said, observing himself in the mirror. "I need to put you on costume duty during next year's Halloween."

Sally accepted the compliment, feeling pleased with herself. If only she *could* take on costuming for Halloween, she thought a little sadly. That would be a dream come true. Too bad Dr. Finkelstein would never allow it.

She pushed the thought aside. She could deal with him later. Right now she and Jack had a little getaway to get to. And she was determined to make the most of it.

Jack pulled her next to him so she could see them both in the glass. She had to admit, they made a dashing pair. Not that they were a couple, she reminded herself, blushing at the idea. Just two like-minded companions going on a trip together. No big deal.

"Well, we look amazing," Jack declared, full of his usual swagger. "But, of course, I had no doubt." He grinned at himself in the glass. "Which means, it's time to get ourselves to Christmas Town and start our fun."

It was still dark when they exited Jack's house and headed down the street in the direction of the graveyard. The town was still quiet, most monsters having long gone back to their homes for a proper post-Halloween rest. Only Undersea Gal was awake, splashing happily in the fountain in the town square. As they passed, she gave them a suspicious look and bared her teeth. Jack waved back happily, then poked Sally in the side.

"See? Our costumes are perfect. Even our friends don't know who we are."

They soon made their way under the archway and into the graveyard. Jack's steps were light and airy, and Sally couldn't help smiling as he dodged each stone, humming to himself as he went. When they passed Zero's grave, the little pup poked his ghostly head up and looked at them sleepily.

"It's just us, old pal," Jack said, patting him on the top of his head. "We're headed back to Christmas Town." He paused, then added, "You want to come?"

Zero yipped excitedly, zooming around the two of them.

Jack reached into his pocket, surprising Sally when he pulled out a tiny red cap that matched his own. He plopped it on Zero's head and laughed.

"Now you fit in, too," he declared. And Zero barked in apparent agreement.

Sally smiled at him, then glanced over at the weed patch at the edge of the graveyard. "Hang on," she said. "Before we go, I'm going to gather a few supplies. Just in case."

Heading toward the weed patch, Sally thought about how she could have definitely used a few potions during her previous trip. She knelt to examine the herbs. After looking them all over, she plucked a few deadly nightshade plants and slipped them into her dress's pockets.

"You never know when we might need someone to go to sleep," she said. She looked over the patch again. "Ooh!" she exclaimed, plucking a few more plants. "Invisibility might also come in handy in a pinch."

Once she had finished, she rejoined Jack and Zero, and together they headed through the graveyard, toward the edge of the Hinterlands. Zero led the way, his nose shining through the darkness, and Jack fell into step behind him, practically dancing down the forest path as if he knew exactly where to go. Once in a while he'd stop and turn back to look at Sally, his hollow eyes seeming to glow in growing anticipation the closer they got to the grove. It made Sally's heart squeeze a little. He was so excited. She just hoped Christmas Town would be everything he wanted it to be and more.

It wasn't long before they arrived at the familiar grove of holiday trees. Jack ran from one of them to the next, like a kid in a caterpillar store, examining each and every one with equal fascination.

"So you really think these all represent different holiday lands?" he asked, pulling open the door with the large bird on it. "What do you think this one could be?"

"A holiday to honor turkeys?" Sally guessed. Though somehow that didn't sound quite right.

"Maybe," Jack mused. "But why would anyone want to honor a turkey? They're such dumb birds. Really, the only good thing to do is eat them." He closed the door, then headed over to the tree with the heart on it. "This one's probably Dissection Town," he decided. "They spend all year long harvesting organs, and one day a year they gather together to eat them."

Sally made a face. "Or maybe it's Love Town?" she suggested. "And their holiday is filled with lots of romantic proclamations?"

Jack looked disappointed by this idea. He moved on to the tree with the four-leafed plant. "Garden Town," he pronounced. "They're completely vegetarian. And they hate turkeys with a passion." He looked up at Sally and smirked. She rolled her eyes.

"You want to try them all, don't you?" she teased.

"Absolutely." Jack moved away from the plant door and straightened. "But one adventure at a time."

He stepped to the door with the decorated pine tree, then reached down, wrapping his gloved hand around the doorknob. As the door creaked open, Sally swallowed hard, her nerves suddenly returning with a vengeance. She closed her eyes, her mind flashing back to the memory of Mr. Jingles's soldiers chasing her through town, their jingle bell spears ringing merrily as they went.

Jingle, jingle.

Jingle, jingle.

What are you doing Sally? Dr. Finkelstein jeered in her head. *Stupid girl! You need to come home, where it's safe.*

"No," Sally growled, squeezing her hands into fists. "I won't."

"You won't what?"

Her eyes flew open, and she realized Jack was staring at her, a worried look on his face. "Nothing," she said quickly. "Everything's fine." She drew in a breath, pushing down her nerves. She was going to do this. For Jack. And for herself, for that matter.

"Come on," she said to Jack, forcing a smile to her face. "Last one in is a rotten apple."

Zero made a beeline for the door, zooming through without hesitation. Sally followed, this time by choice, diving through the door headfirst.

Ready or not, Christmas Town, she thought before everything went black, *here we come.*

CHAPTER THIRTEEN

When Sally came to, everything was white.

It took her a moment to realize why. But once she did, she waved her arms, sweeping the snow away. It had accumulated quite a bit since she'd left Christmas Town, the wind swirling it up into massive drifts. One of which, it appeared, she and Jack had fallen straight into.

Which was probably a good thing, she decided. Since Jack was definitely more brittle-boned than she. And they didn't need an injury cutting their adventure short before it even properly began.

Once she'd surfaced, she dug into the snow until her hands came across something solid and bony. She yanked on it and eventually managed to pull Jack out from under the pile. The look of shock on his face made her want to laugh out loud. And she couldn't resist scooping up a snowball and tossing it lightly in his direction. It hit him square in the chest and he yelped in surprise, which made her giggle.

"Gotcha!" she teased.

A slow smile spread over Jack's face, replacing his initial surprise. He reached down and scooped up his own snowball, then brought it to his nose to sniff it. Then he stuck out his tongue to give it a lick.

"Doesn't taste like much," he remarked, looking a little disappointed.

"You're not supposed to eat it," Sally told him. "It's more of a weather thing. They call it snow and it falls from the sky and accumulates on the ground. It's actually very pretty."

Jack tossed his snowball from hand to hand thoughtfully. "And people throw it at one another?" he asked, looking up.

"Only when they're being naughty," Sally replied, her eyes flashing mischievously. She grabbed a second snowball and tossed it at Jack. He laughed and grabbed another of his own, lobbing both in Sally's direction with a bit too much force. The snowballs hit her in the face, knocking her backward into the snowdrift.

Jack gasped. "I'm sorry!" he cried. "Are you all right?"

Sally grinned wickedly as she sat back up, scooping up a huge pile of snow. "Oh, I'm just fine," she said, standing and stepping closer to Jack, the snow cradled against her chest. "Just fine."

She lunged at him, dumping the snow down the front of his jacket. He cried out in alarm.

"That's freezing!" he protested.

"They do say revenge is a dish best served cold." She gave an impish shrug.

For a moment, Jack stared at her. Then he started to laugh. Soon he was laughing so hard that he was doubled over, clutching his belly with his hands. Sally started to laugh, too. She couldn't help it. And suddenly all her worries seemed very far away.

"I'll think twice before taking you on again," Jack joked.

"You wanted to experience something new," she reminded him. "And this is about as new as it gets."

"Well, I have to say, I love it already," Jack declared, brushing himself off. "And I can't wait to see the rest."

"I can't wait to show you," she said. Then she wagged a finger at him. "But no more snow shenanigans once we get to town. As I said before, we have to be on our nicest behavior when we're around the others."

"I wouldn't dream of acting otherwise," Jack promised, putting his hand over where his heart should have been. "Lead the way." Then he frowned. "Wait, where's Zero?"

"Oh, I'm sure he's around here somewhere," Sally said, glancing around. "Probably off flying with the reindeer again. Seems he also made some good friends in Christmas Town."

"I'm glad," Jack declared. "The little guy deserves his own fun."

Sally nodded and the two of them headed down the path, toward Christmas Town's valley. At least this time Sally knew the way and what to expect. It didn't take long for them to step out onto the edge of the cliff, with Christmas Town shining brightly below them.

Jack stared down into the valley, his mouth dropping open.

"Whoa," he whispered. "Is that . . . ?"

"Christmas Town," Sally pronounced. "It's pretty, right? They really like their festive lights here."

The look on Jack's face told Sally all she needed to know. He was fascinated. He was enthralled. He was completely blown away by everything he was seeing.

Something different. Something new.

And Sally had been the one to show it to him.

"Can we get closer?" he asked, turning to her, his face alight.

"We can," she told him. "But we're going to have to slide. It's too slippery to walk down. At least from this side of the hill." She sat down, preparing herself. Then she looked up at Jack. "If you need to slow down, drag your hands and feet. But not too much or you'll lose your balance and tumble over."

Jack sat next to her, looking a little confused. She patted his arm. "Just follow me," she told him, then pushed herself off the hill. Soon she was once again sliding down the slope, fast and furious, though this time in a much more controlled descent. But the exhilarating feeling of the wind whipping at her face was exactly the same. Like she was flying. Already her immediate return had been well worth it.

Once she'd glided to a stop at the bottom of the hill, she turned her head to glance back at Jack, to see how he was faring. The expression on Jack's face as he slid down made her want to laugh out loud all over again. He looked terrified. But also enchanted. His arms and legs waved madly until he lost his balance and began tumbling down the hill in wild summersaults. When he reached the bottom, he leapt to his feet, his eyes wide with astonishment.

"Can we do that again?"

She patted him on the arm. "Maybe later," she said. "Right now, we've got much to see." She pointed to a large clock positioned on a tower in town. "Remember we've only got two hours," she said. "Let's try to make the most of it."

Together, they headed into town, under the archway and down the well-lit cobblestone streets. Sally could tell Jack was trying to remain calm and unassuming but that it was proving difficult with all the wonders that appeared around him. He ran to a shop window, pressing his bearded face against the glass. Then he pulled away just as fast and dashed over to the next.

"Look at this!" he cried. "And this!"

Sally chuckled. If only the residents of Halloween Town could have seen him now. The celebrated Pumpkin King—acting like a baby nightmare experiencing his first Halloween.

She led him into the town square, where she'd accidentally scared everyone half to death the day before. The large Christmas tree was still there, shining brightly, but the stage had been disassembled and there were no longer any signs of the talent show remaining. Sally wondered if Abigail had gone to Santa to plead her case. She really hoped she had. Because if she missed her chance to ride on Santa's sleigh because of Sally, well, Sally would never be able to forgive herself.

The sound of singing suddenly rose to her ears. She turned to see that a group of elves, dressed in matching red-and-green scarves, had gathered in front of the tree and were singing what must have been a Christmas song. Something about a man made out of snow who evidently came to life, much to the delight of the young children in town. It was a jaunty tune, much more chipper than the macabre melodies the zombie band favored back home, and Sally caught Jack bopping along to the music. He'd always enjoyed a catchy number.

After the elves had finished their song, one of them walked around town holding out a hat tipped upside down. On the hat were the words CHRISTMAS CAROLERS, which Sally assumed was the name of their band. She watched curiously as several residents threw little coins into the hat.

Jack looked on approvingly. "I have to say, I'm impressed. Though I could suggest a few tweaks," he added, holding up a hand before Sally could speak. "The toys could be much scarier, for example. If they really want to impress the children. And those animals over there?" He pointed to a small herd of reindeer like the ones Zero had been hanging out with during their first visit. A couple practiced leaping into the air, soaring in a circle, then touching down. "They have far too much fur, don't you think? Imagine them as skeletons! That'd make them much more interesting. And probably more aerodynamic, too."

Sally rolled her eyes. Jack just couldn't help himself, could he? But then that was why he was so good at his job, she supposed. He never stopped working to make things bigger and better.

Still, she didn't think they'd appreciate his grand ideas around here. After all, it wasn't very *nice* to criticize.

Speaking of . . . Sally's heart leapt as she caught sight of a few tin soldiers marching into the square. She grabbed Jack by the hand, yanking him in the opposite direction while trying to remain calm. They might have been disguised, but she didn't want to press her luck.

"What's wrong?" Jack asked.

"Nothing. Let's, um . . . head inside this shop," she said, pointing to a random building in front of them. "Just for a few moments."

Jack followed her into the light-trimmed building, which turned out to be a small restaurant. It was similar to those they had in Halloween Town, though in typical Christmas custom, this one appeared to sell sweets instead of slugs.

A little old woman with pointy ears, dressed in a red-checkered apron, greeted them cheerfully. "Well, hello!" she exclaimed. "Welcome to the Chocolate Café. My name's Mabel. It's so good to have new customers." Before they could say anything, she'd ushered them over to a nearby table, luckily away from the window, and pushed large plastic menus into their hands. Sally scanned hers, impressed by the number of options, all unfamiliar but each looking more delicious than the last.

"What would you recommend, Mabel?" Jack asked, looking up at the woman with a polite smile on his face.

Mabel practically beamed. "Well, everything's good here," she assured Jack. "But we're famous for our hot chocolate." She pointed to a photo on the menu of something brown in a steaming mug. "I, myself, prefer it with extra marshmallows and whipped cream."

Sally raised her eyebrows, putting two and two together. This must have been the place Abigail was talking about during her first visit. The one she'd wanted to take Sally to herself. It was too bad Sally had no way to tell her new friend she was back. Maybe Abigail could have joined them and gotten to meet Jack. She was pretty sure Jack would like Abigail and vice versa.

"I'm sorry," Jack said. "It all looks amazing. But I'm afraid we don't have any money."

The woman frowned, just for a moment, and Sally thought she caught her steal a quick glance toward the window. Then she waved her hand dismissively. "Ah! It's on the house. Order whatever you like! No one goes hungry in my café." Her smile returned, though it appeared a bit more forced.

"Sounds great to me!" Jack declared.

Sally bit her lower lip. "That's very kind of you," she said. "However, we really don't—"

But the woman was already taking their menus and walking back behind the counter, where she began to operate a silver machine. Sally watched her a moment before turning back to Jack.

"The people here are certainly nice," he said, looking impressed. "I can't imagine anyone in Halloween Town giving away free drinks. I thought we might have to go out and sing for a while, then pass around a hat." He shook his head. "So nice."

Sally nodded slowly. But inside her leaves churned. That was it, wasn't it? she realized. Why the woman looked so stressed. She *had* to be nice. Or she might be taken.

Sally stole another glance behind the counter. The woman was filling the mugs, humming as she worked. The same tune, she realized, as the carolers had been singing earlier—the one about the man made of snow. But somehow her hum was a little too high-pitched, a little off-key.

Sally's mind flashed back to the people she'd met on her first visit. She hadn't noticed it then; she'd been too touched by their friendliness and generosity. But had it been out of the goodness of their hearts that she'd been given things like a warm cape and sugarplums? Or was it only part of a dark charade? Residents acting out of fear, not genuine kindness.

Not in the true spirit of Christmas.

Mabel returned a moment later, carrying two steaming mugs with tiny Christmas trees imprinted on them. As she set them down on the table, Jack observed the thick brown liquid inside with a thoughtful look.

"Reminds me of mud mog from back home!" He brought the cup to his lips and downed a huge gulp. Then he coughed and spit chocolate all over the table. The woman startled, looking horrified.

"Are you all right?" she asked. Her gaze shot back to the window. "Is something wrong?"

"He's fine," Sally said, trying to make eye contact with her. *"Everything's fine."*

The woman still looked wary but ran to get a rag to wipe up the mess. When she returned, Jack gave her an apologetic look.

"I'm so sorry," he said. "It's lovely, really. Just . . . different than I expected, is all. A lot more . . . hot?"

"Well, it is called *hot* chocolate," Sally said, trying to keep her voice light. "Just give it a moment to cool and I'm sure it'll be great." She took the rag from the woman and continued to wipe up the table. "Thank you," she said again. "This is all so *nice* of you."

The woman's shoulders drooped. She headed quickly back behind the counter, busying herself with some dishes. Sally watched her for a moment longer, a stirring of pity swirling inside her. What must it be like to have to live like this? To always be on guard? To never be able to relax and have fun, without worrying about someone judging you for things outside of your control?

But there was nothing she could do about that now. All she could do was act like everything was fine and hope it would relax their host and not cause her any more worry. She brought the hot chocolate slowly to her lips, breathing on it to cool it down before taking a sip. She sighed dreamily as the thick chocolate slid down her throat, sweet and delicious.

"Yum," she said. "Try it again, Jack. You're going to like it."

Jack did as he was told, this time taking a much smaller sip. His mouth curled to a grin as he set the cup back down. "Well, that's pretty good," he admitted. "It's like someone took a pile of Halloween candy and melted it down, then added milk." He sniffed the cup. "Though it'd be better if they used the expired kind. Then we might get some actual curdles."

He took another sip, managing to get a blob of whipped cream stuck in his fake beard. Sally giggled, then grabbed the rag to blot his face.

"You're a mess," she teased. And he smiled back at her.

"I know," he said. "But you love me anyway, right?"

Sally felt her cheeks go red and she quickly grabbed her mug again, bringing it to her face to hide it. She knew Jack was just being silly. But the way he was smiling at her—as if, in that very moment, she was the only other person in the world—well, it felt far too lovely.

Even in her wildest dreams, Sally could have never imagined a moment like this. Sitting in a small café, across from the Pumpkin King, laughing and joking as if they didn't have a care in the world. And if somehow it was all only a dream? Well, she hoped she would never wake up.

Jack set his mug down. "That settles it. We must get the recipe for this hot chocolate. We can bring it back to Halloween Town. It'll be perfect for next year's festivities. In fact, all of this would be perfect. We could make it our new theme!" He stroked his fake beard. "Yes! I'm seeing it all now! Christmas in Halloween Town. It'll be a sensation! Of course, we'd make it much scarier," he amended. "Maybe maggots instead of marshmallows? Glow worms strung together as lights? Oh, and maybe you can use

Dr. Finkelstein's lab to whip us up some of those flying creatures we saw earlier—in skeletal form, of course. They'll be
a definite hit."

Sally shook her head in mirth. She held up her hand.
"All great ideas," she said. "But maybe slow down a little?
This is supposed to be your break, remember?"

Jack leaned back in his chair. "I know. You're right. I
just can't help myself." He snorted lightly. "This is why
I needed you to come with me. Imagine if I had discovered
this place all by myself. Who knows how much damage I'd
have managed to do?"

"I can't even imagine," Sally said. "Good thing you
have me to keep you in line."

"Good thing indeed," Jack said, reaching across the
table and placing his hand over hers. His expression turned
serious and when he met her eyes with his own, Sally's
breath hitched.

"Thank you for bringing me here," he said softly. "This
was exactly what I needed."

Sally nodded, not trusting herself to speak. She couldn't
believe she'd almost chickened out and stayed behind.
Missed out on this special day with Jack. Seeing the light in
his eyes. Hearing the joy in his voice. Just the two of them
together.

No one knew where they were. No one knew what they were doing. And the only thing that mattered was that they were doing it together.

Maybe she needed to face her fears more often. . . .

CHAPTER FOURTEEN

After the hot chocolates, they thanked Mabel and headed out of the shop, back into town. Luckily the soldiers were no longer anywhere to be seen and Sally couldn't hear any bells, either.

"So what's next?" Jack asked eagerly. "What haven't I seen yet?"

Sally grinned, an idea forming in her mind. "Come on," she said, her eyes twinkling. "I've got just the thing!"

She grabbed Jack by the hand, dragging him over to the frozen swamp she'd seen during her first visit to Christmas Town. Her heart began to pound with anticipation. This was going to be great.

"What are they doing?" Jack asked, watching the

elves glide across the ice, his head cocked with curiosity.

"It's called ice-skating," Sally explained. "And it's supposed to be really fun. My friend Abigail told me all about it."

"Ice-skating," Jack repeated. "What an inspired idea. And, I imagine, far less sticky than swamp swimming."

"Come on," Sally said, glancing at the clock tower. "We've got just under an hour left. I think that'll be enough time."

They headed over to the man standing at the side of the pond who seemed to be giving out the ice skates. Sally wondered again about money, but the man simply handed over a pair of skates to each of them, saying they just needed to return them when they were finished.

How very nice, Sally couldn't help thinking.

Jack enthusiastically kicked off his boots and slipped his feet into the strange shoes. But when he tried to stand up on the ice, he immediately lost his balance, his legs going in opposite directions. He landed hard on the ground, letting out a loud *oof* as he did. Sally tried not to laugh at the shocked look on his face.

"Let me help you," she said, reaching out to pull him back up, only to have him immediately fall again, this time dragging her down with him. They landed on the ice in a tangle of limbs, and Sally was once again grateful for her cloth body and soft stuffing.

"This is harder than it looks," Jack muttered, rubbing his knee.

Sally gave him a sympathetic look. "We could try something else . . ." she suggested, not wanting to bruise his ego along with his backside.

But Jack only shook his head, his dark eyes glistening. "Are you kidding?" he cried. "I'm not letting some silly ice skates defeat me!"

Of course you won't, Sally thought fondly, watching him scramble to his feet again, wobbling a bit but somehow managing to stay upright this time. Jack didn't let anything defeat him. It was one of the things she'd always admired about him.

If anyone could learn to ice-skate, it'd be Jack.

As Jack tentatively walked out onto the ice, Sally settled down on the bench to slip on her own skates. They felt odd on her feet, almost too tight at her ankles, and when she stood up she felt ten feet tall. She took a tentative step, then another, allowing her knees to bend slightly to help with her balance. And soon she was gliding across the pond, scraping the ice gently with her blades to move herself along as the wind tickled her face.

This was even better than sliding down that hill! No wonder Abigail had wanted so badly to try it.

She looked back at Jack. He was some distance behind

her, waving his arms madly in the air, still trying to stay upright. Sally made a gentle turn, then headed back to him, grabbing him by the arm to steady him.

"Bend your knees," she told him. "Lean your torso just slightly forward. . . ."

Jack followed directions, finally finding his balance. Sally smiled and let him go. But he grabbed on to her hand again, squeezing it in his own.

"For balance," he said, flashing her a grin. Sally felt her leaves flutter.

And so they began to ice-skate together across the pond, holding hands. And while Jack almost fell at least three more times, he always managed to right himself just at the last moment.

"I think I'm getting the hang of it," he declared. "And you, Sally . . ." He looked at her with admiration. "You are a natural."

Sally blushed. "Why, thank you, Jack," she said. "I actually—"

"Sally? Are you Sally?"

Sally startled at the sudden voice calling her name. She lost her balance and almost fell, but Jack held her upright. After she recovered, she turned around, surprised to see a doll that looked just like Abigail, but with blond hair, waving at her from the side of the pond. Sally glanced at Jack, then shrugged and started skating over, knowing the doll probably couldn't come to her without risk of breaking.

"Hi!" she said once she reached her. "Yes, I'm Sally. I don't think we've met."

"I'm Tammy." The doll looked her up and down. To Sally's surprise her eyes narrowed. "I thought it might be you," she added. "You still have Abigail's dress, I see."

Sally frowned. "Well, yes," she said. "And she still has mine." She wondered fleetingly if exchanging clothes might be considered naughty. It was hard to know in this place. All she knew for certain was the doll was looking at her as if Sally were something slimy stuck to the bottom of her shoe.

Sally cleared her throat. "Are you friends with Abigail?" she asked hopefully. "Do you happen to know where she is? I'd love to introduce her to someone." She waved at Jack, who was waiting for her at the center of the pond.

The doll raised two perfectly arched eyebrows. "Actually, I have no idea where Abigail is," she said angrily. "No one does."

A sudden chill slid down Sally's back. "What do you mean?"

"Abigail's missing," the doll said flatly. "And I'm pretty sure it's all your fault."

CHAPTER FIFTEEN

Sally stared at Tammy, her heart pounding. "What? How did this happen?"

But even as she asked, she realized with a sinking feeling that she already knew. Someone must have seen Abigail helping her escape the soldiers. Someone must have reported it back to Mr. Jingles.

And now Abigail was in trouble.

Tammy paced back and forth, wringing her hands as she walked. "She should have just let them take you away. You deserved to be taken after what you did at the talent show. But Abigail . . ." She trailed off, looking dismayed. "She's so nice. *Too* nice," she added bitterly. "I mean, who just goes and helps a stranger? And not just *any* stranger.

The one who stole her chance to audition for Santa's sleigh." She shot Sally a reproachful look.

Not that Sally could blame her. Tammy wasn't wrong. Sally had broken the laws of the land, even if she hadn't known she was doing it. And Abigail had stuck her neck out for her, even after Sally's stunt had ruined her own opportunities.

She hung her head, shame washing over her. "I should have never interfered," she murmured.

"You shouldn't have come to Christmas Town at all," Tammy corrected. "Seriously, why are you even here?" She gave Sally a snotty once-over. "I can tell you right now, you don't stand a chance of cutting the line and getting yourself on Santa's sleigh." She laughed bitterly. "I mean, could you imagine? Some little girl waking up on Christmas morning to find *you* under her tree? She'd probably run away screaming in fright."

"Well, I should certainly hope so," Sally agreed, a little confused. For what could be better than that? Then again, that hadn't been a positive reaction back at the talent show. "In any case, you don't have to worry," Sally added. "The last thing I want is to become some child's toy. Now can we please talk about Abigail?"

"What's going on?" Jack asked, clumsily skating over to the two of them. He peered from one doll to the other while trying to balance on his skates. Tammy glared back at him, crossing her arms over her chest.

"Remember I told you about my friend Abigail?" Sally asked, ignoring Tammy. "It seems she's missing. Tammy thinks Mr. Jingles's men might have taken her away because she helped me escape him earlier."

Jack frowned. "That's not good."

"You think?" Tammy asked sarcastically. "She should have never helped you."

"It's too late for that now," Sally reminded her. "So how about we figure out how to help Abigail instead? Do you know where they might have taken her?"

"Perhaps some kind of jail?" Jack suggested. "Why, we could stage a jailbreak. That could be even more fun than ice-skating." He rubbed his bottom ruefully. "And probably a lot less painful."

"There's no jail in Christmas Town," Tammy told them. She screwed up her face. "Everything here is *nice*, remember?"

Sally sighed. "Okay. That means they must be taking them somewhere else," she decided. "Somewhere outside of town maybe?"

Tammy gave a reluctant shrug. "All anyone knows is that once you're picked up by Mr. Jingles's crew, you're never seen or heard from . . . again." Her voice hitched on the last word, a crack in her angry shell. Despite what she might think of Sally, she clearly cared for Abigail. And she was worried.

It made Sally worry, too. And the guilt began to tangle in her chest. Abigail had likely saved her life. Would she be made to pay for that good deed with her own life?

No. Sally couldn't let that happen. She *wouldn't*.

She turned to Jack, looking up into his eyes. "We have to help her."

Jack frowned. He glanced over at Tammy. Then at the clock tower. Their time was almost up. "I thought you wanted to keep a low profile," he reminded her. "And not overstay our welcome."

"That was before," Sally declared. "But this changes things. Tammy's right—it's my fault Abigail was taken away. Which means I have to fix it."

"But you don't even know where they took her!"

She waved him off. "I'll figure it out somehow," she said stubbornly. "Whatever it takes!"

"Sally—"

"You can go home if you want. But I'm staying."

Without waiting for an answer, Sally skated over to the bench and started yanking off her ice skates. Jack stumbled after her, somehow managing to half fall the entire way. He dropped down on the bench and pulled Sally's hands away from her laces. She looked up at him, steeling herself for another argument.

Instead he nodded his head sadly. "You're right," he said. "You're absolutely right. I'm not going anywhere, either. Not until we find your friend and make sure she's safe."

Relief and gratitude flooded Sally. She hadn't wanted to admit—even to herself—how much she didn't want to do this alone. "Thank you, Jack," she said, her voice hoarse. "But you really don't have to. . . ."

"You didn't have to come with me, either," he reminded her. "But you did." He reached out, cupping her chin in his hand, turning her face to him. To meet her eyes with his own. "Think of it as my chance to return the favor," he added, his voice deceptively light. But she could hear the solemnness just below the surface. He was taking this seriously. And she appreciated that, more than he could know.

Sally heard a throat clearing. She looked up, realizing Tammy had followed them to the bench. "So what are you going to do?" the doll asked skeptically.

Sally thought about it for a second. "Does Mr. Jingles have an office somewhere?" she asked. "Maybe we can break in and look for clues. He must have some records of where he's taking people, right?"

Tammy raised her hand, pointing up the hill. "He works

there," she said flatly. "In Santa's workshop. But you'll never get in. It's guarded and locked up tight."

Sally's heart sank as she remembered the guards at the door. This might prove harder than she thought.

Still, she wasn't about to give up. After all, how many times had she broken out of Dr. Finkelstein's lab? Surely she could figure out a way to break *into* a place. "Let us worry about that," she told Tammy. "In the meantime, you should head home. People have seen you with us now. And if we go down, I don't want to take you with us."

Tammy looked at her for a moment, then gave a grudging snort. "You're a brave toy," she said. "I'll give you that." She paused, then added, "Just be careful, all right? A lot of people underestimate Christmas Town. But nightmares can lie in the dreamiest of places."

"Well, that's good," Sally declared, flashing Jack a look. "Because it just so happens we have a lot of experience with nightmares."

CHAPTER SIXTEEN

After saying goodbye to Tammy and making her promise again to lie low for the time being, Sally and Jack returned their skates to the man by the side of the pond. He thanked them and asked how they enjoyed their time on the ice. Sally tried to sound enthusiastic when she answered—they *had* loved skating, after all—but she was pretty sure she came off sounding as fake as some of the "nice" people of Christmas Town. And by the time they started walking away, an almost overwhelming wave of despair washed over her.

She'd only wanted a change. Had she destroyed someone's life in the process?

"It's going to be all right, Sally," Jack insisted, slinging an arm around her shoulders and giving her a sympathetic look. Sally glanced up him, wondering why he suddenly looked so blurry. Until she felt the splash of tears falling from her eyes and onto her cheeks.

"I hope so," she said. "Abigail was so kind to me. I can't let anything happen to her."

"You won't. *We* won't," Jack declared. He rose to his full height, patting his chest with his hands. "After all, I'm Jack Skellington, the Pumpkin King. And you're Scary Sally, the doll who can single-handedly frighten away an entire town just by using her head." He bared his teeth menacingly. "They have no idea who they're dealing with."

A chill spun down Sally's back as she caught the fierce look on Jack's face. It was the kind of swagger he usually reserved for Halloween night, and she had always been enthralled by it. That confidence! That conviction! That look that told her he seriously believed he could achieve anything—if he just put his mind to it.

And maybe Sally could, too.

"I suppose we *did* want an adventure," she said wryly.

Jack snorted. "I'll say," he agreed. He reached up, straightening his beard. "Now come on. Let's go storm this Christmas castle."

And so together, they headed out of the center of town and up the path on the side of the hill that led to Santa's workshop, hoping their disguises would hold. On the way up, they passed others coming down and tried their best to act normally, giving overly cheery waves and happy greetings and wishes for a merry Christmas as they went, as if nothing were amiss.

As if they were oh so nice.

"I can't imagine having to live like this," Sally muttered after they waved hello to a man leading one of those flying antler creatures down the hill. "Being forced to be so cheerful all the time, even when I'm stressed and worried? And being stressed and worried because I'm forced to be so cheerful all the time."

"Indeed. I think my jaw would drop off if I had to smile as much as these people do," Jack agreed with a grimace. Then a thoughtful look came over his face. "Makes me appreciate Halloween Town," he added softly.

"Me too," Sally declared. "Imperfection never looked so good." She paused and added, "Though they do make a mean hot chocolate here."

"You're not wrong," Jack agreed with a laugh. "And then there's the ice-skating, too. I'd like to try that again— once I'm fully healed, of course." He rubbed his bottom and Sally gave him a sympathetic look.

"Poor Jack," she said. "First you scald yourself, then you almost break yourself."

"Bah! Just a bone wound," he assured her. "I'll be fine."

They soon arrived at the front gates of Santa's workshop. Just like before, it was guarded by two identical tin soldiers holding jingle bell–tipped spears. Of course, this time Sally didn't have Joey to help them get through the front door. And she was pretty sure they weren't going to just allow her entry, even if she asked nicely.

She grabbed Jack and pulled him behind a large snowdrift so they could better observe the scene. She scanned the building, noting a back door on the other side. It wasn't guarded, but that probably meant it was locked. And all the bottom-floor windows had red-and-white-striped bars on them. To make matters worse, she spotted two more guards patrolling the building's perimeter.

"How are we supposed to sneak in?" Sally asked, feeling discouraged.

Jack stroked his fake beard. "What if we simply stormed the front gates?" he asked. "You said they can't stomach even the simplest of scares. I could set my body on fire and then run at them screaming. I bet they'd scatter like crows in a cornfield."

"Possibly effective, but not exactly subtle," Sally pointed out. "And we don't want them to know what we're up to. If they get suspicious, they could move Abigail from wherever it is they're keeping her. Someplace we'd never be able to find her."

"Right. Good point," Jack agreed, though he looked a little disappointed. He'd always been one for dramatic entrances. "What do you suggest we do instead?"

Sally frowned, thinking hard. Her eyes settled on the barred windows. "Look there," she said, pointing. "I bet I can slip through those if I squish myself enough. Then I can go unlock the back door and let you in."

"That could work," Jack agreed. "But what about the patrol? What if they see you?"

Sally pursed her lips. Good point. She had the ingredients to mix an invisibility potion, but she'd need a stove of some sort to make it. If only she'd thought of this when they were still at the bottom of the hill.

She watched the guards continue their march around the building. She just needed a momentary distraction. . . .

She turned to Jack. "You're going to take care of the guards," she told him. "But not in the scary way you're thinking," she added quickly, catching his face. "You're going to be nice."

Jack raised his eyebrows. "Nice? Me?"

"It's not that hard, I promise. Just walk right up to them and tell them what a good job they're doing. Praise them for their hard work and . . ." She paused, an idea forming in her mind. "Give them some of these."

She reached into her bag and pulled out the leftover

sugarplums she'd saved from her first visit, then held them out to Jack. He observed them skeptically.

"Do I need to make them say trick or treat first?"

Sally shook her head. "Nope. And definitely no tricks, either—even if you think you can get away with them."

"You're no fun," Jack lamented. But his eyes twinkled. He grabbed the sugarplums from her hand. "Okay, I've got it. Just leave it to me."

"Good luck," Sally said. "And be careful."

Jack gave her a short salute, then slipped out from behind the snowbank. Sally watched nervously as he waltzed over to the guards with perfect Jack-style nonchalance. When the guards noticed him, they jerked to attention, raising their spears. Sally drew in a shaky breath. Here went nothing.

Come on, Jack. You can do this.

"Why, hello, good fellows!" Jack cried cheerfully. "It's so *nice* to see you today!" He reached out, grabbing each soldier by the hand in turn and giving them a vigorous shake before releasing them. The soldiers looked at him warily, as if taken aback by his boldness.

But Jack smiled widely. "You've been working so hard, haven't you?" he asked. "I've been watching. And I'm so impressed. In fact, I think you deserve a reward for all this hard work. Which is why I'm here. I've come to give you candy. And don't worry," he added quickly. "I have no tricks up my sleeves. I'm just really, really nice."

Sally stifled a groan, hoping he wasn't about to roll up his sleeves to demonstrate the aforementioned lack of tricks. If the soldiers caught sight of his lack of skin, they were going to start asking questions. Or maybe even take him down on the spot.

But luckily Jack resisted illustrating his point and instead pulled out his bag of treats. And before Sally knew it, the guards had set down their spears and were sampling the sugarplums with eager faces.

"These are really good!" the first one exclaimed.

"I haven't had sugarplums since I was a kid," added the other. "Where did you find them?"

"Oh, I can't give away all my secrets, now, can I?" Jack said with a laugh, slapping the soldier on the back. "But you enjoy them. And while you do, tell me all about your day. It must be so exhausting to be so important."

"Oh, it is," agreed the first soldier, his mouth full of candy. "You have no idea. Especially this morning when . . ."

He kept talking, but Sally was no longer listening. They were sufficiently distracted now, which meant it was time to make her move. Quickly and quietly, she made her way over to a window near the back of the factory, as close to the unguarded door as she could find.

Unfortunately, when she got there, she realized the bars on the windows were narrower than she'd estimated from far away. And try as she might, there was no way to slip her entire body through. Her arms and legs could squeeze, but her head was just too large.

She frowned in dismay. Was this not going to work after all?

"So how've you been doing these days?" she could hear Jack asking the soldiers. "How nice would you say you've been . . . on a scale of one to ten? No judgment, of course!"

Sally bit her lower lip, her mind racing. *Come on, think! What would you do if you were trying to escape Dr. Finkelstein?*

Suddenly she had an idea. She hoisted up her frilly dress, her fingers fumbling for a thread in her leg joint. Once she'd found one, she yanked on it hard, trying not to wince at the ripping sound as her stitches broke away. A moment later, her lower leg detached from her body and fell to the ground. She then repeated the process with her left arm. Once it was free, she got out her needle and thread and sewed her arm to her leg.

It wasn't a perfect job by any means. And the

result looked like a very odd experiment straight out of Dr. Finkelstein's lab. But she was pretty sure it would serve its purpose—and that was all that mattered.

Balancing on one foot, she leaned against the wall, then grabbed her leg-and-arm creation and shoved it through the narrow bars.

"Go find the door in the back," she whispered. "I'll meet you there!"

The hand gave her a thumbs-up. Then it turned to start hopping through the dark room. Sally felt a flutter of hope. This might actually work!

She headed toward the back door, hopping on her remaining leg. It wasn't easy—especially in the snow—and she almost fell a few times and had to slow down. When she finally reached the door, she tried the handle.

At first it didn't turn, and Sally worried that someone had discovered her creation bounding down the halls and had put a stop to it. But her fears proved unfounded, and soon the door creaked open from the inside, her hand/leg bouncing up and down in excitement.

Sally let out a breath of relief. "Good job," she said, grabbing her appendages and hopping them back over to stand behind another snowdrift. She sat down, ignoring the cold on her bottom as she quickly reattached her arm and leg to her body. It was a rush job and would have to be redone soon, but it would serve for the time being. Until she could get somewhere safe.

She had just finished tying up the thread when a sudden shadow crossed over her. She gasped, looking up, only to sigh in relief as she realized it was Jack.

"What are you doing?" he asked. "Is this really a good time for a sit-down?"

Sally rolled her eyes, scrambling to her feet. "Come on," she said. "The door's unlocked. If we're going to do this, it needs to be now."

"Lead the way," Jack declared. "I'm right behind you."

CHAPTER SEVENTEEN

The door Sally had unlocked turned out to lead into a small kitchen, which was luckily empty when they entered, though it looked frequently used. There were old-fashioned gadgets strewn across the counter: a hand mixer, a butter churner, and several piles of strange metal objects that seemed to be fashioned into various shapes like stars, stockings, and trees. Sally sniffed the air; something was baking, too. And it smelled good.

Her eyes lit up as she spotted the stove. "Keep an eye on the door," she told Jack. "I'll need a minute to whip up an invisibility potion for us. It'll help us get through the rest of the workshop without being spotted."

"Of course," Jack said, walking over and peering into the

oven. "But you might want to be quick about it. Whatever's in here has a timer set to go off in five minutes."

Sally nodded, quickly reaching under a cabinet and pulling out a pot. She filled it with water from the sink, then hurried over to the stovetop. She dumped the herbs into the pot and stirred vigorously while Jack paced the room, keeping an eye on the door.

Soon the potion began to bubble and turn green. Sally took it off the stove, hoping she'd let it simmer long enough, then began to pour it into a couple of mugs she'd found nearby. Her hands shook a little as she worked, her nerves jangling as she pushed a now-filled cup to Jack.

"Here you go. You need to—"

BING!

The timer went off. Sally swallowed hard. "Down it! Now!"

The door began to open. Sally chugged her potion, then yanked Jack down behind the counter to give it a few moments to kick in. Meanwhile, two elves pushed through the door, wearing matching red aprons covered in white powder that looked more like flour than snow. One had a beard and the other was completely bald.

"I can't believe he ordered another batch," the bearded one complained as he opened the oven and pulled out a tray of what appeared to be little cookies cut in the same shapes as the metal objects Sally had noticed earlier. "At this rate we're not going to have any dough left for our post-Christmas cookie swap."

"You better stop whining about that if you know what's good for you," the bald elf scolded, wagging his finger at his friend. "Or you'll find yourself on the naughty list. And doughless cookie swaps will be the least of your problems."

The bearded elf shuddered. "Don't even joke about that!" He glanced around the kitchen, as if half expecting some spy might be listening. For a moment, his gaze rested right on Sally and Jack and she squeezed her eyes shut, sure they'd been seen. But then he turned away, as if nothing were amiss. Sally's shoulders slumped in relief. The potion had worked.

The elf turned back to his friend. "That reminds me, Frank and Fred have gone missing."

"Oh, no. Are you serious?"

"They didn't show up to their shifts this morning. And no one saw them last night, either."

The bald elf groaned. "Seriously, if we lose any more elves, we won't have to worry about Santa's cookie con-sumption. He won't have any presents ready to deliver."

"Yeah, well, tell that to Mr. Jingles," the bearded elf replied, rolling his eyes as he set the tray on the counter and began scooping the cookies onto a plate. "I'm sure he'd love to hear your constructive criticism."

"Yeah, right. I've got a vacation planned after this holiday and I'm not losing my deposit because I'm in some prison for speaking up." He shook his head. "Just lie low. It's not worth it."

He grabbed the plate of cookies and headed toward the door, beckoning for his friend to follow. "Now come on. We can't keep the big guy waiting." He smirked. "It wouldn't be *nice.*"

The bearded elf laughed, and together they headed back out of the room. Once they were gone, Sally and Jack rose to their feet. Sally's legs felt a bit wobbly, but her brain was spinning fast.

"That was close," she said with a shaky laugh.

"That was amazing," Jack countered. "I had no idea you could make yourself invisible. What a useful trick. I mean, just think of the possibilities for next Halloween! Instead of setting myself on fire, I could make myself disappear." He nodded to himself. "It'd be great. And a lot less potential for charring."

"We can think about that later," Sally said. "Right now we have work to do. The potion won't last long. We need to get to Jingles's office, and fast."

They headed out of the room, through the same door the two men had just exited, and into a sterile white hallway that branched out in three directions. Luckily there were little plaques on the wall that helpfully pointed out which hallway went where.

"'Stables,' 'Toy Making,' 'Wrapping Room' . . ." Sally tapped her finger down the signs. She stopped at the last one. "'Executive Offices.' I bet that's where we'll find something."

Jack nodded. "Lead the way."

They took a right turn into another hallway, dodging elves hurrying in the other direction who luckily couldn't see them, then continued to follow the signs toward the offices until they reached a set of doors, each labeled with their occupant's name. At the very end of the hall there was a door off by itself, far grander than the others, complete with a large jingle bell serving as a knocker.

"That must be our man," Jack declared. "We just have to hope he's not home."

Sally approached the door on tiptoes, putting her ear to the wood, trying to listen for some sign that the room beyond was occupied. But she heard nothing. Not a single jingle. She shrugged at Jack before remembering he couldn't see the gesture.

"I think we're all right," she said. "Come on. We need

to make this quick. The potion isn't going to last much longer."

She reached for the handle, then pushed the door open slowly, just in case she was wrong about the office being vacant. But it revealed itself to be empty and they slipped inside, closing the door behind them. Jack gave a low whistle as he looked around the room.

"This is quite the place," he observed. "Must be good to be the judge."

Sally couldn't help agreeing. The entire room was decked out in heavy expensive-looking furniture, complete with a set of built-in bookcases with an actual ladder on a rail to help reach the top shelves. There was a large fireplace in one corner, with a massive stone hearth, and in the center of the room was a mahogany desk strewn with papers, with a chair behind it that resembled a throne. And to complete the room, a life-size replica of Santa's nice and naughty lists had been hung on the wall behind the desk.

Except . . . Sally frowned, squinting at the lists. They weren't exactly the same, were they?

"Take a look at this," she said, moving closer. She dragged a finger down the nice, then naughty list. "These aren't the same names as the ones in Santa's office."

"How can you tell?"

"Well, for one thing, I definitely remember another Sally on his list. She was three down from the top in Santa's nice column. Also, these names are quite different—Snowflake, Elfie, Sparkle, Holly. There's even a Rodney the Reindeer and a Roger Robot. And . . ." She gasped softly, reading the last name on the naughty list.

"What is it?" Jack asked, striding over.

"Abigail," she read, then swallowed hard. "So it's true. They did put her on the naughty list for helping me." She felt a sinking feeling in her stomach. "That's so unfair."

"We can debate fairness later," Jack reminded her. "Right now we have to figure out where they've taken her." She could hear him walking across the room and rummaging through some papers. "He's got to have something about it written down, right? Perhaps we can find an arrest report."

"I hope so," Sally said, joining Jack at the desk. "Because if we can't—"

She never got a chance to finish her sentence because her ears caught voices on approach. The papers Jack was presumably holding fluttered back to the desk; he'd heard them, too.

"They're coming this way," he whispered. "Do you think our invisibility will hold?"

"I don't know how much longer we have," Sally confessed. "Find somewhere to hide."

She looked wildly around the room. Should they go under the desk? But no, it was open on both ends. And none of the windows had any curtains.

"What about in here?" Jack asked. For a moment Sally didn't know where he was pointing to, seeing as he was invisible. But then she watched a poker rise from the fireplace stand and point into the hearth.

"What are you . . . ?" she started to ask, then her eyes widened as she realized what he was suggesting. "Jack Skellington! We cannot climb up a chimney!" she protested.

"Why not? From what you told me, the big guy uses them as egresses all the time."

"I know but . . ." Sally tried, then winced. The voices were getting closer. They were running out of time.

"Okay, fine," she said. "But I'm going on record to say this is a very bad idea."

"Duly noted," Jack said. "Now come on. I'll give you a boost up."

They ran to the fireplace, ducking under the mantel to climb into the hearth itself. It was actually bigger than Sally had imagined it to be, but that didn't make it spacious by any means.

She gingerly shinnied her way up, using Jack's hand as a

stepstool and the interior bricks as handholds. Inch by inch, she climbed, trying very hard to stave off her growing claustrophobia as she became enveloped in blackness. How on earth did Santa manage this on a regular basis?

There must be an easier way to get into people's houses, she thought wryly. *Why don't people just leave their doors unlocked for the poor man?*

She could feel Jack's hands on her ankles as he made his own way up into the chimney behind her. "Can you climb up any farther?" he asked, coughing a little from the chimney soot. "My legs are still sticking out the bottom."

Sally looked up. Unfortunately, the chimney's flue appeared to be shut, leaving her no more room to maneuver. Something they probably should have thought of before they started their climb. She reached down, grabbing Jack's hand and pulling him up to where she was crouched. It would be an even tighter squeeze with the two of them, but she saw no other way.

"We're going to get cozy," she told him. "I hope that's okay."

She could feel Jack's silent chuckle as his chest pressed against hers, and something hitched in her throat. She still couldn't see him—but she could feel his warm breath on her lips, indicating they were now face to face. A moment later, his foot curled around her ankle, anchoring them.

"Stay still," she whispered, feeling as if her heart was betraying her, beating far too loud. "You don't want to kick down any soot."

Jack's hand curled around hers, squeezing lightly, telling her he understood. For a moment they just crouched there, holding their breaths. Then the door squeaked open, and Sally caught the sound of footsteps heading into the room. The ash from the chimney tickled her nose and she fought back a sneeze.

"So, has our little doll been delivered?" she heard someone with a familiar voice ask with a sickening laugh. Sally scowled. Mr. Jingles. And he was probably talking about Abigail.

Her heart sank. All this time, she hadn't realized how much she'd been holding out hope that this was all a big misunderstanding. That Abigail was just lying low somewhere, keeping safe.

But no. They had her. And it was all Sally's fault.

"Yes, sir. We bused her down this morning. Very upset, as you can imagine. Lots of blubbering. Lots of apologies. Lots of begging to talk to Santa."

"Yes, well, they're all sorry in the end," Mr. Jingles scoffed. "Perhaps they should have considered the price of their actions before they got out of line." Sally could almost hear the sneer in his voice. "Sad, really, that it has to come to this. She seemed like a decent toy. But Santa's work must be protected at all costs. This is Christmas we're talking about, after all! The most important holiday of the year!"

"Of course," his partner agreed. "It's a good thing he put you in charge. Soon no one will dare to be naughty again." He chuckled. "There's not a crime in the world worth committing if it means being sent to that thing." He paused and Sally could almost hear his shudder. "He scares the stockings off my chimney, I'll tell you what."

"Sootfang is definitely a good . . . incentive," Mr. Jingles agreed with a nasty giggle. "I'm sure our naughty little dolly is shaking in her porcelain boots right about now."

Sootfang, Sally mouthed, worry rising inside her. What in the name of Christmas Town was a Sootfang?

"What about the other one?" Mr. Jingles's friend was asking. "That rag doll our little porcelain princess was helping out? The one who shut down the talent show?"

"Bah! She's long gone, from what my informants have told me," Mr. Jingles replied. "She and her little ghost-dog friend headed out of town yesterday, probably back to whatever rathole they crawled out of. Good riddance, too. We don't need the likes of her stirring up folk around here."

"Agreed," his friend replied. "But we'll keep an eye out for her just in case. If she gets some wild idea about coming back here, well, she'll soon learn the true meaning of Christmas."

The two men laughed. The kind of laugh that chilled Sally right down to her leaves. She scowled in her hiding spot. The two of them were evil—pure evil, she decided, fury boiling in her stomach. What she wouldn't do to teach them each a lesson.

Suddenly she felt Jack lean forward, then press his forehead against her own in a silent show of support. He knew this talk would upset her, she realized. He wanted her to know she wasn't alone. Sally closed her eyes, trying to still her anger. Trying not to think about how weirdly comfortable she suddenly felt, trapped in a tiny chimney.

The door squeaked again, and Sally heard more footsteps, this time fading into the distance. Mr. Jingles and his henchman had exited the office. She let out a breath of relief—and the sneeze she'd been holding in.

Once they were sure they weren't coming back, she and Jack climbed down the chimney, coughing and sputtering as they exited, both sucking in large breaths of clean air. Their hiding spot had not left them unscathed, and their costumes were covered in soot, something she could now see since their invisibility potions had completely worn off. And while this look might have been considered "making an effort" back home, here it was likely to draw unwanted attention.

Sally shook herself, trying to brush off as much soot as she could from her dress. "That was close," she muttered.

"And yet, rather cozy," Jack remarked with a sly grin, and something inside Sally involuntarily fluttered.

She waved him off, trying to focus on the task at hand. "Keep searching," she scolded. "We don't know how much time we have left."

She scanned the room, her mind going back to her time spent in Dr. Finkelstein's lab. He was always hiding stuff— secret recipes, directions for his experiments—you name it. He lived in constant paranoia that someone would someday sneak in and steal something important. In fact, one time he even wrote a formula on a wall and then covered it up with wallpaper. . . .

Sally's eyes widened. Her gaze snapped to the naughty and nice lists on the wall. Could Mr. Jingles have done the same?

She walked briskly toward the lists. When she reached them, she took the roll of paper in both hands and pulled on it as hard as she could, tearing it in two.

"Sally! You're a genius!" Jack cried as the paper fell away, revealing a large map behind it. Sally's heart leapt. Could this be what they were looking for? A clue to lead them to wherever Abigail and the others had been taken? Why else would it have been hidden?

She studied the map carefully. At the center was Christmas Town. That was obvious. But there were several other locations marked farther out toward the map's edges. And some kind of road or path winding through all of them. A path that ended at a small black mass at the very northern part of the map. A mass circled with a red pen.

Sally's eyes bulged. "Do you think that's it? Where they're taking them?"

Jack grabbed the map, carefully detaching it from the wall so as not to tear it. "It has to be," he said. He folded the map and stuffed it in his pocket. Then he turned to Sally. "All right. Now let's get out of here before—"

But the words died in his throat as a horrified expression washed over his face.

"What is it?" Sally asked worriedly, realizing he was no longer looking at her.

He was looking at something behind her.

Slowly, with dread, she turned around, her eyes falling on a small elvish woman dressed in a green-and-white apron, standing in the doorway. Sally wasn't sure who looked more surprised—the woman or her.

"Who are you?" the elf demanded. "And what are you doing in Mr. Jingles's workshop?"

"Um . . ." Sally tried to think quick. "We just got turned around! We're looking for the cookie kitchen?"

But, she realized, the woman wasn't listening. She was too busy reaching into her bag and pulling out a small horn. Sally gasped in dismay as the elf brought it to her lips, then blew hard. A trumpet rang out, loud enough to be heard throughout the entire workshop.

"Intruders!" the elf screamed.

CHAPTER EIGHTEEN

Sally stood frozen in place. What were they going to do? How were they going to escape?

Jack, on the other hand, didn't share her hesitation. He sprang into action, leaping forward and shouting "BOO!" at the poor woman while pulling down his beard and revealing his skeletal face. The woman shrieked in terror and staggered backward to avoid the unexpected ghoul charging in her direction. Leaving their path to the doorway clear.

"Come on!" Jack cried, beckoning to Sally. "I think we've overstayed our welcome!"

Sally didn't need a second invitation. She ran past the poor woman, who was sobbing and screaming about ghosts and goblins, and sprinted through the door and out of the office. She followed Jack down the hall as she tried to remember how to get back to the kitchen with the door leading outside. It wasn't going to be easy now that they were visible to all.

Jack moved fast with his long limbs, and Sally soon started falling behind. Not only were her legs shorter, but the left one had been hastily reattached after her break-in scheme and wasn't working to its full potential.

"Jack! Wait! Please!" she begged, hobbling down the hall. She could feel her stitches straining as she limped, getting worse and worse with each step. She tried to keep pushing herself forward, but eventually her leg gave out altogether, coming out from under her—literally. Sally's body was flung forward, her palms skidding across the tiled floor until she landed in a heap.

Jack was at her side in an instant. "Are you all right?" he asked.

"I'm not hurt. But I can't run like this. . . ." Sally trailed off, crawling across the floor to retrieve her detached leg. She could hear shouting in the distance and cringed. It wouldn't be long before their pursuers caught up to them. And this time there was no chimney in which to hide.

"Just go," she urged Jack. "Leave me."

"What? Absolutely not!" Jack looked horrified by the suggestion. "I'll carry you."

"You won't be able to run fast enough if you do. We'll both be caught!"

"Then I'll talk our way out of it."

Sally shook her head. "That's too much of a risk at this point. They're going to see my leg and know we don't belong. Plus that woman saw your face. She's not going to be quiet about it." She bit her lower lip, looking around, her mind racing. There had to be someplace to hide! But the hall stretched out in both directions, long and straight and empty.

Come on, think! she scolded herself. *You've escaped Dr. Finkelstein's lab a thousand times. What would you do if you were there now?*

But her mind remained blank. And her leaves rustled with growing fear. She bent her head back, staring up at the ceiling helplessly. . . .

And then she saw it. Saw exactly how they could escape.

"I've got it!" she cried. "Lift me up."

Jack followed her gaze, frowning. "I don't understand."

"The ceiling. Look! There's a grate to let in air. If we push on it, we can crawl up through it. It probably leads to a ventilation tunnel where we can hide."

"All right," Jack agreed, though he still looked a little doubtful. Sally supposed she couldn't blame him; she wasn't a hundred percent sure it would work, either. But it was something at least. A chance.

Jack reached down, scooping Sally up and making sure she had hold of her detached leg.

Then he rose to his full height, lifting her up to the ceiling grate above, and Sally pushed on it as hard as she could. At first it didn't give, and she worried maybe it was locked in place. But she tried again, even harder this time, and at last she was able to jar it free, leaving a big hole for them to climb through. Sally grabbed the edges of the hole and hoisted herself up into the ceiling. Then she reached down, holding out her hand.

"Come on," she said. "I'll pull you up."

Jack grabbed on to her hand. She gripped his tightly in her own (the good one that hadn't been recently reattached), then closed her eyes and pulled as hard as she could. She could hear more seams ripping, and for a moment she was sure she would drop him and it would all be over. But she held on tight anyway. She knew Jack would have done the same, had their positions been reversed.

Finally Jack was able to grab hold of the ceiling, and Sally allowed herself to let go. He swung his legs up, shoving them into the tunnel and almost kicking Sally in the face in the process.

"Sorry!" he cried as he scrambled to right himself. It was a tight squeeze for a tall skeleton like him, and he had to basically fold himself up to fit.

"I'm fine," Sally assured him as she quickly replaced the grate, sliding it into position just as elves came around the corner below.

"Where are they?"

"They couldn't have gone far!"

"Keep looking! That way!"

Sally glanced at Jack. He put a finger to his mouth. They waited, silent and still, until the footsteps faded into the distance. Only then did Sally let out a breath of relief.

"Okay," she said. "I think we're safe. For now anyways."

"We should keep moving though," Jack urged. "If you can bear crawling through these tight shafts, I assume one of them eventually leads outside."

Sally nodded in the darkness. She didn't love the idea of spelunking through this cramped space. It was almost as bad as being stuck in a chimney. But she knew they had no choice.

"All right," she said. "But first I have to sew my leg back on. Properly this time, so it doesn't come apart again." She reached for her leg, her hands still shaking from residual adrenaline after their near escape. She hoped she'd be able to thread her needle.

Jack placed a hand over her arm. "Allow me," he said, and Sally's eyes widened as he carefully aligned her lower leg with the stub of her knee.

"I can do that—" she started. But Jack put a finger to her lips.

"I know you can," he said, meeting her eyes with his own. "But right now your hands are still trembling from trying to help me up and I don't want you to hurt yourself. So why don't you just rest for a second? Allow me to make myself useful for once." He wagged a playful finger at her. "You don't get to save the day every time, you know."

Sally tried to laugh, but it came out more like a choke as grateful tears began to well in her eyes. A part of her still wanted to argue, to insist she could do it herself. But then, Jack already knew that, didn't he? Even in the darkness she could see his confidence in her, reflected in his dark eyes.

Sally had always hated when Dr. Finkelstein had sewed her back together. It made her feel weak. Helpless. Yet another thing he didn't trust her to do on her own. Another way to retain control.

But Jack wasn't trying to control her, she realized. He was trying to help her. And wasn't it nice, sometimes, to lean on another? To trust that someone cared enough to do the job right?

Jack's mouth quirked. "Don't worry. I know how to sew. Maybe not as well as you. But you can poke me if I do something wrong."

She nodded slowly, reaching into her pocket for her needle and thread and handing them over to Jack. "Don't mess it up, Pumpkin King," she joked, trying to keep the mood light, though her voice sounded a little froggy. "Who knows the next time I might need to use it to flee from jokers with jingle bells?"

Or this Sootfang, she thought with a small shudder. *Whatever it was.*

Jack got to work, sewing with care. Making sure each and every stitch was even and tight. Sally watched, hardly able to breathe as the needle wove in and out of her fabric. And she couldn't help a small tremble as his fingers brushed across her leg.

He looked up immediately, his eyes rimmed with concern. "Did I hurt you?" he asked worriedly.

She shook her head wordlessly. It did hurt a little, of course—it always did. But so much less than when Dr. Finkelstein would carelessly jab his needle into her cloth, without caring how she was feeling or even if his stitches would hold for the long haul.

But Jack was different. Meticulous. Gentle. And instead of feeling uncomfortable, she felt a strange warmth settle in her stomach.

Soon Jack finished, giving her a shy smile as he tied off

the last stitch. And from the look on his face, she realized he'd felt something, too. Maybe it wasn't exactly the same. Maybe not as strong. But something.

Which made her feel even warmer.

"Better?" he asked.

"Much," she agreed. "Thank you."

"I'm at your service," he said with a mock salute. Then he grinned goofily. "Now come on. Let's get out of here."

They began crawling through the ventilation tunnels on their hands and knees. Which was a lot easier for Sally, who could scrunch herself down to an acceptable size. Jack had a harder time and kept banging his head on the shaft's ceiling.

"Are you okay?" she asked, after he'd done it a third time.

"Never better," he joked. "Why, when we get home, I might just start looking for other dark tight tunnels to crawl through for fun." He banged his head again and grunted.

"Well, you wanted an adventure," Sally teased.

"Not exactly what I had pictured in my head," Jack snorted. "Not that I mind," he added quickly, shooting a glance back at Sally. "I'm glad we're going to be able to help your friend."

"Yeah, well, I hope we can," Sally murmured. Now that they weren't in immediate danger, the full weight of their mission had begun to sink heavily onto her shoulders. They had a map, but would that be enough to find Abigail? And even if they did free her, where would they take her?

"What's wrong?" Jack asked. They'd reached an inter-section in the air shafts, which gave him enough space to turn and look at her. "We've got the map. We're going to do this."

"I know," she said. "I mean, yes, we're going to rescue her—I have no doubt. But, Jack, what happens after? You heard Mr. Jingles and his friend. There's no way they're going to just let her come back to live in Christmas Town. She'll be a fugitive! And there's certainly no way Santa will let her ride on his sleigh. Which means she'll never get a child of her own."

Jack made a face. "Why does she want one of those any-way? Children are so . . . sticky. And they don't take care of their things at all."

"I don't know *why* she wants it," Sally admitted. "But she does. And we need to support her. Whether we under-stand her or not."

Jack was silent for a moment. "Did anyone ever tell you how amazing you are?" he asked in a soft voice.

Sally's cheeks heated. "Oh, please. Stop."

"I'm being serious!" Jack protested. "And I can't believe you don't see it. You're brave, you're resourceful, you can break into buildings, and you can turn people invisible.

You're smart, but you're also kind. You care about other people and you're always trying to help them. I mean, you barely know this Abigail doll. But you're willing to risk everything for her." He shook his head. "I wish more people were like you. The world would be a much better place."

Sally's stomach summersaulted at the admiration she heard in his voice. No one had ever seen these things in her before. They'd only seen her as Dr. Finkelstein's creation, a simple rag doll who never joined them on Halloween. But Jack saw something beyond the rags. He saw the doll she could be, if only given a chance.

He thought that doll was amazing.

"Well, thank you," she said awkwardly, not sure of the proper response to such praise. "You're not so bad yourself, I suppose," she added with a small grin. "But of course you already know that. All of Halloween Town knows that."

She expected him to smile at this. But instead he looked grave. "Maybe that's part of my problem," he said slowly. "They all love me for what I do for them. But hardly anyone knows the real me. It's like they see me as this great Pumpkin King! Larger than life! Someone to rule over them and inspire them and give them a night to remember." He hung his head. "But then daylight always comes. And I find myself all alone. Without any real friends."

Sally's heart wrenched at the pain she heard in his

voice. She knew it too well, that terrible empty feeling that stemmed from loneliness. That desperate desire to be close to something—someone. Someone who understood you. Someone who allowed you to be yourself without any strings attached.

Perhaps, all along, it hadn't been freedom or adventure they'd truly craved that night in the graveyard, she thought suddenly. Perhaps it had been connection.

She looked up, realizing Jack's face was near hers. He gave her a timid smile, reaching out to brush a lock of yarn from her eyes. Sally felt her leaves swirl, and her first instinct was to jerk away, laugh, break from the moment and make it all a joke.

But no. That was the coward's way out. She needed to face her fears. To be the Sally she so desperately wanted to be. The Sally she saw reflected in Jack's dark eyes.

"Jack . . ." she whispered. His name felt like a prayer on her lips. "Oh, Jack."

"Sally . . ."

Jack closed his eyes. Tilted his head. Began to lean closer. Sally's breath caught in her throat as she realized what he was about to do. Drawing in all her courage, she closed her own eyes and—

CRACK!

Suddenly the air shaft gave way. The floor fell out from

under them, and they found themselves tumbling down through the ceiling. Sally shrieked, trying to grab on to something—anything—to keep herself from falling. But it was no use. They crashed into the room below.

And the next thing she knew? Sally was looking up straight into the eyes of Santa Claus.

CHAPTER NINETEEN

"Ho ho ho! What do we have here?"

Sally scrambled to her feet, her cheeks burning and her heart pounding. Was this really happening? Seriously, of all places to crash-land, did it have to be Santa's office? Any second now, he'd probably be on the phone to Jingles, demanding they be taken away.

Her eyes darted around the room, searching for somewhere to run. But the only exit was directly behind Santa and there was no practical way to reach it.

"S-Santa," she stammered, trying to brush herself off as she addressed him. She must have looked a total fright, with all the chimney soot now embellished with cobwebs and dust from the vents. She glanced over at Jack, who wasn't faring much better himself as he rose unsteadily to his feet. He seemed shaken and he was rubbing his back with his hand, as if he'd bruised it in the fall. Worse, his hat was gone and his beard was askew, revealing his whole face in all its skeletal glory. "I can explain."

Santa raised a bushy eyebrow. "This ought to be good."

Sally cocked her head. Did she catch a hint of amusement in his voice? That was unexpected. He should be furious with them for breaking into his workshop, let alone crashing through his ceiling. After all, that was about as naughty as you could possibly get.

She drew in a breath, her mind racing as to how she could justify any of this. But before she could speak, Jack stepped forward, surprising her by thrusting out his hand toward Santa.

"Allow me to introduce myself," he said gallantly. "My name is Jack Skellington. They call me the Pumpkin King." He looked curiously at Santa. "And you are . . . ?"

Santa frowned, seeming taken aback. "Why, I'm Santa . . . Claus," he stammered.

"Of course!" Jack acknowledged. "Sandy Claws. I knew you must be! I've heard all about you—they say you're the big man himself." He pumped Santa's hand up and down. "The leader of Christmas Town." He dropped his hand and smiled. "I guess you can say I hold a similar position, back where I'm from. We call it Halloween Town. It has a bit of a different ambiance, of course," he added, giving Santa a knowing look.

"Of . . . course," Santa repeated doubtfully.

"Anyway, I have to tell you, I admire what you've done to the place. It's quite stellar. Especially that hot chocolate— wow! That stuff is intense. I simply must get the recipe. And the ice-skating? An absolute thrill, though a bit dangerous, I have to say." He chuckled. "When I have more time, I'd love to sit down with you and hear all about what you've got going on. One holiday leader to another, you know?"

Sally swallowed hard, not sure what was happening. Santa was looking up—way up—at Jack with an expression on his bearded face that told her he had no idea what to think of this unexpected diplomatic visitor from a neighboring holiday town. And he wasn't sure what to do with him.

"Look, we didn't mean to intrude," she tried. "And we're very sorry about the ceiling."

"Though, it's not that bad, really," Jack broke in, giving the ceiling a critical once-over. "If you want, I could send some vampires over. They'd have it patched up in no time."

"Vampires?" Santa repeated.

"Oh, they're like those elves you have here," Jack replied nonchalantly. "But with pointy teeth instead of pointy ears.

Surprisingly good at drywalling, too. Who would have thought?"

Sally glanced nervously at the door behind Santa. She wondered where Mr. Jingles and his men were now. Were they looking for them? What if they decided to check in here?

She realized Jack was still talking. "Anyway, we don't want to keep you," he was saying. "I know it's crunch time for you right now, and believe me, I understand. Those last weeks before the big event? Brutal!" He shuddered. "But come January, you look me up, okay? I'll even have some notes for you, if you want them. Ways to make things better. Not that Christmas doesn't sound great and all, as it is, but there's always room for improvement, am I right?" He winked at Santa, and Sally cringed. *Don't go too far, Jack.*

But to her relief, Santa laughed. "You know, that's something I say to my elves," he told Jack. "Always room for improvement." Then his expression sobered. "Though it's hard to improve anything when you're hanging on by the skin of your teeth. These days it feels as if I can barely pull off Christmas at all, let alone make it as good as it can possibly be." He sighed. "I hate the idea of disappointing the children. They deserve the best Christmas ever." He shrugged sheepishly. "It's just a lot of pressure. And not a lot of thanks. I mean, half of them don't even believe in me—even after I spend all that time traveling around the world to personally deliver presents under their trees!"

"I get it," Jack assured him, laying a hand on his shoulder. "I can't tell you how many times parents have undermined my efforts by telling children there aren't any monsters under their beds or in their closets. Some of them even go as far as to tell them monsters don't exist at all!" He snorted with indignation. "It's a thankless job to be sure. You give, give, give, and no one appreciates it. It's actually why I'm here," he added brightly. "Sally and I are on a little holiday. And let me tell you, it's been glorious. You should try it sometime. I can't tell you how good it feels to just relax and enjoy yourself."

Santa nodded slowly. "You know," he said. "That's not a bad idea. Maybe after Christmas I'll carve out some me time." He looked up at Jack. "Maybe I'll even come try out your town. If you wouldn't mind, of course."

"Absolutely," Jack agreed. "You're always welcome!"

"Speaking of Halloween Town . . ." Sally gave him a pointed look. "Don't you think it might be time to get going?"

Jack nodded. "Right. Of course. We've got to get back. We've been gone so long—everyone's bound to be missing us by now. So we'll go *right there*. We're not going to dawdle at all in Christmas Town or any of the surrounding areas, you know. Because we'll be *back home*."

And with that, Jack gave Santa a short bow, then waltzed over to the office window and pulled it open. He started unscrewing the candy cane bars.

Santa frowned. "I have a door, you know."

But Jack waved him off. "Bah! Doors! So overrated. That's why you prefer chimneys, am I right? And we, in Halloween Town, like to exit by the window." He beamed. "Why, it's practically a tradition."

"Yes!" Sally broke in, running over to help him with the bars. "A definite tradition."

As she worked, she scanned the area outside. Luckily she didn't see any soldiers nearby. They were probably all inside, looking for them. Drawing in a breath, she hoisted herself through the opening, then waited for Jack to join her on the other side. A moment later, Santa stuck his head through.

"Goodbye!" he called. "Nice to meet you. Have a merry Christmas!"

"Merry Christmas to you, too!" Jack replied. "I'll see you in the New Year!"

Sally watched as Santa ducked back inside, closing the window behind him. She and Jack exchanged looks.

"Good job," Sally said. "I thought for sure we were goners."

"Me too," Jack agreed with a laugh. "Thank goodness that Sandy Claws is a reasonable chap."

"*Santa Claus,*" Sally corrected, scratching her head thoughtfully. "And he does seem nice, doesn't he? As if he's a genuinely good person, unlike some of the others we've met who seem to be nice just for show." She paused, then added, "Which really makes me wonder what is going on with Mr. Jingles. I can't imagine Santa approving of his methods."

"Agreed. I was actually going to question him about that," Jack said. "But I thought it could get awkward. Especially if he *does* know what's going on and has signed off on it."

"No, you handled it right," Sally assured him. She shook her head, remembering Jack's quick improvisation. "In fact, you were amazing in there."

Jack waved a dismissive hand. "It's not that hard, really. Just takes a little practice. Treat people with respect, talk to them like they matter. That'll get you what you want every time."

"I'll keep that in mind," Sally said, and gave him a smile. "Now come on. We've got our map. Let's go find Abigail."

CHAPTER TWENTY

Since it would have been too risky to head back through Christmas Town, they decided to skirt around the village from above, following the train tracks and ducking behind trees when the train went by, just in case. As they walked, Jack consulted the map, pointing out various landmarks as they passed them.

"We just need to get to that sign over there," he said. "There we'll find another path that leads to the top of the hill. From there we should be able to cut through the forest—you know, the one we came in at. On the other side of that, there should be another valley. We drop down into it to find our next trail." He folded up the map and slipped it into his pocket. "I'm not going to lie—it looks far. But I'm sure we can make it."

Sally nodded, forcing herself to pick up the pace. Jack had done a good job on her leg and it felt very secure, which helped. Soon they found themselves heading under a red-and-white-striped archway with a cheery sign on top. YOU ARE NOW LEAVING CHRISTMAS TOWN! it read, next to a picture of a smiling face in a jingle bell hat. STAY NICE!

Stay nice . . . or else, Sally thought ruefully as they stepped under the archway.

She wondered if Abigail had passed through this very spot earlier, seen the same sign. Of course, she had probably been stuffed in a sack, so she couldn't have read it. But what if she had? Would she have recognized the hypocrisy of her hometown—of being convicted as naughty, when she'd only been nice? Or did she regret helping Sally? Did she wish Sally was in her position instead?

And that was if she was still alive at all. They still had no idea what this Sootfang was and what it did to those Jingles took to it. . . .

Sally pressed her lips together. No. She couldn't think like that. She had to believe Abigail was still out there. That there was still hope for a rescue.

She felt a sudden gust of wind behind her. She turned

around, her eyes lighting up as she caught sight of Zero zooming into view. The ghost dog was panting hard; he must have flown fast to catch up with them. He looked from Jack to Sally, questioningly, as if to ask, *Time to go home?*

"Not yet, old pal," Jack said, reaching out to scratch the dog's ears. "We've got a mission first. But you can head home anytime. Don't worry about us."

Zero gave a bark that sounded rather reproachful. Sally laughed and bonked him playfully on the nose.

"All right, then," she said. "We're glad to have you along."

They headed up the hill, Zero floating ahead, and soon they found themselves back in the familiar forest where their adventure had begun. When they reached the grove of holiday trees, Sally caught Jack giving a longing look to the jack-o'-lantern one before turning away.

She bit her lower lip. She knew what she had to say, even if she didn't want to say it. "What about you?" she asked gently. "Do you need to get home? I won't be upset if you do. I know you have important duties back in Halloween Town. Why, they're probably all panicking that you're missing. Sending out search parties . . ."

Jack snorted. "Oh, I'm sure of it. The Mayor's head is likely spinning in circles at this point."

"Meanwhile, the only person missing me will be

Dr. Finkelstein," Sally said, scrunching up her nose in distaste. "And only because he didn't wake up to a piping hot cockroach waffle breakfast this morning and can't find anyone to rub his warts."

"Well, *I'd* miss you," Jack assured her with a grin. "But lucky for me, I don't have to. Because you're right here with me. And"—he added, holding up a hand before Sally could speak—"there's no place I'd rather be."

Sally felt a blush rise to her face. She turned away, hoping Jack hadn't noticed. "Trust me, I'd rather have you with me," she said. "But a lot of people depend on you."

He reached out, touching Sally's shoulder. When she looked up, she found herself caught in his dark hollow gaze. "They can wait," he said in a voice rich with conviction. "Your friend cannot."

Sally drew in a shaky breath as Jack's hand tightened on her shoulder, sending what felt like sparks of electricity down her arm. As she struggled to maintain her composure, he reached out with his other hand, pulling her into a warm embrace.

At first, Sally felt frozen in place, shocked by the unexpected gesture.

This closeness that wasn't forced on them by a tight chimney but rather was sought out freely. But it felt too good, and soon she found herself relaxing into his hold.

Wrapping her own arms around his back, feeling his bones at her fingertips as she cradled her head against his chest.

There's no place I'd rather be, his voice seemed to whisper in her head.

Oh, Jack, she thought once again. *I know exactly how you feel.*

CHAPTER TWENTY-ONE

After heading out of the grove of holiday trees, they walked through the rest of the forest, leading farther away from Christmas Town and down the other side of the hill. Luckily the snow wasn't quite so deep on this side, which made for a much easier journey.

As they walked, they chatted easily, distracting each other from the seriousness of their mission. Jack told silly stories about past Halloweens, and Sally offered up a few potion recipes. Meanwhile, Zero zoomed ahead happily, chasing the occasional rabbit that had the misfortune of walking by at the wrong moment.

When they reached the bottom of the hill, the path

forked in two directions. Jack pulled out the map and consulted it. He pointed to the left.

"It looks as if we should go that way," he said. "Through that grove of trees. It'll lead us right to the Nog Bog, which is the next marker on the map."

"The Nog Bog," Sally repeated. "Sounds like something we'd have back in Halloween Town."

Jack laughed. "Definitely. Though there it'd be the Belch Bog. And it'd be full of burping mud that reeked of rotten onions."

"And it'd be a spa!" Sally added, joining in on the game. "Mud baths for monsters."

"You'll come out smelling worse than when you went in," Jack declared. "Money back guarantee."

"But it's very exclusive," Sally told him. "Only the scariest of monsters could ever hope to score an invite."

"Absolutely!" Jack agreed, looking shocked at the mere suggestion otherwise. "You have to have a three-star scare rating—at minimum—to even be considered." He winked at Sally. "But don't worry. I know a guy."

Sally rolled her eyes. "How lucky."

Jack grinned, grabbing the hat off her head and stuffing it over his skull, then dancing away when Sally tried to grab it back. She couldn't help laughing.

"Keep it," she told him.

"Won't you be cold?" he asked.

She waved him off. "I have more stuffing than you. I can take it."

He rocked into her playfully, his bony hip connecting with her own. She smiled back at him, feeling a tad guilty she was having so much fun, given the circumstances. But then Abigail wouldn't want her to be miserable, would she? And being worried and stressed wasn't going to make the rescue go any faster.

She and Jack continued down the path, toward the grove of trees, brainstorming names for their new monster spa as they went. Jack's long legs made for long strides, but every time Sally began to fall behind, he slowed his pace to allow her to catch up. It was funny, she thought, as she scrambled to reach him; he was so different than she'd ever imagined him to be. All those times she'd watched him waltz into town on Halloween night in all his pumpkin glory—she'd always been so impressed. He'd been like a rock star to her, larger than life.

But he was also just a simple guy, it turned out. With hopes and dreams and desires, just like everyone else.

And she liked that Jack. Maybe even more than the illustrious Pumpkin King.

She sighed dreamily, stealing a glance up at his face. Up until now, almost all her life had been spent alone, save for

Dr. Finkelstein, who had never tried to please her or make her laugh. And he certainly couldn't care less about her feelings. It was always what Sally could do for him, and never what he could do for Sally.

What would it have been like to have a friend like Jack around all that time? To have someone who treated her like an equal—a partner instead of a possession. A friendship built out of mutual respect. A bond created by love, not fear.

She frowned. *Love?* Where had that come from?

She turned her head away, concentrating on the path. She needed to stop this line of thinking, and fast. Before she got carried away. Yes, Jack was nice. He treated her with respect. Maybe he was even starting to care for her a little bit. But then, he cared for all the residents of Halloween Town.

It didn't mean he was in love.

She scowled, squeezing her hands into fists. *You need to stop,* she scolded herself. *Right now. If you do something stupid like fall in love, you'll risk falling alone. And it could ruin any hopes for the future of this friendship.*

When this adventure was over, they'd go back to Halloween Town. Jack would be the Pumpkin King again, throwing himself into planning next Halloween. And she . . . well, she'd have to figure out the rest of her life. Would they even have time to spend together if they wanted to? And if so, could she risk this blossoming friendship by suggesting something more? What if Jack didn't feel the same?

Just be glad Jack's here now. Let the future worry about itself.

"I have a question," Jack said suddenly, innocently breaking through her troubled thoughts. "Why have you never joined us on the Halloween preparations back home? I mean, no judgment at all," he added quickly, holding up his hands. "I know it's not everyone's thing. But I bet you'd be really good at it. I mean sewing, potion making. Not to mention you scared the residents of Christmas Town right out of their gourds!"

"They're not exactly a tough crowd," she joked. Then she shrugged. "But I'd love to be part of Halloween. In fact, it's always been one of my dearest dreams."

"Well then, why don't you?"

She gave him a dry look. "Have you met Dr. Finkelstein?"

Jack scowled. "That guy," he spit out. "Where does he get off telling you what to do?"

"Because I'm his creation. He brought me to life."

"So what? You have to devote that life to him forever? Seems pretty unreasonable, if you ask me."

"I know. It's just . . . well, he claims I'm not capable of taking care of myself." Sally wrinkled her nose.

"Well, clearly that's not true," Jack said. "I mean, look at you here! You've single-handedly scared a crowd, escaped a madman, broken into a high-security warehouse, and then found a way to escape again. Now you're trekking through the wilderness on a rescue mission. If that's not capable, then I don't know the definition."

Sally found her lips curling into a smile. "Well, when you put it that way," she said, "I do sound pretty great."

Jack stopped walking. He turned to Sally and reached out, taking her two hands in his own. "One thing I've learned. If you want people to believe in you, you have to know your own worth." He paused, then added, "And, Sally, you're more than worthy."

His bony hands, cold and hard, squeezed hers. But somehow they felt soft and warm all the same. Sally swallowed, trying to will her own hands to squeeze back in return. To let him know, without words, how much she appreciated his confidence in her. Never in her life had she had anyone believe in her before. And it felt almost too good.

Just don't take it too far. Don't confuse kindness with something more.

If you fall in love with him, it'll be too late.

Oh, dear. What if it already was?

With effort she jerked her hands away, stuffing them in her dress pockets. Jack frowned, a confused and hurt expression falling over his face. But luckily he didn't ask what was wrong. He seemed to sense somehow that she wasn't ready to say.

She swallowed hard, forcing her gaze back to the path. "Look," she said. "I think I see the edge of the forest. Which means we must be close to the Nog Bog." She started walking quickly toward the clearing ahead. "Come on. Let's see if—"

Suddenly the ground seemed to shift under her feet, as if it was no longer solid. Sally cried out in surprise and dismay, flailing her arms as she began to sink. But there was nothing to grab on to. And Jack was still standing where they'd stopped—too far away to help.

The Nog Bog, she thought in horror. They'd found it, all right.

And it was quickly pulling her under.

CHAPTER TWENTY-TWO

"Help!" Sally cried, waving her arms. She was sinking fast and could feel the slime oozing into her stitches, dragging her down. Being a rag doll had its advantages. But none of those advantages involved getting soaking wet. Liquid seeped too easily through the weave of Sally's fabric skin, saturating her stuffing and making her body too heavy to move. Which was why she usually stayed inside when it rained back home.

And this wasn't just rainwater, either. The liquid she found herself sinking into was much thicker. So thick she could grab handfuls of it and let it ooze from her fingers in slimy streams.

It also smelled disturbingly like eggs and cinnamon.

She dug her hands into the mud, trying to claw her way free, but the more she struggled, the more she sank. And soon she found herself up to her waist in the bog, with no obvious way to get out. Above her, Zero whined anxiously, floating in circles.

"Stop moving!" Jack commanded. She looked up to see he'd stepped over to the bog, though he remained a short distance away. Which was smart—she didn't need him falling in, too. But at the same time Sally desperately wished he were closer.

"This stuff is like quicksand," he called out to her. "The more you struggle, the more it's going to pull you under."

Sally closed her eyes for a moment, trying to reset her mind. It would do no good to panic, she reminded herself. When she opened her eyes again, she tried to stay still, as Jack had suggested. But that proved easier said than done since there was nothing solid for her feet to rest on, which made it almost impossible to keep her balance.

"Can you reach my hand?" Jack asked, lying down on the ground and stretching out his arm as far as it would go. Sally drew in a breath and attempted to move closer to him.

Closer. Closer . . .

"You can do it, Sally," Jack urged. His face was even more ashen than normal, and a bead of sweat dripped down his skull. He crawled his way toward her, as close as he dared, trying to make it easier for her to reach him. Sucking in a breath, she stretched her arm out. . . .

And she grabbed hold of a firm grasp!

Relief flooded through her as she clamped her hand down on his. She'd done it. And now he'd be able to pull her out. In just a moment, she would be lying on the ground by Jack's side, laughing about the whole ordeal.

But the bog, it seemed, had other ideas. And when Jack pulled on her hand, the bog wouldn't let go. He tried again, grunting in determination. But he couldn't manage to yank her free. Instead he started sliding forward himself.

"Let go!" she cried, frantically trying to untangle her fingers from his. "It'll pull you in, too!"

Jack gritted his teeth, attempting once more, this time with added force. Her ears caught the sound of ripping seams.

"Stop!" she begged. "You'll tear off my arm."

With a moan, Jack did as he was told, and Sally slid backward, sinking even deeper than she had been before. She was now up to her neck in the stuff. And Jack seemed even farther way. He gave her an anguished look.

"I'm so sorry," he cried. "I thought I could . . ."

"It's not your fault," she assured him. "We just have to think of another way."

She drew in a slow breath, trying to remain as still as possible as her brain whirled with possibilities. She'd worked with a lot of potions over the years, she reminded herself. Some with a similar consistency to this. Heavier liquids would always float to the bottom, she remembered. Which meant she needed to find a way to get lighter.

She considered detaching an arm or leg but quickly dismissed the idea. She might end up losing it in the bog.

Think! she begged herself.

It was then that she remembered Halloween Town's resident Undersea Gal. The one who lived in the fountain at the center of town. When she emerged from the fountain's depths, she would often float on her back. Maybe that gave her some kind of buoyancy?

Could it work for Sally, too?

She gritted her teeth, trying to muster the courage to move. If this didn't work—or if she did it wrong—the bog would take her again, this time completely submerging her in its depths. But then that would eventually happen anyway, she realized, even if she stayed in one place.

Might as well go out swinging.

Moving as slowly as possible so as not to disturb the bog, she gingerly pulled on one foot, dislodging it from the sludge and allowing it to slowly rise from the depths. The bog bubbled and splashed in her face as she maneuvered, forcing her to swallow a good mouthful of liquid, which turned out to taste like a sugary egg dusted with cinnamon.

Well, if this doesn't work, at least my ending will be sweet, she though wryly.

She heard a noise behind her and turned her head carefully. Jack was a short way away, wrestling with a large tree branch, trying to bend it in her direction. Unfortunately, it wasn't quite long enough for her to reach it. At least not yet . . .

Drawing in another breath, she dislodged her second leg from the slime, kicking it up and pushing out with her back at the same time, until she was in a supine position, staring up at the sky. Floating on her back, just like Undersea Gal in her fountain.

But just as she was about to celebrate her achievement, she started to sink again, the bog sucking her under. She had a moment of panic as her face dipped below the surface, but she forced herself not to struggle and to trust her buoyancy to bring her back up again. Which luckily happened a moment later, and she let out a breath of relief.

"Are you all right?" Jack called. "Can you make it over to the branch?"

"I'm going to try."

She waited until her body felt stable again. Then, ever so gently and still floating on her back, she began to paddle toward the branch Jack was bending. It was a slow process—every time she tried to go faster, she began to sink again. But eventually, inch by inch, she managed to make some headway. Until finally she could reach up and wrap her hand around the branch.

"Good," Jack said, his voice barely a whisper. "Now try to turn yourself over and grab it with your other hand as well. You'll need a really good grip to make this work."

She nodded grimly, clutching the branch tightly while attempting to turn, then grabbing the wood with her other hand as she twisted.

"I've got it!" she cried triumphantly. "Let go. Now!"

Jack stepped away from the branch. It snapped backward with great force—enough force to send her flying out of the bog and into the air. She screamed as her sticky fingers slipped on the branch about ten feet off the ground and she was sure she was about to fall. But then she felt Jack's arms lock onto her waist, gripping her tightly against him.

"I've got you," he murmured. "You can let go."

She did as she was told, releasing the tree and falling into Jack's arms. The shift in weight caused him to lose his footing and they both went tumbling to the forest floor, luckily away from the bog. For a moment they just lay there, a tangle of soaking wet limbs and dry bones. Then Sally rolled off Jack, sucking in huge breaths of air as tears of relief streamed down her face.

"Are you all right?" Jack asked, leaning over her, his eyes wide and worried.

She nodded, finding herself quite unable to speak. But Jack got the message. And his expression filled with relief. He reached down, tracing her cheek with a gentle finger, removing a blob of bog from her face.

"I thought I'd lost you," he said. "I didn't know what to do. I'm not used to not knowing what to do," he added, looking a little embarrassed.

"I know," she said, smiling up at him. "I was scared, too."

Jack cleared his throat and sat up, removing Abigail's hat and running a hand over his head. "That was smart, floating like that," he said.

"Thanks. But it wouldn't have been enough if you didn't get that branch to me," she told him. With effort, she managed to sit up, looking down at her sorry self. If she'd had bones, she would have been soaked right to them.

"I'm disgusting," she said with a brittle laugh. She tried to lift her arm. "And I can barely move. I need to be rinsed off and squeezed out before I can keep going."

"I saw a small cabin a little way back," Jack told her. "Maybe there's someone there who can help us."

Sally considered this. "But what if they're friends with Mr. Jingles and they turn us in?"

"I think we're going to have to take that risk," Jack said honestly. And Sally realized he was right.

"Okay," she said. "Let's try the cabin." She tried to stand but sank to the ground again. "Or maybe not . . ." She made a face. "I'm too heavy to even move. Maybe if I wait to dry out a bit—"

But Jack wasn't listening. He was leaning toward her, wrapping his arms around her.

"You're going to get all gooey!" she protested, a little alarmed at the idea of being carried.

"I'm from Halloween Town," he reminded her. "I like gooey. Now stop squirming and let me do this!"

Sally was too exhausted to put up a fight. Also, she had to admit, it felt pretty cozy to be carried in Jack's arms— not that she'd ever admit it aloud. She settled in, resting her weary head against his shoulder as he carried her down the forest path.

You wanted a change, she thought. But she'd never imagined anything like this.

CHAPTER TWENTY-THREE

When they arrived at the cottage, Jack shifted Sally in his arms so he could rap on the splintered wooden door. "Anyone home?" he called out.

But there was no answer. Jack waited another moment, then shrugged, kicking open the door with his foot. It gave way easily, revealing a small dark room beyond. Sally sneezed as a cloud of dust bloomed in the air.

"I think it's fair to say no one's home," Jack declared. "And more so, no one's *been* home in quite some time." He chuckled. "Guess that means it's ours for now."

He walked into the dwelling, still carrying Sally in his arms. Zero flew in behind them, sniffing curiously. The place was small and humble and much plainer than the brightly colored dwellings they'd found in Christmas Town proper. There was a faded holly-patterned sofa facing a large fireplace and a small antiquated kitchenette set up against one wall. Two doors led off the main room, presumably a bedroom and bathroom, and the floors were made of solid wood.

"Feels almost like home," Sally joked. "Bonus! There's even spiderwebs!" She pointed to the beautiful silvery strands draped across the otherwise plain lighting fixture hanging from the ceiling.

"Marvelous!" Jack said appreciatively. "Hopefully there's some actual spiders around, too. Then I can whip us up a nice stew."

He lowered Sally down on a wooden chair by the kitchenette, then set off to explore the cottage. Sally watched him go, smiling a little to herself. It was funny; after a near-death experience like she'd had, she probably shouldn't have felt so cozy. Maybe it was the adrenaline wearing off.

Or maybe it was just Jack.

He returned a moment later, carrying a big bucket. "No running water," he announced. "And no bathtub, either, unfortunately. So I'm going to scoop up some snow from outside. Then I'll make a fire and melt it in that cauldron," he added, pointing to the large pot sitting in the hearth. "If my calculations are correct, the snow will melt into water, and you'll be able to rinse yourself off."

Sally nodded, relieved. She was really getting sick of being so sticky. "Thank you," she said.

Jack gave her a salute, then headed outside, Zero at his heels. He returned a few moments later with a bucket of snow. Setting it aside, he began to work on lighting a fire in the hearth, then poured the snow into the cauldron.

"It's working!" he cried excitedly. Then his expression changed. "Wait, that's all?"

"What is?" Sally asked curiously.

He tipped the cauldron so she could see. The mountain of snow he'd brought in had turned into water, just as he'd predicted. But it was a lot less than it had been in its solid form.

"We're going to need more snow. A lot more snow."

Jack trudged outside, then returned again with his snow bucket. This time he didn't wait for it to melt before heading out for another batch. Zero snorted, as if to say he was done with this nonsense, curling into a ball on the edge of the sofa and nodding off. But Jack continued his trek, back and forth, back and forth, until Sally started feeling bad for him.

"I should be helping," she protested.

"You rest." He shook a finger at her. "I've got this all under control."

And out he went again. And again. Until finally they had enough water to fill the cauldron. Triumphant, he pulled it off the fire and set it in front of Sally, along with a big fluffy sponge he must have found in the bathroom.

"All right," he said. "While you wash yourself off, I'll see what I can find in this kitchen to eat."

"Thank you," Sally said, and reached for the sponge as Jack began rummaging through the cabinets. Her stomach growled in anticipation and she realized that besides the hot chocolate earlier, they hadn't eaten all day.

She stuck the sponge in the water. It was still a bit cold, but it was heavenly to feel the nog running out of her cloth skin. She wrung her arm out as best she could, then repeated the process with the other arm. The bucket's water soon clouded, and she realized she was going to need a second batch.

"Sorry," she said to Jack. But he just waved her off and began the process all over again, not uttering a single word of complaint. Which warmed her heart even more.

It took three buckets in the end, but finally Sally was clean. She was still damp, of course, and would be for some time, but she was able to rise from her chair and walk normally, and that was good enough for now.

She wandered into the kitchen area, breathing in the delicious scent coming from the stove. Jack stood stirring something in a small pot. He grinned as he watched her approach.

"Feeling better?" he asked.

"Like a new doll," she assured him. "What are you cooking? It smells delicious."

Jack shrugged. "I couldn't find any spiders, so we're trying this." He held up a can. "Something called Christmas hash. I've never heard of it, have you?"

Sally shook her head. "But I'm so hungry I could pretty much eat anything at this point. Even the witches' slug stew." She wrinkled her nose at the thought.

"Hey, don't knock the slug stew," Jack protested as he scooped a portion of the hash from the pot and plopped it into a bowl, then added a spoon. "It'll do in a pinch."

"You'd have to pinch me pretty hard," Sally shot back, rolling her eyes. She took the bowl from Jack and spooned the hash into her mouth. "Mm," she said. "My compliments to the chef."

Jack waved her off, but he looked pleased all the same. He joined her at the table with his own bowl, sitting across from her and taking a large bite.

"Actually, you're right," he admitted. "It's pretty good. Though I still think it could use a few spiders."

"Fair," Sally said, and took another bite. "But we can't have everything, can we?"

"I suppose not," Jack agreed. "Just . . . almost everything." He smiled at Sally warmly.

Sally opened her mouth to reply, but at that moment something flashed at the window.

She turned to look, surprised to see the sky had darkened since they'd been in the cottage, and it appeared a storm was rolling in. A rumble of thunder rose to her ears, confirming her theory, and the wind began to howl in a high-pitched whine. Zero lifted his head from the couch, panting nervously as his eyes darted to the window, then to the two of them.

"Wow," Sally said, setting down her spoon. "We're lucky we found this place. I would not want to be out in that."

Jack nodded. "Definitely not," he agreed. "Also, it's getting cold. And, let's face it, handsome as I might be, I don't exactly have much meat on my bones to keep me warm." He shivered to demonstrate his point.

"I'm a little cold myself," Sally said. "Not to mention, still damp. Maybe we should call it day. We can stay here tonight and I can dry out, and then we can leave first thing in the morning. Hopefully the storm will have passed by then."

"Good idea," Jack agreed, pushing away from his chair.

"And let's finish our food by the fire." He headed over to sit on the floor by the hearth. He held out his hands, warming them in front of the flames. "I just hope Santa doesn't choose to swing by tonight," he joked. "He'll end up burning his bottom."

"I think Santa only does the chimney thing on Christmas," Sally said with a laugh, coming over to sit by his side. "And besides, we're not exactly on the nice list these days."

She stared into the flames, enjoying the heat on her damp cloth. The flames danced happily as the wind whipped up outside. Soon Sally found herself yawning.

"Am I boring you?" Jack teased, echoing her own joke from back on Spiral Hill when he'd been the one to be yawning.

"Not at all," she said with a laugh. "It's definitely not the company. It's just been a very long twenty-four hours." She yawned again. "Also, I want to wake up as early as possible tomorrow. Abigail's already waited too long, and who knows how they're treating her."

"Agreed. I'm tired, too," Jack admitted. "Let me see what this place has for bedding. We should sleep by the fire so we'll stay warm."

"Allow me," Sally insisted, standing up and shaking out

her legs. "I'm feeling much better now. And you've done enough."

"If you're sure," Jack said, stretching out his feet in front of the fire. Sally smiled at him, then walked into the bedroom, which was indeed frigid compared with the living room. Much better to curl up in front of the fire . . . with Jack.

Her insides tingled a little at the thought. Hopefully she'd be able to sleep.

Looking around the room, she wondered who had once called it home and where they were now. Whoever it was hadn't been here for a while, based on the amount of dust. And yet the bed was rumpled, its covers in disarray, as if it had been slept in the night before. Or as if someone had left in a hurry. There was still trash in the trash can, she noted. And the framed picture on the wall was askew.

Curious, she walked over to straighten it, peering at the photo inside the frame as she did. It was of a small group of men and women, smiling happily in front of what looked like a large cave. They carried pickaxes and shovels and looked quite filthy. At the same time, they were smiling into the camera, as if proud of a hard day's work.

Were these coal miners? she wondered suddenly, thinking back to her first conversation with Santa. He'd said something about bad children getting coal in their stockings. Which meant there had to be some kind of mine nearby. Perhaps the elf who had lived here worked it.

But that didn't explain where they were now.

As she backed away from the photo, she stepped on something sharp. She looked down to find a ceramic shard that appeared to have come from a broken lamp on the floor nearby. She frowned. How had that happened? She reached down, taking the shard in her hands and turning it over, gasping a little as she found a red stain on the other side.

Was that blood?

"Um, Jack?" she called out worriedly. "Can you come in here for a second?"

And suddenly everything went black.

CHAPTER TWENTY-FOUR

"No! Please, no!"

Sally looked up, her eyes widening in shock. The room was no longer empty. A man and a woman huddled in the bed, dressed in nightclothes and stocking caps, identical looks of fear on their faces. When Sally turned around to see what was scaring them, she caught sight of two soldiers storming into the room, their jingle bell spears jangling angrily.

She leapt backward to avoid being trampled. But to her surprise one of the soldiers walked right through her—as if she were a ghost.

As if *he* were a ghost, her mind corrected.

It was another vision, she realized. This time of

something that had happened before. Right here in this room.

Biting her lower lip, she forced herself to turn back to the scene. The soldiers had reached the bed and were flanking it. The woman had her arms out, trying to block them.

"Please! My husband's done nothing wrong!" she begged, tears streaming down her rosy cheeks.

"Really?" snorted the first guard. "Then what's this?" He reached into his pocket and pulled out what appeared to be a letter. On the envelope were the words *To Santa*, and it had been roughly torn open.

"I don't know! We've never seen it before!" the woman cried.

Her husband sighed, laying a hand on her arm. "It's all right, Flora," he said. "I'm not ashamed of what I've done." His eyes flashed fire as they rose to the soldiers. "In fact, I'm quite proud. Someone has to let Santa know what's really going on in his land. What's really happening to the folks Mr. Jingles takes away. Trapped and suffering in that miserable coal cave! With that monster he calls a warden!"

Suddenly Mr. Jingles himself appeared in the room. He stood over the bed, his lips curled in a sneer. "Well, I'm sorry to say Mr. Claus will not be receiving that particular letter," he said coldly. "You should be ashamed of yourself for attempting to bother him with such trifles. Do you know how busy the man is? He's single-handedly trying to save Christmas! Which is why he put me in place to uphold the law and keep people like you away!"

"Upholding the law is one thing," the man argued, not willing to back down. "But this is too much. It's cruel and unusual. No crime is terrible enough to warrant that place. That . . . creature. Except maybe your own."

Jingles laughed heartily. "Look at you, little man. You're so brave," he said. "I'd like to see how brave you'll be when you're face to face with Sootfang himself." He turned to his soldiers. "Take him away."

"No! Please!" Flora begged. As the soldier closed in on her husband, she tried to shove him away. But the soldier grabbed the lamp off the nightstand and smashed it against the wall. Flora recoiled in horror, managing to tumble off the bed.

"Flora!" her husband cried, alarmed. Then he turned to Mr. Jingles and his men. "You won't get away with this!" he growled. "One way or another, we will stop you."

Suddenly he turned to Sally, as if seeing her for the first time. His eyes, dark and pleading, met her own. "Please help us. You're the only one left who can. This place, it's the key to everything." His eyes flickered around the room to the corner before he gazed at her once more, beseechingly. "Please. Before it's too late!"

Sally swallowed hard. "Tell me," she said. "What is Sootfang?"

The man's eyes bulged from his head. His entire body shook with fear. "Sootfang," he said in a shaky voice. "Sootfang is—"

"Sally? Is everything okay?"

Sally jerked from her vision, the room falling back into place. A rumpled bed, a broken lamp. A picture frame askew. Jack standing in the door, looking at her, brow knit in concern.

Her shoulders slumped. "Sorry," she said. "I just . . . well, I had a vision. I have them sometimes. Usually when I least expect them." She realized her hands were shaking furiously and she shoved them behind her back, feeling a little embarrassed.

Jack walked over to her and pulled her down to sit on the bed. His eyes searched her face. "What did you see?" he asked. "Was it something about this place?"

She nodded woodenly, then explained her vision. "It was so awful," she said when she had finished. "They were so frightened. And they were trying to do the right thing. To let Santa know what was really going on. But

Mr. Jingles . . ." She looked up at the picture frame. At the happy people who used to live here in peace.

"They mentioned a coal cave," she added. "It sounded like that's where Mr. Jingles is taking people when they're arrested. He must be using it as a prison. I think the elf I saw worked there and discovered what was happening. He tried to blow the whistle but . . ." She trailed off miserably.

"What an odd punishment," Jack remarked. "I mean, back home those caves are highly sought-after vacation destinations."

"Well, it's clearly not a great place here," Sally said, thinking back to the terror she'd seen in the man's eyes. Suddenly she remembered his words. She rose from the bed and looked around the room. She peered under the bed, behind the curtain, in the closet. What answers lay here? Then she remembered the man's flickering glance. She turned to the spot he seemed to have indicated and noticed the plain nightstand next to the bed. Her heart was beating very fast as she strode over and pulled open the drawer. . . .

And discovered a key inside. *The key is an actual key.*

"What is that?" Jack asked as she lifted it from the drawer. "How did you know that was there?"

"The man in my vision told me," she said. "He asked me to help them. He said I was the only one who could."

Her legs gave out under her. Jack leapt up, leading her back to the main room.

"Come on," he said. "Let's warm you up."

Zero whined nervously as they entered, zooming over to Sally and licking her cheek. She spotted the map they'd been using to get here, lying on the table. She walked over to it and studied the black mound at the edge that had been circled. "That's got to be the coal cave," Sally said. "At least we know now what to expect."

Except . . . did they? Her mind flashed back to the terror in the couple's eyes. What exactly did this key open? Who was Sootfang?

And what could he do?

"I will say I'm glad Santa isn't a part of this," she added, walking back over to the fire. She realized she never did grab any pillows or blankets. "He seemed so great. I'd hate to think he knew this was going on and wasn't doing anything about it."

"Do you think we need to go back and tell him?" Jack asked.

"Tell him what? That I had a vision?" Sally wrinkled her nose. "He's not necessarily going to believe us. Not if we don't have proof." She glanced at the crackling flames. "Also, I don't want to waste any more time. We have no idea what these people are suffering. Or how long they have left."

"You're right," Jack agreed. "We'll keep with our plan to head out tomorrow morning bright and early. And we won't stop again until we find that cave."

And Sootfang, Sally thought, but didn't say aloud. *Sootfang, who will be waiting.*

CHAPTER TWENTY-FIVE

"Wakey, wakey!"

Sally groaned at the far-too-chipper voice chirping in her ears early the next morning. It was almost as irritating as the bright light shining down on her face. She yanked at her blanket, pulling it over her eyes.

"Five more minutes, Dr. Finkelstein," she muttered. "Just five more . . ."

"It's not Dr. Finkelstein," replied an amused voice. "And also, may I remind you? You were the one who wanted to wake up at dawn."

That did it. Sally's eyes flew open. She shoved the blanket off her face. Looking up, she found an oddly dressed Jack Skellington standing over her, watching her expectantly.

She blinked. "What in the Halloween Town horrors are you wearing?"

Jack had changed out of his filthy chimney-soot-covered suit from the night before and stood before her in some kind of sweater featuring a litter of kittens wearing Santa hats and frolicking around a rainbow-colored Christmas tree. It was so cheerful it was almost hard to look at.

"I don't know exactly," Jack admitted. "But it sure is ugly. And oddly . . . charming . . . at the same time."

Sally raised an eyebrow. "If you say so. . . ."

Jack gave an impish shrug. "How did you sleep?"

"Good, I think," she replied, rubbing her eyes with her fists. "It feels like I only laid my head down a minute ago."

"You must have needed it," Jack said. Then he pointed to the window. "And look. We've had more snow."

Sally had to squint to look, everything was so bright. But sure enough, the storm seemed to have passed, leaving the forest dressed in blankets of white. It was beautiful.

And also worrisome.

"What are we going to do?" she asked, rising to her feet and walking over to the window. "We're not going to be able to see any of the bog pits under the snow."

Jack nodded. "I thought of that." He headed over to the table to peer down at the map he'd laid out across its surface. "I think we're going to have to take the long route.

Up these mountains, see? It looks as if there's a ridge here along the cliffside that crosses the entire length of the bog. It may take a little longer, but we'll be able to clear the bog without worrying about falling in again."

"Right." Sally pressed her lips together. "What about this?" she asked, pointing to a label next to the ridge. "'The Caroler Cliffs'? What do you think that means?"

"Maybe like the carolers back in Christmas Town?" Jack suggested. "Perhaps we'll be serenaded with songs along our way. That'll be pleasant."

Sally wasn't so sure. While she appreciated Jack's never-ending optimism and bravado when it came to dangers untold, she had learned her lesson with the bog. The world outside Christmas Town wasn't always what it appeared. And they needed to remain vigilant. One near-death experience was quite enough, thank you very much.

But then she also wasn't eager to fall into the bog again, and the map showed no other obvious path. So she told Jack to give her a moment, then headed into the bedroom to find herself some new clothes, too.

She came out a little later in a red woolen dress with faux fur trim and decorative black buttons going down the front of it. It fit like a glove, even if it was a bit too short. She'd added a pair of black trousers underneath so she wouldn't be cold.

"You look great," Jack said.

Sally blushed as she took the boots he was holding out for her and sat down in a chair to slide them on her feet. She added a heavy woolen scarf around her neck to keep out the wind, and Jack plopped Abigail's big floppy hat—which had been spared from the bog since he'd been wearing it at the time—on her head.

"Don't you need something on *your* head?" Sally asked Jack worriedly. "Or at least your ears?"

"I don't have any ears," he reminded her with a grin, boxing the sides of his skull with his hands.

"Oh, yeah. I never thought of that. How do you hear?" she asked curiously.

"Something called bone conduction. My skull transmits sounds to my brain."

"I had no idea."

"Stick with me," Jack joked. "I have all sorts of wondrous, weird, and altogether useless facts at my disposal."

Sally started to laugh, but it ended in more of a sigh. While it was pleasant to banter back and forth with Jack, they needed to stay focused. They had a big journey ahead of them and Sally had no idea what they were in for at the end.

"Come on," she said. "Let's get going."

Together Sally, Jack, and Zero headed outside, into the

wintry forest. As Sally closed the door to the cottage, she gave it a sympathetic look. "Thank you for last night," she murmured. "And I'm sorry you lost your people. We'll do our best to find them for you. So you can be a home again."

They set out into the woods, Zero floating happily behind them. Sally followed the map toward the ridge as best she could, which wasn't easy, considering the snowfall had covered any hint of a trail. They walked carefully, too, testing the ground in front of them with long sticks to make sure they didn't accidentally hit any more bogs.

About a half hour in, they caught sight of a steep slope rising before them. Sally pointed excitedly.

"There! That must lead to the Caroler Cliffs!"

"Definitely," Jack agreed, picking up his pace. Sally trudged after him, a little nervous about starting their ascent. It was slippery enough on the flat ground. What was it going to be like up at the top?

Of course they didn't have much choice, so they began to climb the steep and narrow path. Soon the hill crested, revealing the Nog Bog in the valley below them. The whole thing was covered in snow, so they couldn't see any actual bogs, but Sally shuddered all the same, reminded of her experience the day before. That horrible feeling of sinking fast and not being able to do anything about it. Whatever the Caroler Cliffs turned out to be, they couldn't be as bad as that.

At least she hoped not. . . .

"I wonder where these so-called carolers are," Jack mused, as if reading her mind. "I was hoping to hear some music!"

"Maybe the bad weather kept them away," Sally suggested. She looked out onto the ridge and winced, all relief of avoiding the Nog Bog fading fast. At this elevation, the wind was blowing quite hard, and she wasn't thrilled about the idea of crossing something so narrow and icy—musically accompanied or not.

Jack scratched his chin. "Disappointing, really," he decided. "I would have loved to have discovered some new twisted tunes to torment everyone with back home." He shrugged. "Oh well. Perhaps I'll come up with one of my own to pass the time."

Before Sally could suggest that they might be better off focusing on the slippery slopes rather than singing, Jack broke out into a song he called "Freaky the Snowman," using the same melody the carolers had sung back in Christmas Town. Of course he changed the words up a bit, singing about a snowman who, thanks to a magical hat, came to life to torment little children. Though at least justice was served in the end, Sally supposed, when the sun came out the next day, melting the snowman where he stood.

"But!" Jack added, waving a menacing finger in Sally's direction. "He'll be back again . . . someday."

"Oooh," Sally moaned playfully. She waggled her eyebrows. "So scary!"

Jack grinned. "All right, your turn," he said. "You have a song for us?"

"Oh, no!" Sally protested, holding up her hands. "There is no way I'm going to—"

Her words were cut short as another voice rose to her ears in song. It was high-pitched, pretty, and perfectly on key. Singing something about silver bells, if she wasn't mistaken.

"What's that?" Jack asked, stopping dead in his tracks, so quickly that Sally almost slammed into him and knocked them both off the cliff. "It's . . . beautiful."

"Our carolers maybe?" Sally suggested. "They probably heard you and decided they'd better help."

"Or they were so impressed by my tune they felt they should return the favor," Jack suggested. He cupped a hand around his mouth. "Go ahead, then," he called out. "I'm all ears!" Then he grinned goofily at Sally. "Well, all skull, actually," he amended. "But I'm listening all the same!"

The voice rose again, as if in response, this time

accompanied by another, just as beautiful, joining in on the chorus. Jack smiled, clearly delighted, and continued heading up the path, his steps a little quicker than they had been earlier. Sally followed as close as she dared, wary of him stopping short again. The path had narrowed considerably and left room only for walking single file. Which would have been challenging in any weather. But this ice made it downright treacherous.

"Slow down!" she begged Jack, straining her voice to be heard over the growing chorus. Two more voices had joined the song and it was becoming far too loud for Sally's liking. She yanked Abigail's hat tighter over her ears to block it out as best she could. Beside her, Zero whined nervously.

"Seriously!" she called. "If you slip off this cliff and die, I'm not coming to your funeral!"

She waited for Jack's comeback. Something about him already being dead, most likely. But to her surprise, he didn't even turn around. Meanwhile, another voice had joined the chorus, this one a deep baritone in stark contrast with the sweet sopranos. The voice was so deep, in fact, that Sally could almost feel it vibrating beneath her feet, and she prayed it wouldn't cause an avalanche.

Agitated, she picked at the faux fur on her dress, pulling a piece of it free and rolling it into two balls of fluff, which she stuck in her ears to mute the sound. Then she did the same for Zero. The voices finally began to fade, and she let out a breath of relief. Enough was enough.

Now she just had to catch up with Jack. He was even farther away now, his long thin body seeming to sway in perfect rhythm to the song. He seemed so engrossed by it, in fact, she half wondered if he was about to break into a full-on dance.

"Be careful!" she couldn't help calling out. "It's slippery!"

But again, he didn't answer. And he didn't stop swaying. Maybe he couldn't hear her over the growing number of carolers joining the never-ending song. Sally could no longer tell just how many voices were singing at this point, though it sounded like quite a lot. She stuffed a little more fluff in her ears, then did the same for poor Zero.

Meanwhile, Jack was still going. Gritting her teeth, she picked up her pace, forcing herself to go as fast as she dared in an attempt to catch up. But somehow, she found the quicker she walked, the farther away Jack seemed to get. She frowned. Was he purposely trying to outrun her?

What was wrong with him?

Was it something to do with the music?

Was it some kind of spell?

She quickened her steps again, trying her best to run without slipping. "Jack!" she begged. "Please! Stop! Now!"

And then, suddenly, he did. Stopped so short it was as if he'd slammed into a solid wall. Sally watched in a mixture of confusion and fear as he slowly turned in the direction of the singing. His face was completely blank as he stood at the very edge of the cliff, his eyes dropping to the abyss below. Sally gasped in horror as he lifted his foot.

"Jack! No!"

She lunged at him, throwing her entire weight on top of him and knocking him to the ground. He struggled to free himself, still trying to crawl toward the cliff's edge.

"It's so beautiful," Sally heard him murmur. "It's just so . . . beautiful."

Desperate, Sally clamped her hands over the sides of his head. "Block it out, Jack!" she begged. "Don't listen to it."

He turned and stared at her as if he hadn't even been aware she was there, lying on top of him, pinning him down. He cocked his head, puzzled, but Sally held on tight, tears slipping down her cloth cheeks and splashing onto his skull.

"Jack, please!" she cried. "Listen to the sound of my voice."

Suddenly his eyes seemed to come back into focus. He swallowed hard, staring up at her with confusion. "Sally?" he asked. "What are you doing? Why are you on top of me?"

Sally choked out a sob of relief. "It's the carolers, Jack!"

she explained. "I think their song is like a spell. You . . ." She swallowed hard. "You almost walked off a cliff."

Jack's eyes grew wide as saucers. He turned from Sally, looking down into the ravine below. "I . . . did?" he asked. "I don't remember. I just remember the song. That beautiful song . . ."

Sally winced. What was she going to do? He didn't have ears like she and Zero to stuff faux fur into. . . .

"Look, Jack, I need to let go for a second. I'm going to pull off my scarf and I'm going to wrap it around your head. Hopefully it'll work to mute the sound enough for you to resist it."

Jack nodded wordlessly. Sally drew in a shaky breath, then let go of his head, still clamping herself down on top of him so he couldn't move. She quickly unwrapped her scarf and tied it around his head, making sure to secure it tightly under his chin.

Jack blinked. He looked up at Sally.

"Okay," he said. "I think I'm okay."

Sally exhaled a sigh of relief. She rolled off Jack, rising to her feet. He followed her lead, the scarf tight against his skull. Then, together, they began walking the ridge again, not speaking until they reached the other side and descended the opposite hill about an hour later.

Once on solid ground, Sally removed the fluff from her ears. The sounds of the carolers had faded into a distant hum. *Not even a good song,* she thought bitterly. Worse than "Freaky the Snowman." Not that she was about to admit that to Jack.

Jack pulled the scarf from his head, handing it back to Sally. He took a long shaky breath. "Death by chorus. That's a new one. And pretty creepy, too. Even for the likes of me." He tapped his chin thoughtfully. "Maybe we need to try to incorporate something like that next Halloween."

Sally groaned. Of course that would be Jack's takeaway from his near-death experience. "I mean, it certainly terrified me when you tried to walk off a cliff," she said wryly.

Jack frowned. "But it didn't affect you," he pointed out. "I wonder why."

Sally held out the two piles of fluff. He nodded, looking impressed. "Smart," he said. "I'm glad you thought of that. Otherwise, I'd be at the bottom of a ravine right now." He gave her an affectionate look. "You saved my life, Sally. Thank you."

"Well, I had to return the favor," she pointed out with a sly smile. "After yesterday and all. You can't expect to be the hero all the time, Jack Skellington."

He laughed heartily. "We make a good team, you and

I," he declared, slinging an arm around her. "Now come on. We've only got one more area to cross before we reach this coal cave. I wonder who's going to be the hero this time."

"Maybe we won't need a hero," Sally declared, pressing her hands together in a prayer gesture. "Maybe it'll be just a walk in the graveyard."

Jack grinned. "Sally being optimistic, I like it!"

"Well, don't get too used to it," she replied, pointing up at the sky. Dark clouds had gathered, low and thick. Another storm was on the way. And this time they didn't have a cozy cottage to retreat to until it passed.

This did not seem good.

CHAPTER TWENTY-SIX

Before she had come to Christmas Town, Sally had always enjoyed storms. She liked the way the darkness fell over the land and the tingle of electricity crackled in the air. Thunder rumbling in the distance was a comforting purr. And as long as she was in her bed and not out in it, she enjoyed watching the rain pour down outside her window.

But here, it was a different matter entirely and a lot grimmer—and not in a good way, either. The air felt heavier somehow, almost suffocatingly so. And it was becoming difficult to take in a good deep breath without feeling as if she would choke. The clouds hung thick and low in the sky, and it looked as if, any minute now, they would open up and bury Sally and Jack in snow.

It didn't help that there was no shelter here. No trees, no cottages—literally just an empty wasteland that seemed to stretch out forever in all directions. Without anything to slow it down, the wind whipped furiously through the space, cold and sharp. And Sally was beginning to envy Jack's ugly sweater.

"How much farther?" she asked, yelling over the storm.

"I'm not sure," Jack said, staring down at the map. The wind whipped at the paper, making it difficult to read. "It's hard to get a good perspective from this. But you can see the outline of that mountain over there, right?" He pointed into the distance. "I'm guessing that's where our cave is."

Sally nodded grimly. Of course it was. About as far away as one could get from their current location. But there was nothing they could do but keep trudging through the snow in that general direction, hoping it was actually closer than it appeared.

You can do this, she told herself. *Abigail and the others need you to do this.*

To make matters worse, more snow started to fall. Lightly at first, then more heavily. Soon the wind picked up again, howling across the vacant field. It was so strong that at one point it almost blew Sally off her feet.

"Hang on," she said to Jack. Reaching down, she picked

up a few small but heavy stones in one hand. Then, with the other, she plucked at her stitches, just enough to make small holes in her legs so she could stuff the rocks inside of them to weigh herself down.

"There," she said. "That should help."

Jack nodded. "I wish I could do that, too," he admitted.

"Just hang on to me," Sally said, grabbing him by the arm. "We'll keep each other grounded."

"Wait," Jack said. "Where'd Zero go?"

Sally looked around the windy snow-covered field, her mouth dipping into a frown. "I don't know," she said worriedly. "He was here a minute ago. Wasn't he?" She tried to remember the last time she'd caught sight of the ghost dog. She'd been so distracted by everything.

"Zero?" Jack called out. "Are you there, buddy?"

But there was no response.

Worry prickled at Sally's cloth. Where was he? Had the wind blown him away? And if so, how would he be able to find them again? He was so small. So light. She cringed. *Please don't let anything happen to him!*

"Come on," Jack said, pulling her along. "Zero's smart. And he's very capable of taking care of himself. I'm sure he'll be fine."

Sally wasn't sure at all, but she realized there was nothing they could do. They could barely see two feet in front of their faces with the snow now swirling thick and heavy around them. All they could do was keep pushing forward, hoping to get through the field to find some shelter on the other side.

Hoping sweet little Zero could do the same.

"How do we even know we're going in the right direction?" she asked, squinting into the storm. They could no longer see the mountain in the distance, the visibility was so poor.

"I'm . . . not sure," Jack said, sounding doubtful. "I mean, I think we are. . . ." He scratched his skull, and Sally caught a flicker of fear in his eyes.

"Maybe we need to stop," she suggested, starting to feel desperate. "At least until the storm ends. Or the fog lifts. Otherwise, we could be walking miles in the wrong direction."

"I don't know if that's a good idea," Jack said, his voice quaking as he spoke. He was cold, Sally realized. He might have had a sweater, but other than that he was all bones. No stuffing to keep him warm. If they stopped moving, it would get even worse.

"Okay, we'll keep going," she said, rubbing his arm with her gloved hand, trying to warm him up as best she could. She could feel his whole body trembling underneath her fingers and it filled her with dread. "I'm sure we'll come out of it soon," she added, trying the optimistic thing again, even if she didn't feel it.

But all the optimism in the world couldn't stop a blizzard from raging, and it only seemed to be growing more furious. And as the sky grew darker, Sally started to wonder if their little trip was about to come to a very abrupt and terrible end.

What would Halloween Town think if they never returned? If they vanished into thin air, never to be heard from again? They would send search parties, of course. But there was no way anyone would ever find them out here.

Stop it, she scolded herself. *This isn't helping. You've been through so much. You can get through this, too.*

Somehow . . .

Suddenly Sally frowned, her eyes catching a weird flash of light above. *Was that lightning?* she thought miserably. As if things weren't bad enough already.

But then lightning would have flashed and disappeared, she realized, confused as she continued to watch the sky. This was more of a steady glow. And it was . . . orange, not white.

"What is that?" she whispered, tightening her grip on Jack's arm. "Do you see it?"

"I do," Jack said. "I don't know what it is, but there's definitely something there." He paused, then added. "Do you think it could be—"

ARF! ARF!

"Zero?" Sally exclaimed. "I think it's Zero!" She cocked her head. "And . . . he's not alone, either!"

CHAPTER TWENTY-SEVEN

Sally couldn't believe it. It was Zero and an entire team of reindeer, flying through the storm, dragging along Santa's sleigh, just as they'd been doing above Christmas Town during her first visit. The pup must have gone back for them, realizing that Sally and Jack were having trouble navigating the storm. And thanks to his glowing nose, he was able to lead the way, coming to a graceful landing right in front of them.

Sally cried out, running to the dog and throwing her arms around him. "Oh, Zero!" she said. "Thank you so much!"

"We thought you were lost," Jack told him. "Silly us."

Zero gave a sharp bark, as if to say, *Give me a little*

credit. Jack laughed and patted the top of his head. The ghost dog zoomed over to the sleigh and barked again. Sally looked at Jack.

"I guess Zero decided it was his turn to play the hero," she remarked as she climbed on board. Jack joined her, and together they covered themselves up with the thick blankets they found inside. Sally let out a long breath of relief. She was still cold, but it was so much better than before.

"Not that this isn't great and all," Jack said after getting settled. "But what if he's trying to take us back to Christmas Town? I don't think he really knows why we're out here or what we're trying to find."

Sally frowned. That was a good point. Zero could lead a sleigh, but he didn't necessarily know where to go.

Suddenly an idea occurred to her. She climbed out of the sleigh and ran over to the ghost dog. She reached to her head, pulling off Abigail's hat, trying to ignore the sting of the wind against her now unprotected ears. She held it out to Zero.

"Do you smell that?" she asked. "That's Abigail. It's very important that we find her," she told the dog. "Do you think you can get us to her?"

She held her breath as Zero sniffed the hat curiously. Then he barked twice, nodding his head back to the sleigh.

Sally ran back and rejoined Jack, hoping Zero had understood. Hoping he could locate Abigail if he did.

Once she was settled back in, Zero woofed at the reindeer. They began to run as a team and before Sally could even register what was happening, they suddenly leapt into the air, flying through the sky. Sally gasped and grabbed on to Jack for support as the sleigh jerked up with the team.

"Brilliant!" Jack cried. "What a way to travel!"

Sally couldn't help agreeing—as long as she didn't look down. They were flying high above the storm, the snow swirling below them but no longer in their faces. There was still wind, of course, but it was exhilarating now—the kind of wind she'd felt against her face when sliding down the hill.

She realized she was still clutching Jack's arm, but he didn't seem to mind, so she didn't move. Ahead of them she could see Zero's nose shining brightly through it all.

Finally they began to descend, dropping down on the far end of the plain, just short of a grove of trees offering some shelter from the storm. Sally let out a breath of relief as the sleigh settled on the ground and she was able to climb out, leaning against one of the nearby trees for support, her legs still a little heavy from the stones she'd stuck in them.

"Good old Zero," Jack exclaimed, joining her and

helping her remove her rocks. He smiled at the ghost dog. "Who's a good boy?"

Zero barked happily, as if to say, *It's definitely me*, then took off again, leaving his team of reindeer and their sleigh grounded as he headed deeper into the woods by himself. He stopped just before ducking out of sight, yipping impatiently.

Jack and Sally exchanged excited looks. He was still on Abigail's trail!

They ran after him, not wanting to lose the dog through the thick forest of trees. They came to a dead end at the base of a mountain—the same mountain they'd seen in the distance when they'd started across the plain. Now it loomed in front of them, large and imposing, like a giant face with a gaping mouth at the very bottom, complete with stalactite fangs.

The coal mine, Sally realized. They'd found it at last.

"Well," Jack said, looking at the cave with admiration. "This is nicer than I'd pictured. For some reason I thought it was going to be draped in those dreadful multicolored lights. But this . . ." He rubbed his chin with his hand. "I can work with this. In fact, maybe we need to re-create something like this back home. Like a haunted house, but a cave. The cave of terrors!" he announced in an overly theatrical voice, as if trying the idea on for size. "The creepy cave of chaos. Coal-filled creepy chaos. Enter if you dare."

Enter if you dare indeed, Sally thought, her cloth prickling as her excitement faded to trepidation. What would they find inside this place? Who was this Sootfang who guarded the prisoners, and what would he do to any intruders who dared breach his territory?

"What are you waiting for?" Jack asked, and Sally broke from her worries to see he'd already waltzed up to cave's mouth as if he didn't have a fear in the world. Zero, on the other hand, seemed to have better sense, hovering at the entrance to the cave, whining softly. Even after Jack called to him and slapped his hand on his thigh, the pup refused to budge.

Great, Sally thought. *Even the flying ghost dog's scared.*

She tried to rouse her courage. Abigail was counting on her, after all. As were the others inside. They'd come this far. They couldn't back out now.

You survived Mr. Jingles, Sally reminded herself. *You survived a sinking bog and a deadly chorus. You survived getting lost in a terrible storm. You can survive this, too. You just have to keep your wits.*

Steeling her nerves, she stepped through the gap between the sharp-looking stalactites and into the mouth of the cave. It was dark and damp inside, but at least the walls kept out the howling wind and it wasn't snowing. (Sally realized her standards had gotten pretty low at this point.)

Zero whined again. Jack gave him a sympathetic look. "It's okay, buddy," he assured him. "Why don't you take the sleigh back while we do this? Someone's bound to be missing it by now. We'll meet you in Christmas Town when we're done here." He smiled at the dog. "You did good," he assured him. "It's time for you to rest."

Zero gave a small yip, looking relieved. Sally watched, a little envious, as he zoomed away from the cave, soon vanishing from sight. She turned back to Jack.

"What about you?" he asked. "Do you want to wait here? I can go in first and see what I can find."

"Not a chance," Sally said, crossing her arms over her chest. "We came here together. We're staying together."

Swallowing her fear, she followed Jack through the dark cave, heading down a rough passageway strewn with a mixture of ice and rocks. Along the path was an iron rail, assumedly used by the miners to remove the coal by cart. But there were no miners here now. And from the rusty look of the iron, there hadn't been any for some time.

Sally frowned. "I wonder where they're being kept," she murmured. "These mining caves can be miles deep and have entire labyrinths of tunnels. We need to make sure we don't get lost, wandering around the place."

"I know," Jack agreed. "I wish Zero had come in. He could have at least guided us." He paused, frowning. "Wait a second."

"What is it?"

"I think I hear something. It sounds like a song of some sort."

"A song?" Sally grimaced, really hoping that didn't mean more cliff carolers.

"Come on," Jack said. "Let's follow it."

"Wait." Sally cocked her head, thinking. "Do you still have those sugarplums?"

Jack reached into his pocket, pulling out the bag. "Hungry?" he asked with raised eyebrows.

"Not exactly." Sally took the bag and set a piece of sugarplum on the ground. "I just want to keep track of where we're going so we can get out later."

Jack nodded approvingly. "You're full of good ideas, aren't you?" he remarked. "Why, you almost remind me of myself!"

"And yet so much more humble," Sally shot back with a grin, breaking off another piece. There weren't too many left at this point, so she needed to be frugal. "Now come on. Let's go."

They traveled through the cave in the direction of the sound, weaving down passages to the left and right. A few times they got stuck at dead ends and had to retrace their steps, making Sally very grateful for the sugarplum trail.

Eventually the song grew louder. And when they turned a corner, it grew louder still. Finally they came to a large iron door with a heavy lock. In an instant, Sally realized what she was supposed to do.

"It's definitely coming from in there," Sally declared. She reached into her pocket, pulling out the miner's key. "I hope this works," she muttered as she slid the key into the lock. To her delight it slid in place, and with great effort, she was able to turn it. They heard a click—the door unlocking. She glanced at Jack.

This was it. They were here at last.

But what would they find on the other side?

CHAPTER TWENTY-EIGHT

It took both of them to push the door open; it was that heavy. But eventually it grudgingly gave way, groaning as it did. A surprising amount of bright light spilled out from the other side, blinding them for a moment, after they'd been in the dark for so long. Sally and Jack exchanged curious looks, then stepped inside, mentally preparing themselves for anything.

What they weren't prepared for was nothing.

Sally looked around, confused. The room beyond didn't look like a cave anymore, save for its low rocky ceiling. The rest appeared to have been drywalled over, with plain white walls and a glistening white floor, so shiny she could see herself reflected in it.

But that was it. No décor. No furniture. No mining equipment. No cells with bars on their doors. Not even any cruel and unusual torture devices one might find in a dungeon. Just a blank canvas stretching out in all directions.

"That's odd," Sally couldn't help remarking. "Do you think we're in the right place?"

"It's not like any prison I've ever seen," Jack said, walking over to touch one of the walls. "Not that I've seen a lot, but still. It's rather, well, underwhelming."

"That's the whole point, actually," came a voice behind them.

Jack and Sally whirled around, startled. Stepping out from behind a white wall was a man with a purple beard, wearing plain white coveralls. He was soon followed by others—toys, elves, animals—all wearing matching white garb.

Sally's breath caught in her throat as the group surrounded them, peering at them with curious eyes. Could these be the naughty residents of Christmas Town? Had they found them at last? She scanned the group for Abigail but saw no one that looked like her friend.

Suddenly a cheerful voice broke out over unseen speakers: "Attention, residents. This is your hourly reminder to abandon all hope. If you have any hope remaining, please deposit it in the nearest trash receptacle at your earliest convenience. Thank you and have a terrible day."

Sally looked at Jack in confusion. What was going on here? "I don't understand," she said, addressing the man who had spoken first. "What is this place?" She turned in a slow circle, observing the rest of the group—all of whom appeared, at least at first glance, as if they had properly abandoned all hope long ago, as instructed.

It was then Sally recognized the man who had spoken. He was the same miner whom she'd seen in her vision. The one who had told her about the key.

"Who are you?" the miner asked, giving Sally and Jack a distrustful look. "Is this another one of Jingles's tricks? 'Cause, no offense, we're done with his little reindeer games. Let him do his worst. What does it matter anymore anyway, while we're stuck in here?"

"We're not with Jingles," Sally assured him. "I promise you that. My name is Sally, and this is my friend Jack. We came here looking for a friend of mine who I think was brought here." She scowled. "But it's all been a mistake. She was only helping me. She didn't do anything wrong."

To her surprise, the residents broke into laughter. She cocked her head. "What's so funny?"

The miner shot her an apologetic look before turning to glare at the others. "Don't mind them," he said. "It's just, well, the way you said that. As if the rest of us deserve what we've been given."

Sally's eyes widened. "I didn't mean—"

"It's okay," the man interrupted. "I get it. But just so you know, none of us here were actually bad. At least not intentionally. We're only here because we made mistakes."

"But you can't *make* mistakes anymore in Christmas Town," sneered a robot to his right. Sally suddenly recognized him as the one who had overheated during the talent show. "Not now that Mr. Jingles makes the rules."

The crowd collectively booed at the mention of the judge's name. Definitely not a favorite here. Sally couldn't exactly blame them.

"So wait," Jack interrupted, holding out his arms to silence them. "Are you saying you were *all* wrongfully accused? That none of you did anything wrong?"

"Depends on your definition, I guess," piped in a little old lady, squinting at them as if her glasses had been taken away. "I added pink dye to my husband's soup. It was meant to be a silly prank—he said his lunches were getting boring always being the same. But a nosy neighbor noticed and thought I was being cruel, so they reported me to the authorities."

"I borrowed my neighbor's cookie cutters," called out a man in the back. "Mine were missing and I was on a tight deadline. Problem was, I forgot to return them promptly—I was so wrapped up in finishing my cookie orders in time for Christmas. Three days later, Mr. Jingles's men showed up at my door to take me away."

"Remember me?" a little boy chimed in, walking up to Sally. "I hit you with a snowball and then stuck out my tongue at you." He hung his head. "I'm really sorry about that, by the way. I was just having fun."

Sally gave him a pitying look. "No need to apologize," she assured him.

"Yeah, well, try telling that to Mr. Jingles," a woman beside the boy said, pulling him protectively into her arms. "When I went to him to plead my son's case? He told me if I missed him that much, maybe I should join him here. Next thing I know, I'm being carted away in a sack."

Sally cringed, looking around the room at all the people and animals and toys. None of them were bad at all. None of them deserved to be taken away from their friends and family and sent to live in this sterile place.

The tinny voice over the speaker chimed in again: "Attention, citizens," it droned. "Remember, Christmas paraphernalia is strictly prohibited in this place. If you are caught with anything jolly, it will be confiscated. And you will be sent to the deprivation chamber for three days for Christmas spirit detox."

"This is a very strange prison," Sally couldn't help commenting.

"It's more of an anti-joy chamber," the miner explained. "A place void of anything that might make someone happy. Which means no decorations, no festive lights, no gifts, no mistletoe. Nothing sweet or savory to eat. Nothing."

"Mr. Jingles claims we weren't acting in the Christmas spirit," the snowball boy's mother explained. "So he's taken Christmas away from us forever."

"That's awful," Sally cried, horrified. She couldn't imagine being stuck in this place for any amount of time, never mind forever. It was so . . . blank.

"Well, it isn't Christmas morning, I'll tell you that," declared an elf in the back. "But we find ways to pass the time. We've even formed a Christmas choir."

"A choir?" Sally repeated doubtfully.

"Yup," declared the robot. "Jingles hates singing. But he can't really stop all of us if we all sing at once. It's the best we can do to keep sane in this place." Sally saw the others nod in agreement.

"Well, I, for one, am glad of it," Jack declared. "If you hadn't been singing, we might have never found you."

"So wait, you're not prisoners?" asked the miner, looking shocked. "You came here voluntarily?"

"We didn't have a choice," Sally explained. "As I said before, we need to find my friend. Her name is Abigail. Do any of you know her?"

They looked at one another, shrugging. Then the boy's mother raised a finger.

"I think I know who you mean," she said excitedly. "She just got here, right? She's been sticking to herself mostly, off in a corner. Refuses to put on the white uniform. Or join our choir, even though I heard she has an amazing voice."

She pointed to the back of the room. There, tucked in a corner, was what appeared to be a crumpled heap of rags— in a pattern Sally recognized immediately.

Because she had sewed them herself.

CHAPTER TWENTY-NINE

Excited and filled with relief, Sally left Jack's side to run to her friend. The crowd watched her curiously, parting to give her space. When she finally reached Abigail, she threw her arms around her, hugging her tightly while still remembering to be careful so as not to accidentally break anything.

"I'm so glad I found you," she whispered in Abigail's ear. "When I heard what happened . . ."

She trailed off, realizing Abigail wasn't hugging her back. She just sat there, her head bowed, her body as droopy as a rag doll's.

Sally pulled away, searching Abigail's face with concern. "Are you all right?" she asked. "No, of course you're not," she corrected, realizing the question was ridiculous.

"I'm so sorry, Abigail. When I heard what they'd done to you! And you were only trying to help me."

Abigail gave a small shrug. "I broke the rules," she said in a dull voice that sounded little like her own. "This is what happens when you break the rules."

Sally studied her with worried eyes. The doll's appearance was a far cry from when Sally had first met her back in Christmas Town. She was still wearing Sally's dress, but it was streaked and torn, as if she'd struggled during her capture. Her once blemish-free porcelain skin was smudged with dirt, and her perfect curls were matted and muddy and sticking up at weird angles. And while back in Halloween Town this kind of look would have increased her chances of winning any beauty pageant, Sally knew this couldn't be good for her chances on Santa's sleigh.

It's not right, she thought angrily. *Mr. Jingles cannot get away with this.*

"I'm sorry," she spit out. "But those rules are ridiculous. You shouldn't have to suffer when you've done nothing wrong." She squared her shoulders. "But don't worry. That's why we're here. Jack and I are going to rescue you. To take you away from all of this."

She paused, waiting for Abigail's eyes to light up in relief. For her mouth to lift into a happy smile. Something—anything—to show she understood what Sally was saying.

Instead the doll shook her head mournfully, dropping her gaze to the white floor and avoiding Sally's eyes.

"You shouldn't have bothered," she said sadly.

"No!" Sally protested, alarmed by her friend's unexpected reaction. "Abigail, what are you talking about? You don't deserve to be here! All you did was help me. That's *nice*. An act of selflessness—showing your Christmas spirit. You deserve to be rewarded, not punished."

"Maybe so," Abigail said reluctantly. "But it doesn't make a difference now."

Sally's eyes clouded in confusion. "What are you talking about?"

"Look at me, Sally!" Abigail lashed out angrily. "I'm a mess. I'm filthy and stained and my leg . . ." Her voice caught on the word *leg*, and she trailed off miserably.

"What happened to your leg?" Sally asked worriedly.

Slowly, Abigail reached down and clutched Sally's old dress in her hands. She pulled it up, revealing her right leg. Sally gasped as she saw the huge crack running down the side of it.

"Oh, Abigail," she whispered. "I'm so sorry."

"So now you see," Abigail replied bitterly. "It doesn't matter if I go back to Christmas Town. It doesn't matter if I'm forgiven for what I did. I'm broken now. And no child wants a broken doll for Christmas."

A tear slipped down Sally's cheek, her heart feeling as if it were about to crack like Abigail's leg. It was all she could do not to throw her arms around her friend and assure her that any kid in their right mind would want a doll like her. And if they didn't? If they couldn't see Abigail's value beyond her cracked shell? Well, they weren't worthy of being her child to begin with.

But Abigail was already curling back into herself, her shoulders hunched and her arms hugging her chest. Sally's pity morphed into a righteous fury. How dare Mr. Jingles do this to her.

How dare he do it to any of them.

She rose to her feet and turned back to Jack, her angry steps eating up the distance between them. "We're taking them with us," she declared. "*All* of them. We're going straight back to Christmas Town and we're demanding an audience with Santa Claus. I don't care how difficult it is. He has to know what Mr. Jingles has done."

Jack nodded. "You're right," he said. He turned to the crowd, his expression grim, his shoulders straight. All "skeleton on a mission." Sally watched as he clapped his hands together, as she'd seen him do so many times before in Halloween Town to rally the troops.

"All right, everyone!" he called out in a voice rich with authority. "You heard the doll. Let's move out.

We've got a long journey ahead of us. It's high time we got started."

The crowd cheered, everyone bursting into action, gathering their things, preparing to make a move. Sally watched in growing excitement, her leaves fluttering wildly in her chest. This was really happening. They were doing it! They were going to save them all.

But as quickly as it started, suddenly the activity ground to a halt. The formerly excited faces were shadowed with fear. Confused, Sally turned around to see what had captured their attention. They all seemed to be looking at something behind Jack.

"What is happening?" she whispered.

She watched in growing dread as a large pile of coal rolled through the door. It stopped just behind Jack, then began to take shape. Tiny pieces of rock came together to form small balls. Then bigger ones. Then massive ones that started to stretch into arms and legs. Piece by piece the coal took shape.

The shape of a monster.

Sootfang, Sally realized with horror. And he didn't look pleased.

CHAPTER THIRTY

Sally recoiled as Sootfang, now completely assembled, raised himself to his full height. He was shockingly tall, made of coal, with accents of jagged crystal spikes lining his back, arms, and head. When he opened his mouth, Sally caught a glimpse of razor-sharp spiked teeth.

In other words, he was a total nightmare. The kind straight out of Halloween Town.

Except, apparently, not half as fun.

Sootfang roared in rage and the room shook in response. Rocks rained down from the ceiling and everyone screamed and attempted to take cover. But there was no cover here, of course. And all they could do was huddle together, hands over their heads.

Sootfang didn't seem to notice the frenzied crowd. His eyes had locked on Jack, and he took a heavy step toward him, the white floor cracking under his weight. Jack held up his hands to ward him off, as if he had some magical power to keep a monster at bay.

"Now see here, good sir!" he tried. "I think there's been a bit of a misunderstanding—"

The creature roared, producing another rock shower. Sally cringed, joining the crowd in holding her hands over her head. If he kept this up, he was going to cause a complete cave-in.

"Please!" Jack tried. "Could we possibly take this outside? The acoustics are a bit bad in here and—"

Sootfang angrily swiped a claw at Jack, and the skeleton had to leap backward to avoid being struck. But the creature only stalked forward, closing the gap again, and Sally watched in growing despair as his mouth slowly creaked open, revealing red sparks dancing on a blackened tongue.

Oh, no. Could the coal monster breathe fire, too? That seemed unfair.

As if in answer, Sootfang pulled back his mighty head and roared again, this time shooting fiery flames straight at Jack. The Pumpkin King leapt to the side, just in time to avoid being flambéed, summersaulting to safety as the monster scorched the spot on the floor where he'd been standing a moment before.

Sally groaned in frustration. What were they going to do? Sootfang was bigger than them. He was stronger. He could breathe fire and send rocks raining down. There was no way they were going to be able to match him in battle. And she was pretty sure this was one jam even Jack wouldn't be able to talk his way out of.

Her eyes shot to the door leading out of the cave. If they moved fast, perhaps they'd be able to make it. And maybe the creature wouldn't follow them. Maybe he was only defending his territory and would stop once they got far enough away.

Maybe they could still be safe.

But then, she thought miserably, glancing around the room at the crouching, frightened group, what about everyone else? They were prisoners here. Which meant Sootfang wasn't about to let them escape. How could Sally and Jack just leave them behind, eternal captives in this joyless space? Abandoning them, after they'd promised to save them?

No. She wouldn't do that. She *couldn't*.

"If you could just be reasonable here," she heard Jack say, "I'm sure we could come up with a mutually beneficial agreement."

But Sootfang didn't seem in the mood to bargain. Instead he reached down, scooping Jack up in his massive fist and lifting him closer to his face. Jack struggled to wiggle free, though the creature was too strong and only tightened his grip.

Sally couldn't take it anymore. "No!" she screamed. "Stop it! Now!"

Sootfang's gaze snapped in her direction, as if he was noticing her for the first time. Momentarily distracted, his grip loosened, and Jack dropped down through the gap in his claws, landing hard on the ground. Sootfang looked down at his now empty hand, a puzzled expression on his face as he realized he'd lost his prey. His glowing eyes roamed the cave until they landed on Jack, who was trying to scramble away.

Sootfang slammed his fist against the ceiling of the cavern, producing another avalanche of stone. A large rock crashed down on Jack's unprotected head, and he collapsed instantly, as if he were nothing more than a rag doll himself. Sally screamed in terror as rocks continued to rain down on Jack, covering him almost completely, until all that remained was a single pale leg sticking out from the pile.

No. Tears streamed down Sally's cheeks, almost blinding her with their intensity. *Oh, Jack, no!*

Maybe he's just unconscious, she told herself. *Maybe he'll be okay.*

But the rocks had been so large. So jagged . . .

Sootfang twisted, turning his attention back to the other intruder. Sally stumbled backward, fear spiraling through her as her mind raced through possible escape plans, each more ridiculous than the last. The creature was bigger than her. He was stronger and fiercer—the stuff of pure nightmares. And what was she? Just a rag doll made of wool and old dry leaves. He didn't even need an avalanche to take her down. He could rip her to shreds with just one swipe of his claws.

"Sally!"

The sudden voice startled her out of her panicked state. She whirled around, shocked to find Abigail standing behind her.

"What are you doing?" Sally cried in horror. "Stay back!"

But Abigail shook her head, meeting Sally's eyes with her own. No longer the sad, defeated eyes of earlier, Sally realized in surprise, but rather the ones from the day Sally had first met her. Eyes that flashed with fire.

"Sally," she said, her voice slow and even, "use your head."

What? Sally stared at her before Sootfang roared again,

stomping in their direction. Sally winced and stumbled away, realizing she was running out of time. Any second now he would reach her. He would grab her in his claws. And maybe he'd grab Abigail, too.

Sally had to do something.

Sootfang opened his mouth. Sparks danced again on his blackened tongue.

"Your head, Sally!" Abigail begged. "Now!"

And suddenly Sally understood.

She turned to Sootfang, meeting his eyes with her own. Then she reached up and yanked on her head as hard as she could. She could feel the stitches resisting at first, so she pulled even harder, and at last they snapped free, allowing her to completely decapitate herself.

This is never going to work. It's never going to work.

But there was nothing else she could do. With a cry of rage, she thrust her head in the monster's direction, just as she had in the Christmas Town square.

"LEAVE US ALONE!"

Sootfang leapt backward in shock, almost losing his balance as he stumbled on some fallen rocks. His flames shot from his mouth, going wild and hitting the ceiling instead of Sally or her friend.

Sally watched, too surprised to move. Was this big, bad monster actually so easily frightened? It seemed impossible.

But no, she thought in growing realization, it wasn't fear at all that she saw written on his face as he regained his balance and brushed himself off, but rather a strange look of curiosity.

Curiosity and maybe even hope?

For a moment, Sootfang just looked at her. Just looked and looked until Sally wanted to scream again. Then his mouth creaked open. But instead of shooting fire, this time he spoke.

"You're scary!" he said in a voice filled with wonder.

CHAPTER THIRTY-ONE

Sally was speechless. She stared at the coal monster with the eyes on her still disembodied head. For a moment Sootfang said nothing. Did nothing. Then, out of nowhere, fat tears began to stream down his cheeks.

"Are . . . you all right?" Sally asked, lowering her head to rest it on her neck. It wasn't going to stay that way unless she held it in her hands, but at least the angle was better for addressing someone.

Addressing a monster who had been about to kill her. Who was now, unbelievably, sobbing like a big rock baby.

She watched, still in pure disbelief, as Sootfang sniffled, then plodded over to a small pile of coal and plopped himself down on top of it. Once he was seated, he swiped the tears from his eyes and looked up at Sally with the oddest expression on his face.

"I thought I was the only one," he said in a gravelly voice. "Ever since I was a little lump, I was always different from everyone else in Christmas Town. They're all so small, so covered in . . . skin." He made a face. "When I would walk down the streets, they would gasp at me in horror. Some would even run away screaming."

Yeah, that sounded about right. Sally couldn't help thinking back to Christmas Town's reaction to her own stunt. She couldn't imagine someone like Sootfang wandering the streets without garnering a lot of negative attention.

Out of the corner of her eye, she caught Abigail and some of the others sneaking to the rock pile where Jack had been buried. Abigail gave her a "go on" motion with her hands, and Sally realized they needed her to keep Sootfang distracted until they could make their rescue.

Quickly she turned back to the monster. "That must have been . . . hard for you," she said sympathetically as she slipped her hand into her pocket, searching for her needle and thread. Better to sew her head back on now, just in case things went south again and she needed it reattached for a quick escape.

Sootfang nodded dismally, staring down at his rock knuckles. "Some tried to be nice, of course. They'd invite me to play their reindeer games or come over for a spot of peppermint tea. Which I do like!" he added quickly, as if he thought Sally was about to accuse him of being close-minded. "And I desperately wanted some friends." He sighed deeply. "But when I tried to show them *my* games? Really good ones, too, like hide-and-screech or slip-and-scream? They freaked out on me."

"Slip-and-scream is a classic," Sally found herself agreeing as she quickly stitched her head to her neck.

Sootfang's expression brightened. "I know, right?" he asked. Then he sobered. "But try to tell that to the elves of Christmas Town. No one wanted to play my gruesome games." He shook his head sadly. "And then there was the time I tried to host a dinner party. I spent all day making a slimy slug stew. Only to have everyone refuse to eat it." His mouth dipped into a frown. "A few of them even threw up at the sight of it."

He looked so despondent; Sally found herself almost forgetting he'd been trying to kill them a moment before. Head reattached, she reached out, laying a gentle hand on his rocky arm. "I'm sorry," she said. "That must have been tough."

He looked up at her with bleak, empty eyes. "How did you do it?" he asked pitifully. "How did you survive all this time being so scary?"

Sally stole a glance over at Abigail and the others.

They'd made good progress, and she could see both of Jack's legs and part of his torso now. She swallowed hard, praying he was doing all right under the rubble. That he was just unconscious, but ultimately fine.

She turned back to Sootfang. She needed to keep him talking. "Well, the thing is," she said slowly, "I'm from a much different place. It's called Halloween Town and everyone who lives there is scary—as scary as you or me. In fact, there's even a national holiday where we celebrate our creepiness. Everyone participates and they all try to out-scare each other in the most terrifying ways possible."

Sootfang seemed impressed. "Do they like slimy slug stew?" he asked hopefully.

"Why, it's practically the town's official food," Sally assured him, even though this wasn't exactly the case. "And we actually have two professional hide-and-screech leagues that play each other in a big tournament each year."

"That sounds amazing." Sootfang grinned toothily. "I wish I could go to a place like that. A place where I'd finally belong."

"Well, maybe you can."

Sally whirled around at the sound of another voice, her heart almost bursting from her chest as she saw Jack Skellington rising from the rock pile. Alive and well, even if he was technically dead.

"Jack!" she cried.

"Hello, Sally," he said. He turned to Sootfang, giving him a small bow. "I don't think we've been properly introduced," he said gallantly. "My name is Jack Skellington. They call me the Pumpkin King. And I rule over Halloween Town."

Sootfang's eyes grew very large. He rose to his feet, stomping over to Jack with such force that, for a moment, Sally was nervous he was going to bowl him over. Instead he stopped just in front of Jack and thrust out his rocky hand.

"I'm Sootfang," he said. "Nice to meet you. I'm sorry I tried to kill you."

"Bah! It happens to the best of us," Jack said, shaking his hand up and down.

Sootfang smiled. "Your town sounds really nice, by the way."

"Actually, it's quite naughty," Jack shot back with a wink. "But that's all part of its charm. Honestly, I think you'd really like it there. And the residents would sure like you! They've never seen a real coal monster. Let me tell you, they'd be so impressed."

Sootfang looked from Jack to Sally, his eyes wide with hope. "Could you take me there?" he asked hesitantly.

"Absolutely!" Jack declared. "We can go anytime you like!"

Sally realized it was time to step in. "We'll take you there as a favor," she said, shooting a look at Jack. "But only if you agree to do us a favor in return."

"Of course! Anything you want!" Sootfang gushed. "Whatever it takes! I'll do anything to go to Halloween Town."

"Very well." Sally looked around the cavern. At all the so-called naughty residents of Christmas Town. At Abigail, who was now covered in soot from head to toe and wringing her hands nervously.

"You need to free all these prisoners," Sally said, her voice firm. "Let everyone go. No exceptions. And you must promise to never imprison anyone here ever again."

Sootfang's smile faltered. "Mr. Jingles won't like that," he said nervously.

"Let us deal with Mr. Jingles," Jack proclaimed. "That nasty, jangling judge is on *my* naughty list now. And if he's not scared yet, he will be."

Sootfang looked relieved by the threat. "And then you'll take me to Halloween Town? And you're sure they'll like me there?"

"They'll love you," Jack assured him. "They'll probably try to recruit you for next year's Halloween."

"Of course! I'd be more than happy to pitch in!" Sootfang rubbed his rocky hands together in excitement.

"Very well. I agree to your terms." He looked around the cavern. "You're all free to go!" he called out loudly.

Everyone began to cheer and clap. They surrounded Sally and Jack, all trying to talk at once. Sootfang watched from a short distance away, then waved to Sally to get her attention.

"I need to pack," he said. "Please don't leave without me."

"We wouldn't dream of it," she assured him, and he gave her a toothy grin before running back through the door and into the mine shaft. Sally watched him go for a minute, her heart feeling oddly full.

"Monsters," Jack said. "In the end they're all the same."

She turned to see he had managed to separate himself from the throng and now stood behind her, a big smile on his skeletal face.

"Except you," he added softly. "You constantly surprise me. I thought we were goners. I really did."

"Me too," she admitted. "But I can't take all the credit. It was Abigail. She was the one who knew what to do."

Speaking of . . .

Her eyes roved the cave until she spotted her friend. Abigail was sitting in her corner again, her knees pulled up to her chest. Sally frowned. She walked over to the doll and crouched down to her level.

"Are you all right?" she asked worriedly. "Did you hurt yourself again?"

Abigail sighed deeply. "No," she assured Sally. "And I don't want to seem ungrateful, either. What you've done for Christmas Town?" She smiled sadly. "It's above and beyond. No one's ever going to forget this." She met Sally's eyes with her own, and Sally saw the gratitude shining through her tears. "You're a hero, Sally. A true hero."

Sally scrunched up her face. "Then what's wrong?" she asked. "You can tell me. Whatever it is, I promise I won't judge."

"I know," Abigail said, bowing her head. "It's just . . . I can't help thinking . . . what do I do from here? From this point forward, I mean. What good am I to anyone? I'm just a broken old doll. Useless." Her voice cracked. "I have no place in the world anymore."

Sally's heart ached at the pain she heard in Abigail's voice. She hated the idea that this smart and kind and self-less doll could ever think of herself as useless. That some minor setback that wasn't even her fault could keep her from reaching her dreams.

"Abigail—" she started. But at that moment a shadow loomed over them. She looked up to see Jack standing there, smiling.

"Why don't you come back with us," he suggested

brightly. "Broken dolls are held in high regard in Halloween Town. People find them extremely creepy." He clapped his hands, as if it was already decided. "You'll be a total hit. I'll make sure of it personally!"

Abigail's face crumpled. She sobbed softly. Jack frowned, confused. "What did I say?"

"She doesn't want to be a creepy doll, Jack," Sally reminded him. "And that's perfectly okay," she added to Abigail. "You want the life you want and there's nothing wrong with that. You never have to apologize for having your own dreams."

"Maybe not," Abigail said bitterly. "But I do have to accept that my dreams are now impossible. Santa will never give a child a broken toy. It's against policy. Children want toys that are new and shiny and perfect. He's not going to risk his reputation for a broken doll, especially these days, when it's hard enough to get children to believe in him in the first place." Tears began to roll down her porcelain cheeks. "Which means I'm destined to be alone. Forever and ever."

So much pain. So much sorrow. Sally reached out, taking Abigail's hands in her own and squeezing them as hard as she dared without risking any more cracks in the porcelain.

"You know," she said slowly. "I used to think that way, too. I thought I was trapped in a life I never asked for, with no hope of escaping it. But if this whole journey has taught me anything, it's that I have the power to shape my destiny. I can go after the life I want, no matter how difficult it might feel to achieve. And you can do the same. I know you can! You just can't give up hope."

Abigail sniffed. "You really think so?"

"Absolutely," Sally declared. "You're going to make some little child very happy on Christmas morning. I just know it."

"Oh, Sally!" Abigail looked up at her, eyes shiny with tears. "I don't deserve you."

"Nonsense," Sally scoffed, pulling her friend into a warm embrace. "You deserve everything. And one way or another, I'm going to make sure you get it."

CHAPTER THIRTY-TWO

The walk back to Christmas Town was a lot easier than the trek to the caves had been. The storms had passed and the wind had calmed, and Sootfang knew a secret way through the Nog Bog that wouldn't involve anyone in their group sinking into it. In fact, he even took them to a secret spring where everyone was treated to a refreshing cup of eggnog, straight from the source. Sally had to admit, the stuff was a lot yummier when she wasn't actively drowning in it. Though Jack commented that it was a bit sweet for his tastes and could have used a splash of real mud. Something Soot-fang wholeheartedly agreed with.

In fact, it seemed Sootfang agreed with Jack on almost everything, and the two of them soon became thick as thieves on the journey back. Jack schooled Sootfang on everything he needed to know about Halloween Town, and Sootfang eagerly took in every detail, asking follow-up questions about every story Jack told. Jack was more than happy to answer and kept smiling and laughing as he described the antics of those back home.

It made Sally smile, too. She thought back to Jack in the graveyard, how disillusioned he'd been, how much he'd longed for something different and new. But now it seemed he'd rediscovered his affection for his hometown and was beginning to remember all its many charms. Maybe absence had made the skeleton's heart grow fonder. Or maybe it was the newcomer's excitement that infused his own.

Whatever it was, Sally would take it.

But while Sootfang and Jack were over the top with their mutual admiration society, Abigail remained mostly quiet on the walk back. Sally attempted to engage her in conversation, and each time Abigail answered politely but with as few words as possible, and several times Sally caught the doll self-consciously reaching for her cracked leg when she thought no one was looking. Sally worried that it was hurting her to walk on it. But Abigail refused all offers of help.

Finally Sally couldn't take it anymore. "Can I ask you something?" she said, trying to keep her voice neutral.

Abigail blushed, quickly removing her hand from her

leg. "Sure," she said. Though, in Sally's opinion, she didn't look that sure at all.

Sally continued anyway. Abigail needed to hear this whether she wanted to or not. "When we first met, do you remember telling me you thought I was beautiful?"

"Of course. You *are* beautiful."

"Are you only saying that to make me feel better about myself?"

Abigail looked shocked. "No! Why would I do that?"

Sally held out her arm and pulled up her sleeve. "Look closely," she said. "Do you see all my stitches? They cut across my entire body—even my face."

Abigail looked confused. "I know," she said hesitantly. "So?"

"So you think I'm beautiful?" Sally's eyes locked on Abigail. "Even with my imperfections?"

"They're not imperfections!" Abigail protested. "They're just . . . part of who you are. They make you unique. Special."

"So I'm *better* for my imperfections. Is that what you're saying?" Sally pressed.

Abigail flinched, finally catching on to Sally's game. She closed her eyes for a moment, then opened them again. "Look, I appreciate what you're trying to do, Sally. I really do. But you have to understand, it's different for me. I don't come from a place where people accept you for who you are. And children don't want broken dolls for Christmas."

"How do you know?" Sally asked. "Have you ever met a child?"

"Well, no. I mean, not a human one," Abigail hedged. "But that's just how it is. Everyone knows that everything needs to be perfect on Christmas."

"And look where that belief has gotten *everyone*," Sally shot back, waving a hand at their caravan of elves and toys and animals. "Perhaps the residents of Christmas Town need to relax their standards a bit. Stop thinking of everything as black and white."

"If only it were that simple," Abigail said with a sigh.

"I didn't say it would be simple," Sally pointed out quietly. "The question is whether it's worth trying."

Abigail gave her a fond look. "You're really something, Sally," she said admiringly. "I have to say, Jack's lucky to have you."

Sally turned bright red. "Wait, what?" she cried, horrified by the insinuation. She shook her head fiercely from side to side. "No. Jack and I are *not* together."

"But you want to be," Abigail said matter-of-factly.

"Uh, no!" Sally laughed nervously, glancing over at Jack to make sure he wasn't listening in. Luckily he seemed fully engrossed in telling Sootfang yet another scary story about

Halloween Town that had something to do with purple pumpkins.

Sally turned back to Abigail, who was giving her a knowing look. "It's not that simple," she said with a sigh. "I mean, I'm still trying to figure out how I fit into the world at this point. Let alone how someone else might fit in with me."

"I didn't say it would be simple," Abigail replied with a sly smile. "The question is whether it's worth trying."

Sally chuckled as her own words were thrown back at her. "Okay, fine. I deserve that," she admitted. "And you're right, of course. It's just . . ." She poked her toe in the snow, trying to figure out how to explain it. "For so long I've admired him from afar. How confident he was. How creative. How everyone seemed to love and adore him and worship the ground he walked on. . . ."

"But . . . ?" Abigail pressed.

"I never really knew him," Sally said softly. "Not before this. I think I only liked the idea of who he was. Like, I wanted to *be* him, more than I wanted to be with him."

"And now?"

"And now I think I'm in love with him," she confessed. "And it's strange because what I love about him is the exact opposite of what I always admired. Turns out he's not just brave and bold. He's also caring. He's loyal. Funny. And he has just as many insecurities as me—he's just better at hiding them, I guess."

"Well, he's not so great at hiding how he feels about you," Abigail declared, raising her eyebrows.

Sally gulped, her eyes shooting involuntarily to Jack, who at that moment happened to be stealing a glance over at her. Sally turned away quickly, blushing all over again.

Abigail giggled. "Told you," she whispered. "Jack Skellington's got it bad for you, Sally." Her eyes sparkled with mischief. "The question is . . . what are you going to do about it?"

Sally sighed deeply. That *was* the question, wasn't it? Their trip was quickly coming to an end. And she had no idea what would happen once they returned home. Would things simply go back to how they were? Or would she somehow find the courage to tell Jack how she felt about him and pray Abigail was right that he might feel the same?

Drawing in a breath, she smiled at her friend. "Let's concentrate on saving the day for you first," she said. "*Then* I'll figure out what I'm going to do about Jack Skellington."

CHAPTER THIRTY-THREE

They arrived back in Christmas Town just as the sun was setting and the lights began flickering on. Sally could feel the curious stares of the townsfolk as she and Jack led their ragtag group down the street and toward the main square. Sootfang had elected to stay on the outskirts of town, not feeling quite ready to face the town that had driven him out. He did, however, promise to keep an ear open as backup, should they need him. Hopefully it wouldn't come to that.

"What are you planning?" Jack asked as they turned the corner just before the street opened up into the town square. "Don't you think we should be heading to Santa's workshop if we want to talk to the big guy?"

"No." Sally said firmly. "What I need to say shouldn't be said in the privacy of any office. This is an issue that involves the entire town. I want everyone to witness it."

Jack looked at her thoughtfully and then nodded. "I like it," he said. "Just let me know how I can help."

Sally shot him a grateful smile. She could definitely get used to the idea of having someone on her team. Even if she didn't need him, it was nice to know he was there.

When they reached the town square, Sally didn't pause. She headed straight to the giant Christmas tree in the very center and grabbed a fistful of branches. Then, carefully, she hoisted herself up into the tree.

"Sally! What are you doing?" Abigail asked in a shocked voice. But Sally thought she caught a hint of admiration, as well.

"I'm being naughty," she joked, flashing her friend a wicked smile before pulling herself higher into the tree. She could hear voices rising from down below as the residents of Christmas Town—both nice and naughty—surrounded the tree, pointing and shouting for the others to come check out what was happening. When Sally looked down, she saw Abigail and Jack standing on the sidelines, watching proudly. She gave them a thumbs-up, then continued her climb. She moved her rag doll arms and legs spryly among the tree's limbs, reaching the very top branch and the glowing golden star.

"What in the figgy pudding pie is this?"

A loud, angry voice suddenly rang out from the crowd below. Sally looked down from her perch, delighted to see Mr. Jingles himself marching through the square. He'd brought a full platoon of tin soldiers with him, too, and the soldiers used their spears to push their way into the crowd and march to the bottom of the tree. Even from this high up Sally could see Mr. Jingles's mouth twisted into a fierce scowl, and his normally pale face had darkened to almost purple. He looked up at Sally and waved his jingle bell gavel furiously.

Was this really the man they were all so afraid of? From up here he looked like little more than an angry ant.

"I should have known it was you," he growled. "I should have arrested you the second I saw you. You and your kind have no place here in our beautiful Christmas Town."

Sally put her hand to her mouth in an exaggerated yawn. "Actually," she said, when she had finished, "I think *you're* the one who's overstayed his welcome. You've completely lost the spirit of Christmas and the residents have had enough."

"The spirit of Christmas?" Mr. Jingles scoffed. "Don't make me laugh. What does a pathetic rag doll like you know about Christmas?"

"She knows more than you!" Abigail retorted, surprising Sally by stepping out of the crowd. She shook her finger at Mr. Jingles angrily. "Christmas is supposed to be a time of joy and love. Of coming together as a family and celebrating what makes each of us unique. Christmas is for everyone, Mr. Jingles. Even for those of us who might not be entirely perfect. Or one's idea of perfect."

Sally beamed. She couldn't have said it better herself. "But you've twisted that," she called down. "In your effort to ensure everyone's nice, you've turned the entire town rotten. People should be nice because they respect each other. Not because they're afraid of being taken away and imprisoned. Sure, it might keep the peace short term—get people to fall in line. But in the end, you've only nurtured a spirit of fear and distrust. Which is pretty much the opposite of what I understand Christmas to be."

The crowd erupted in cheers. Along with a few angry shouts, aimed toward Mr. Jingles and his soldiers.

"She's right!" cried a man in the back.

"You've ruined our town. You've alienated friends and neighbors with your little crusade."

"We're not going to take it anymore. Not from you or anyone else!"

BANG!

Mr. Jingles slammed his gavel against a nearby lamppost, so hard the light went out. His face was completely purple at this point and his eyes were bulging from his head.

"Arrest her!" he screamed at his soldiers. "Arrest every one of these traitors!"

The soldiers stepped forward, raising their spears. Though Sally noticed a few of them looked a bit conflicted. As if they weren't sure they wanted to be on the wrong side of this clash, especially since they were clearly outnumbered.

"What are you waiting for?" Mr. Jingles demanded. "Do as I say. Or else you'll be next on my list."

"What, are you going to try to arrest them now, too?" Sally called down to him. "Are you going to arrest the entire town? Good luck with that." She turned to the soldiers. "Think about it. Are you doing this because you think he's right? That these people who are sticking up for their friends and neighbors deserve to be punished? Or are you just acting out of fear like everyone else? Because I will tell you right now, there's nothing to be afraid of anymore. His tyranny is over. There's nothing he can do to you for standing up for what's right."

The soldiers looked at one another. Then, one by one, they turned on Mr. Jingles, raising their spears. Sally watched the judge's face pale as he realized what was happening. And as his own soldiers surrounded him, their spears jangled like music to Sally's ears.

Mr. Jingles shook his gavel again, but this time with less vigor and a lot more trembling. "I will not be treated like this! I am your judge and your jury! Appointed by Santa Claus himself. You just wait until he hears about this!"

"Oh, he's heard, all right. He's heard it all," interrupted a deep voice in the crowd.

The residents of Christmas Town whirled around. Sally gasped as her eyes fell on the figure at the very back of the square. A very familiar hatted figure, standing side by side with Abigail's friend Tammy.

"Ladies and gentlemen," Tammy said grandly, "please give it up for Santa Claus!"

CHAPTER THIRTY-FOUR

The crowd began clapping wildly, respectfully parting as Santa Claus made his way to the center of the square. He looked splendid and regal in his Christmas best: a smart crimson coat trimmed in white, a matching hat on top of his head. As he passed, he shook hands with the eager residents of Christmas Town, even pausing to kiss a few babies as he went—the consummate politician. Sally watched from her perch, noting each and every happy face.

Well, except for Mr. Jingles, that was. He was cowering in fear.

"Sir!" the judge cried, lowering his gavel as Santa stepped closer. "Thank goodness you're here! The entire town has lost the plot. They've threatened my life. They've turned my own soldiers against me." His face twisted as his gaze shot up to Sally. "All because of her," he spit out, pointing at the tree.

"That's a lie!" Abigail burst out. Santa turned to look at her questioningly. She blushed hard under his gaze.

"What do you mean, child?" Santa asked in a kind voice. "You can tell me."

Abigail didn't look entirely convinced. But to her credit, she took a breath, then started to speak. "Sally risked her life to save us, Santa. Even though she barely knew any of us and could have just gone home and forgotten all about us. She didn't," she added, her voice growing in confidence as she spoke. "She saved us all. And if that's considered *naughty*, well, Santa, I guess I don't understand the definition. Because if *this* is considered nice?" She pointed accusingly at Mr. Jingles. "Imprisoning your friends and neighbors because they think or act differently than you? Forcing people to be scared to say anything—do anything— lest they make a mistake and have to pay for it with their lives? If *that* is considered nice behavior"—she shook her head, her tangled curls bouncing off her shoulders—"then I would prefer to be naughty."

For a moment, the crowd was silent. So silent you could have heard a jingle bell drop. Then, one by one, their voices rose in cheers. Until the entire square was yelling and applauding and screaming in support. Abigail looked around in wonder, her eyes wide. Sally smiled atop her tree.

Santa seemed troubled. He scanned the crowd, then looked up at Sally, then down at Abigail and Mr. Jingles. Finally he held up his white-gloved hands, urging everyone to calm down. Once the crowd had settled, he cleared his throat.

"You're right," he said. "You're absolutely right. Christmas is supposed to be a time of joy, not judgment." He stroked his beard. "I think perhaps we've forgotten about that over the last few years."

"But, sir!" Mr. Jingles protested. "I was only trying to carry out your orders! After all, you're the one who came up with the naughty and nice list to begin with."

Santa sighed. "It's true. That was my creation. And it was well-intentioned, I promise you—at least at the beginning. But perhaps I need to rethink my calibrations. After all, no one's entirely nice or entirely naughty. At best, we're a bit of both. Even me," he added with a sly grin. "Like when I sneak into the kitchens late at night and steal a few of Mrs. Claus's freshly baked cookies."

The crowd laughed. A few of them shouted, "Naughty Santa," in teasing voices. Mr. Jingles gripped his gavel tightly, as if he was this close to exploding in rage.

Santa turned to the crowd. "I think I owe you all an apology," he said ruefully. "This whole time I've been working around the clock, so worried about getting all the children of the world to believe in me. And because of that, I've neglected all of you—who already do." He shook his head sadly. "In fact, you not only believe in me, but you support me in my work each and every day. Christmas couldn't happen without all of you. And I'm sorry I've been so wrapped up in things that I haven't properly appreciated that."

He turned to Jingles, giving him a disapproving look. "As for you. You were so concerned with everyone else's behavior, you never stopped to think about your own. From what I can see, that makes you the naughtiest of them all." He held out his hand. "Give me the gavel."

Mr. Jingles hung his head, realizing the game was up. He grudgingly handed over the gavel to Santa Claus.

"What are you going to do to me?" he asked worriedly.

Santa seemed to consider this for a moment. Then he sighed. "Nothing," he said. "I think there's been enough punishment handed out lately. But you need to leave Christmas Town and never come back. There's no place for someone like you in my town."

Mr. Jingles's eyes widened in horror. "But where will I go?"

"Oh, don't worry, I'm sure you'll find someplace *nice*," Santa said wryly. Then he clapped his hands. "Guards. Escort him out of town. And see that he never comes back."

The guards raised their spears. Jingles looked for a moment as if he wanted to run. But eventually he resigned himself to his fate, allowing the soldiers to lead him out of town as the crowd cheered him on his way.

Once he was gone, Sally decided it was time to come down from her tree, and she carefully lowered herself back to the ground. When she reached it, Abigail hobbled over and hugged her tightly.

"Oh, Sally," she said. "You did it. You saved Christmas Town."

"*We* did it," Sally corrected. "And we're not done yet."

She released her friend and made her way through the crowd, stopping when she got to Santa. He looked at her with admiration in his eyes.

"Thank you," he said. "You've made me see the light. And from now on, I promise you everything will change. I won't ever get so caught up in my work that I forget the purpose of it all. Not only for the children of the world. But also everyone here. We all deserve a merry Christmas."

"Agreed," Sally said with a smile. "Not to mention a holiday break every once in a while. If you can ever allow yourself to get away, Halloween Town is always open to you. Right, Jack?" she asked, glancing over at the Pumpkin King.

"Absolutely!" Jack declared. "I'll show you around personally."

"There is still one more thing, though," Sally said. "Before we go. There's a certain . . . someone I'd like to properly introduce you to. Someone really special."

Santa cocked his head. "And who might that be?"

Sally beckoned for Abigail to step forward. Abigail shook her head, her face pale with nerves. But Sally wasn't about to give up and waved her forward again. Finally Abigail gave in and trudged to her side, looking as if she were about to face an executioner.

"This is Abigail," Sally said to Santa. "She saved my life when Mr. Jingles sent his soldiers after me. And she was severely punished for doing so."

"I'm sorry to hear that," Santa said. "Saving a stranger's life should be considered an act of heroism. You should have been lauded, not punished."

"Thank you, sir," Abigail said meekly.

"That's not all," Sally continued. "When she was arrested, they hurt her. They broke her leg." She reached down, pulling up Abigail's dress to show the crack in the porcelain. Abigail cringed, turning her face away.

"That's terrible!" Santa exclaimed, examining the leg. "It looks painful, too."

"It was a little bit at first," Abigail squeaked. "But it's fine. . . ."

"Abigail thinks that because she's broken, she won't get her ultimate wish," Sally explained to Santa. "To ride on your sleigh this Christmas Eve and be given to a child."

Santa stroked his beard thoughtfully. "Well, traditionally toys do have to be perfect to earn a spot on my sleigh," he mused. "It's the way it's always been, you see."

Abigail hung her head, not looking surprised. But Sally lifted her chin.

"Well, maybe you should reconsider your definition of *perfect*," she shot back. "Abigail is an amazing doll. She's smart and she's kind and she's a good friend, too. There's no crack in the world that could make her any less perfect in my eyes. And I'm sure the little children around the world would agree, if they only got the chance to know her."

Abigail burst into tears. "Oh, Sally," she murmured. Then she turned to Santa. "It's okay. You don't have to take me. I'll find something else here. I'll—"

Santa held up a hand, stopping her. "You really want to go on my sleigh?" he asked. "You want a child of your own?"

Abigail nodded meekly. "It's my greatest dream, Santa."

"Okay." Santa reached out, touching her arm with his hand. "I've got an idea. When you're finished here, meet me back at my workshop. But don't dawdle," he added. "If we're going to get you ready in time for Christmas, we have to move fast."

Abigail's eyes shone with surprise, mixed with a dash of desperate hope. "Yes, sir," she said. "I'll come straight-away. Thank you. Thank you so much! You don't know how much this means to me!"

Santa smiled knowingly. "I think I have an idea, actu-ally," he said. Then he turned to Jack and Sally. "Would you like to join us, as well? I believe the missus has been cooking up quite the pre-Christmas feast. I'd love to have you join me in eating it."

"Sounds amazing," Jack assured him. "But I'm afraid we must be heading home. After all, Halloween won't plan itself, you know. I've got three hundred and sixty-two days left. There's no time to lose."

"I understand completely," Santa said, slapping Jack on the back. "Just . . . try to remember to enjoy yourself once in a while, too. You deserve it, just like me."

And with that, he turned and headed back up the hill. The crowd watched him go, then began to disperse, still chattering wildly about all that had taken place that day. Sally noticed several of them hugging their once-exiled friends and neighbors and welcoming them back to town. It appeared the spirit of Christmas was returning to Christmas Town. And this year hopefully everyone—whether they were nice . . . or maybe a little naughty—would have their dreams come true.

Sally turned back to Abigail, who was still standing beside her, watching the scene. "You still here?" she teased. "Don't you have a date at Santa's workshop?"

Abigail threw her arms around Sally, pulling her into a strong hug. "Thank you, Sally," she whispered. "I'll never be able to repay you for all you've done for me."

"No repayment necessary," Sally assured her, hugging her back. "I'm just happy I could help. And please keep in touch. I want to hear all about the amazing child who's lucky enough to end up with you."

"I will," Abigail promised. "As long as *you* tell me what happens between you and Jack." She gave Sally a knowing look, and Sally's cheeks heated.

"Did I hear my name?" Jack asked, ambling toward them.

"Not everything is about you, Jack Skellington," Sally scolded, then winked at Abigail. Jack looked from doll to doll.

"I feel like I'm missing something," he said.

"I'll fill you in later," Sally assured him. "Right now, I think it's time to go home."

"Agreed," Jack said. "I'm ready when you are." And, as if on cue, Zero appeared at his side, zipping around them and yipping happily. Sally reached out and booped his nose before turning back to Abigail.

"I'll miss you," she said.

"I'll miss you, too, Sally," Abigail replied, smiling wistfully. "Stay safe. And have the best Halloween ever."

The girls hugged once again, and once again tears welled in Sally's eyes. But this time they weren't sad tears. More like tears of joy.

Abigail was going to get her happy ending. The new life she deserved. Sally couldn't have been more thrilled for her.

But now it was time to go home. To get started on her own happily ever after.

CHAPTER THIRTY-FIVE

After saying goodbye to their new friends and promising to visit again someday, Jack and Sally, along with Zero and Sootfang, headed out of Christmas Town. Sootfang proved himself immediately useful by allowing them to ride on his shoulders as he climbed up the hill, using his rocky claws to dig into the slippery slopes, and it didn't take long before they reached the grove of holiday trees where their adventure had first begun.

Once inside, Jack turned in a slow circle, examining each tree in turn. "So many adventures," he mused, "just waiting to be had."

"Well, they'll have to wait a little longer," Sally replied

with a smirk. "I, for one, have had my fill of adventure for the time being."

"I suppose you're right," Jack said. Then he shot her a grin. "But another time maybe? You'll come with me, and we'll explore them all?"

Sally's leaves rustled. "Sure, Jack. That would be great," she said casually, as if it were no big deal. But inside, she felt like dancing.

We'll explore them all.

Another time.

Another time with Jack.

And once again Sally found herself wondering just what would happen when they returned to Halloween Town. Sure, they'd still be friendly with each other. And Sally would definitely volunteer to help him with next Halloween, whether it be with mixing potions or sewing costumes or even just incorporating a couple of Christmas themes into the works. After all, that was what she'd always wanted, right? To have the freedom to take part in Halloween? It had always been her only dream. So why did it no longer feel like enough?

Why did she suddenly want something more?

Another time maybe? You'll come with me?

"I'd go anywhere with you, Jack Skellington," she whispered.

He turned, cocking his head. "Did you say something?"

"Nope," she shot back quickly, taking purposeful steps toward the jack-o'-lantern tree. Jack ran to catch up to her, then gallantly opened the door.

"Ladies first," he said. "I need to help Sootfang disassemble himself a bit so he can fit through the door." He gestured to the creature, who waved back cheerfully as he began to break apart into small lumps of coal.

"All right, then," Sally said. "I'll see you on the other side."

She leaned toward the door, breathing in deeply, rejoicing in the moldy scent of death and decay that lingered on the other side. *Ah, home,* she thought as she dove headfirst into the abyss.

After tumbling through blackness, she arrived just like before, this time plopping down in a nice thick pile of fallen leaves. She laughed in delight as she rolled in the pile for a moment, enjoying the feeling of fall tickling her cloth skin.

A disassembled Sootfang came next, followed by Zero. Jack came down last, disappearing into the same pile of leaves as Sally had. He emerged a moment later, popping up with force and thrusting out his arms as he did, sending leaves flying in all directions.

"Boo!" he yelled loudly, and everyone jumped a mile, then laughed. Sally shoved him playfully back into the pile of leaves. Jack's dark eyes seemed to sparkle as he lay there, looking up at the orange autumn sky. "Oh, it is good to be home," he declared. And Sally agreed with him. There was so much she loved about Christmas Town. But Halloween Town was pretty great, too. And it was okay, she decided, to like both for what they were. If she'd learned anything from this adventure, it was that one thing didn't have to define you. You got to define yourself—in any manner you saw fit.

Which was exactly what she planned to do.

Once Sootfang had reassembled himself, they headed down the wooded trail and back into the graveyard, passing Spiral Hill and stopping at Zero's tombstone. The ghost dog looked a little sad and barked twice, as if to say he'd miss the adventure. Sally gave him a scratch on the top of his head.

"Who's a good boy?" Sally asked fondly.

Zero barked happily, evidently satisfied by this. He dove into the ground, disappearing from view.

The remaining three of them headed under the archway back into Halloween Town. Once inside, Sootfang let out a low whistle. "Whoa," he exclaimed, his eyes bulging from his head as he looked around at all the creepy buildings and dead trees and spiderwebs hanging from every lamppost. "This is amazing. I can't believe it exists! It's like something out of a dream!"

"Don't you mean a *nightmare*?" Jack asked with a knowing look.

Before Sootfang could respond, excited voices rose in the air.

"Look! There they are!"

"It's Jack! And Sally!"

"They're back!"

Suddenly the three of them found themselves surrounded by a hearty mix of monsters and nightmares, vampires and corpses, zombies and clowns. In fact, what seemed to be the entirety of Halloween Town were pushing and shoving one another in an effort to reach them. They were all talking excitedly, lobbing out questions so fast that neither Sally nor Jack had time to answer before the next one came volleying in.

"Where have you been?"

"Why did you leave?"

"What are you wearing?"

"Are you all right?"

"Who's that monster with you?"

"Does he celebrate Halloween?"

Jack held up his hands good-naturedly. "Everyone, please!" he begged. "We'll be happy to answer each one of your questions. But I need you to give us some space.

We're a bit exhausted, you see. We've had quite the adventure."

"An adventure?" asked Corpse Kid, looking up at Jack with awe. "What kind of adventure?"

Jack leapt onto the steps of the town hall and cleared his throat. "I'm glad you asked," he said grandly, the consummate showman. "Our journey began with a grove of painted trees, which led to a magical land of cold white powder and a rainbow of lights. A land where everyone gets presents wrapped up in shiny paper and tied with big red bows. There's candy and cookies everywhere you look. Not to mention something called hot chocolate, which is almost deadly it's so delicious."

"Ooh! Do you actually die when you drink it?" asked the Clown with the Tear Away Face.

"Are the cookies made with real caterpillars?" a witch added hopefully.

"Do the presents explode when you try to open them?" piped in one of the vampires.

"No, nothing like that," Sally assured them with a laugh. "In fact, there's nothing gross or gory in Christmas Town at all."

The crowd's excitement was dampened. "Well, that doesn't sound like very much fun," the Mayor said with a dismissive huff, spinning his head around to show his disapproval.

"Is it really an adventure if there're no caterpillar cookies?" muttered one witch to the other. "I'm just asking."

Jack frowned. "But it's fun!" he insisted. "It's tremendously fun! You can skate on icy ponds and eat canes made of candy and—"

He was losing their interest fast, Sally realized. But then, maybe that was for the best. The last thing Christmas Town needed was a massive invasion of nightmare tourists. They couldn't even deal with a single doll's disembodied head.

"I'm telling you, it's magical!" Jack continued, not as willing to give this up. "In fact, I was thinking maybe we could find a way to re-create it here! Could you imagine? Christmas in Halloween Town?"

"Or we could just focus on making next year's Halloween festive for everyone," Sally suggested kindly, laying a hand on his arm.

Jack sighed. "I suppose you're right," he relented. Then he brightened. "But speaking of Halloween! I want to introduce you to our new friend. Everyone, meet Sootfang the coal creature. Sootfang—this is everyone."

They all turned to look at the new monster. Sootfang lifted his hand and waved shyly to the crowd. For a moment, they just stared at him. Then their faces broke into smiles, and they rushed at him, surrounding him and examining him with delight.

"Wow! Look at those spikes!"

"And your claws! They're so sharp! I bet you could cut rock with them."

"I can also breathe fire," Sootfang added eagerly. "Watch!"

He lifted his face to the sky. Then he opened his mouth, blowing a plume of smoke and fire from it. Everyone oohed and aahed in appreciation.

"That's so amazing!"

"Imagine what we can do with something like that on Halloween!"

"You might be our scariest monster yet!"

Sootfang's coal cheeks turned bright red. A toothy grin spread across his face. "Really?" he asked. "You like that I'm scary?"

Everyone laughed at this, as if he'd said the funniest thing in the world. "Of course we like it," declared Corpse Kid. "I mean, look at all of us. Scary is definitely our thing."

Sally opened her mouth to agree, but before she could speak, she found herself being yanked backward so hard it almost caused her to lose her balance. She whirled around, horrified to find Dr. Finkelstein had wheeled himself up behind her and was digging his ragged fingernails into her soft cloth.

"There you are!" he growled. "How dare you just take off on me like this? I was worried sick!" He began dragging her by the arm. "You come back with me right now. You are never leaving my lab again. Do you hear me? *Never!*"

Jack stepped up, squaring his shoulders. "Now see here, Doctor," he started. "Sally is—"

Sally laid a hand on his arm, silencing him. She appreciated his willingness to stand up for her. But this was something she had to do herself.

"No, Dr. Finkelstein," she said firmly. "I'm not going back with you to your lab. Not now. Not ever. From this day on, I'm going to live my own life as my own doll, standing on my own two feet. I'll find an apartment. I'll get a job— I have all sorts of employable skills, after all. I don't need you anymore. In fact, I probably never did."

Dr. Finkelstein's face twisted in rage. It looked as if his eyeballs might pop from his head. "Now, Sally!" he scolded. "Think about what you're saying! You want to live alone? You can't do that! You're not ready!"

"Oh, I'm more than ready," Sally declared. "And if you have a problem with that? You can take it up with my new friend." She gestured to Sootfang, who had stepped up beside her and was glaring at Dr. Finkelstein as if he were a maggot he was looking forward to devouring for dinner.

Dr. Finkelstein shrank back a bit. He squeezed his hands into fists. He opened his mouth, then shut it again. Finally he grunted and began wheeling himself away.

"Goodbye, Dr. Finkelstein," Sally called after him. "Have a nice life!"

Jack laid a hand on her shoulder. "That was pure artistry," he declared. "I couldn't have done it better myself."

Sally giggled. "Why, thank you, Jack Skellington. I figured I spent so much time sticking up for people in Christmas Town, it was high time I should do the same for myself." She turned to Sootfang. "And thank you," she added, "for the backup."

"Anytime!" Sootfang said happily.

At that moment, Lock, Shock, and Barrel pushed their way through the crowd, stopping in front of Sootfang. "Come on," Lock said, putting out his hand to the coal creature. "We want to show you around. Introduce you to everyone."

"How do you feel about bugs?" asked Barrel.

"I love bugs," Sootfang declared. "They were my best friends in the coal cave! Well, when I wasn't eating them, of course," he added sheepishly.

The three gruesome trick-or-treaters laughed and told him they understood completely, then began to drag him down the street. Sootfang shot a helpless but happy look back at Jack and Sally. Jack gave him two thumbs-up, urging him on.

"I think he's going to fit right in," Sally declared.

"Absolutely," Jack agreed. Then he gave her a curious look. "So now that you have your freedom, what do you plan to do with it?"

"Well, I was thinking I might set up a little shop myself. For potions. Or sewing. The sky's the limit!" she added with a grin.

"It certainly is," Jack agreed. "And once you open, I'll be first in line."

"I'm counting on it," she said. "But first things first. I need to find myself an apartment so I can sleep for about a week. I think there's one available above the slug stew shop. I'll go apply straightaway."

"A brilliant plan," Jack said. "I could use a weeklong rest myself." He paused, then added, "But when you do wake up, will you meet me in the graveyard? On Spiral Hill? If you're not busy living your grand new life, that is."

Sally pretended to consider this. Then she grinned. "I'm sure I can find a way to squeeze you in, Pumpkin King."

CHAPTER THIRTY-SIX

One week later

The moon was full and orange when Sally awoke from her long autumn nap. She stretched her arms over her head, yawning sleepily as she looked around her new apartment. It was small—only one room, with a bed, a chair and table, and a kitchenette. And only three spiders in the rafters to decorate. But it was hers. All hers. And that was what mattered.

For the first time in her life, she was free.

After stepping out of bed, she got dressed, slipping on her new patchwork dress and enjoying the feel of the soft cotton against her cloth skin. She'd sewed it together out of fabric she'd found in the dumpster—the remnants of old and discarded costumes—and was pretty proud of how it had come out. Christmas clothing was cute and all, but Abigail had been right—it was extremely itchy. Not to mention a little boring. No dress should be limited to just one pattern or color, she thought with a smile. Which was why her new shop's name was so perfect: Patterns and Potions by Sally. Her opening was in three days and she couldn't wait.

But first she had a promise to keep.

Once dressed, she headed out the door and down the exterior stairs. The tall witch was in her slug soup shop and greeted Sally cheerfully, offering her a spoonful. Turned out it was actually pretty good for a change, and she wondered if Sootfang had shared his recipe.

After saying goodbye to the witch, she headed across town, her steps light and airy. It still felt a little strange to be wandering about like this, without having to poison anyone's soup. For the first time in her life, she could go anywhere— do anything. And no one could tell her otherwise.

Of course, at the moment, there was only one place she wanted to be.

As she headed toward the graveyard, she passed various monsters and nightmares, some hard at work on early Halloween preparations, while others were just hanging around causing mischief. She found Sootfang on the town hall steps, deeply involved in a game of creepy-crawly cards with the vampires, and he gave her a toothy grin as she passed.

"Having fun?" she asked.

"The best time ever!" he cried. "Even if some of them cheat." He cast a knowing look at a vampire, who shrugged and threw down a card that had clearly come from his cloak.

"I did warn you," Sally said. "We're all a bit naughty here."

Sootfang laughed and went back to his game. Sally continued, soon finding herself passing Dr. Finkelstein's laboratory. She noticed a flash of light coming from his lab's window and wondered if he was already at work on her replacement. If so, she needed to have a talk with the new doll as soon as possible. Teach her all about deadly night-shade, frog's breath, and the joys of freedom.

After passing the lab, she headed down under the arch-way at the edge of town and into the graveyard. She smiled as she looked up and found Jack, just where she'd hoped he'd be, sitting atop Spiral Hill, silhouetted by a full moon, Zero floating by his side.

Sally sighed dreamily as she headed his way, passing the toppled gravestone that had started this whole adven-ture. How different things might have turned out if it hadn't broken just in time. If she'd remained in the shadows. If Jack had remained sad. Would they still have found Christmas

Town in the end? Would they still have gotten their happily ever after?

But those thoughts were for another day. Jack had spotted her and was waving her over with eager hands. She picked up her pace, climbing Spiral Hill, careful not to slip. When she reached Jack, he held out his hands, clasping them around her own. His touch was cool as always. Maybe a little clammy. But it sent a warmth through Sally's entire body all the same.

"Can you believe it was only a week and a half ago we sat right here in this very spot?" Jack asked, his voice filled with wonder. "And I was whining about wanting an adventure?" He chuckled. "Well, mission accomplished I suppose. Thanks to you."

Sally's heart swelled at the gratitude she saw radiating in his eyes. "We both needed a change," she reminded him, trying to keep her composure. "And I'm glad we found one together."

"Me too," Jack agreed, staring out into the dark night as a few bats crossed the moon. "I can't remember the last time I had so much fun. Halloween is great and all, but I like knowing there's more out there."

"I do, too," Sally agreed. "But I also like it here. Especially now that I'm free. No more being cooped up in my room. No more being told what to do." She looked up at the moon happily. "I can do anything I want. And I might just do it all."

Jack gazed at her with eyes filled with affection. "I hope you do." He paused, then added, "I bet there's nothing in the world—even all the holiday ones—that you can't do if you set your mind to it."

Sally felt a blush rise to her cheeks. But she forced herself not to look away. Instead she lifted her chin, staring back into Jack's beautiful endless black eyes.

"There is one thing I've been considering doing actually," she said.

"Oh?" Jack cocked his head, curious. "And what might that be?"

Sally bit her lower lip. She couldn't believe she was about to say this. But then, how could she not? Hadn't she learned the value of speaking up? Of going after what she wanted? It was the only way, she knew now, to make one's dreams a reality.

"Well, to start, Jack Skellington," she said, forcing herself to smile slyly, as if it were no big deal, "I'd really like to kiss you."

Jack's jaw dropped. And for a split second Sally almost took it back—told him she was joking, that it was all a silly

Halloween prank. But before she could speak, a look came over Jack's face. A dreamy look. A look that told her he wanted the very same thing.

And so she didn't take it back. And she didn't step away. Instead she closed her eyes, feeling her thick lashes brush softly against her woolen cheeks, and she leaned forward, tilting her head to the side, her lips brushing softly over Jack's own.

A simple kiss between a rag doll and a Pumpkin King. And perhaps the beginning of their most amazing adventure yet. Not in another world far away this time, but right here, right now, just the two of them, silhouetted in the moonlight on top of Spiral Hill.

As if it was simply meant to be.

"Oh, Sally," Jack murmured against her mouth, seeming unwilling to pull away, even to speak. His arms wrapped around her, pulling her close. "This is even better than Christmas."

Sally giggled—she couldn't help it. And soon they were both laughing and kissing as Zero spun around them, yipping happily. And as visions of sugarplums danced through Sally's head, she realized that this wasn't actually her happily ever after at all. But only the beginning of her story.

She couldn't wait to find out what would happen next.

EPILOGUE

Christmas morning

"He came! Mommy, he came!"

Abigail opened one eye, then the other, at the sound of a child's voice in the room. She couldn't see anything, of course, since Santa had wrapped her up in a colorful box with a bow and set her gently on his sleigh. But the sense of movement had ended some time ago, and she was pretty sure she had heard Santa whisper, "Good luck, Abigail," as he set her down under what she assumed was a Christmas tree in someone's home.

After that, all she could do was wait. And worry.

Now, at last, someone was awake. A child, squealing in delight at all the packages Santa had left her. Abigail felt her box being picked up and shaken, rather forcefully. Her head smacked against the sides, and she was half-afraid she might crack again.

"Easy with that, Miranda," came another voice, this one older. "It might be breakable."

"Sorry!" Abigail felt the box being set down again, this time much more gently. "I wouldn't want to break my present. Not before opening it! I want it to be perfect!"

Abigail winced, the child's innocent words stabbing her like a dagger straight to the heart.

Perfect.

And suddenly she wasn't just worried, she was terribly afraid. *I knew it. I told Sally from the start. No little girl wants a broken doll for Christmas.*

Her mind whirled with panic. The box she was in started feeling way too small. If only there were a way to escape, she thought. To run away and never return. Anything to avoid seeing the disappointment in little Miranda's eyes when she opened her box and found a defective doll with a broken leg held together by a metal brace.

Abigail didn't think she could bear it.

Oh, why had she agreed to this? Why had she allowed herself to hope? She should have stayed in Christmas Town. Found a job. Found a life. Or she could have gone with Sally to Halloween Town even. They liked weird, ugly things there.

But no. She had forced herself to hope. To chase her ridiculous dream. And now it was turning out to be a nightmare.

"Well, aren't you going to open your present?" the adult asked, her tone filled with amusement.

"Can I, Mommy? I don't have to wait for everyone else to wake up?"

"Yes, sweetie. But just one present."

"Oh, thank you, Mommy! Thank you so much. I'm going to open this one! It's the nicest wrapped. And it's from Santa. Santa always brings the most perfect presents. And I asked him for something very special this year. I really hope he remembered."

"Well, there's only one way to find out," her mother said. "Go ahead. Open it."

Abigail felt her box being lifted again, followed by the sound of wrapping paper being ripped to shreds. A moment later, the top of the box opened, letting in a blast of light, and Abigail found herself face to face with a little girl with curly auburn hair and green eyes. A girl who looked a lot like her.

A girl who was currently squealing with excitement.

"Mommy! It's the doll I wanted! Look, Mommy! She has green eyes just like me. And curly hair and—"

Abigail felt herself being pulled from the box. Soon she was eye to eye with Miranda—who was staring at her with a shocked look on her face.

"Mommy," she whispered. "Look at her leg."

And there it was. Abigail's heart plummeted. *Look at her leg.* She swallowed hard, waiting for the rest to follow. The tears that would fall. The disappointment radiating in the child's eyes.

But oddly, the words about returning her didn't come. Instead Miranda laid Abigail gently in her lap, carefully examining her brace with surprisingly tender fingers. And when Abigail did dare to look up again, she found Miranda's eyes were not filled with sadness or anger or disappointment at all, but rather a sense of awe.

"She has a brace, Mommy," she murmured, "just like me."

It was then Abigail saw it. The girl had braces on her legs and little crutches leaning against a nearby table. And Abigail realized in shock that the tears forming in Miranda's eyes were not tears of disappointment or anger at all but tears of pure joy.

Miranda pulled Abigail into her arms, embracing her gently, taking great care not to jar her leg. "You're just like me," she whispered in Abigail's ear. "I'm so lucky to have you."

Abigail's heart soared. Suddenly she realized Sally had been right all along. That she wasn't just a broken doll. She wasn't broken at all. She was exactly how she was meant to be.

The perfect doll for this perfect little girl.

Hello, Miranda, she thought. *I've been waiting for you a long time. Maybe forever.*

"What are you going to name her, Miranda?" her mother asked, coming over to examine Abigail. "A doll this precious needs a good name."

Miranda nodded. She looked down at Abigail, and a smile spread across her face. "Her name is Abigail," she said, reading the little card Santa had pinned to Abigail's chest. "And she's so very nice. I just know the two of us are going to be the best of friends."

And in that moment, Abigail knew it, too. Without a doubt in her mind.

Oh, Sally, she thought, her mind floating back to the rag doll who had changed everything. *Thanks to you, I finally got my happy ending and it's even better than I ever dreamed. I wonder if you've found yours, as well.*

But deep down she realized she already knew. There was no way a doll like Sally would rest until she'd gotten everything she wanted. Sally had found a way to be just as happy as Abigail was; she just knew it.

And hopefully she'd get to hear all about it next Halloween.